Paying
Davy Jones

© Millie Vigor 2014
First published in Great Britain 2014

ISBN 978-0-7198-1326-9

Robert Hale Limited
Clerkenwell House
Clerkenwell Green
London EC1R 0HT

www.halebooks.com

2 4 6 8 10 9 7 5 3 1

Typeset in Palatino
Printed in Great Britain by Berforts Information Press Ltd

Paying Davy Jones

MILLIE VIGOR

ROBERT HALE · LONDON

Dedication

This is for the 'oilies', the men who work on oil rigs.
They are a vital link in the production of oil for
our central heating.

Acknowledgements

My thanks go to friends who had oil-related jobs and who were happy to answer my questions. To the man in planning, the one from the RSPB, to Paul Rutherford of D-S-R for legal advice and to the Rebel Writers for their comments and criticism. My grateful thanks to all at Robert Hale Ltd, especially Amanda Keats who straightened out the kinks in my typescript and Ruby Bamber who put up with my emails.

One

1979

'NO!' screamed Catherine as a lorry came hurtling towards her. Eyes wide with fear, she swung her car on to the grass verge and held tight to the steering wheel as, bucking and jolting, it careered along until it skidded to a stop. The engine coughed and died, but the car was off the road and she was safe. 'Idiot!' she yelled at the lorry driver when he grinned at her as his vehicle roared past. Heart pounding and on the verge of tears she watched, in her wing mirror, as the lorry disappeared from sight. Breathing deeply she willed her heart to calm down. Her fear turned to anger as it did; anger with herself for panicking and with the lorry driver for being irresponsible.

Lack of width in Shetland's roads had never been a problem before. Traffic had moved at the leisurely pace of everything else on the islands. But when plans to bring North Sea oil ashore meant that an oil terminal had to be built, construction companies came to do the work and brought heavy machinery with them, lorries too, and these were frequently to be met with on the narrow roads. Not all drivers were as fast or had such a devil-may-care attitude as the one Catherine had just encountered, but they were as liable to cause accidents as the little hill sheep that still roamed free.

In control and ready to move on, Catherine turned the ignition key, put the car in gear and drove away. She was going to Lerwick, fishing port, harbour and centre of trade for the cluster of scattered islands that made up Shetland. When she reached the town she parked her car and, pulling up the collar of her coat – it was the middle of March, but winter was refusing to give up and wet snow was falling – she hurried along Commercial Street.

The town was busy and from others on the street she heard accents far removed from the lilt of the Shetland dialect she was so used to. Apart from English and the twang of a Scottish tongue, foreign languages that had once been centred on the harbour, where continental fishing boats tied up, were now to be heard every-where. Immigrant labour – needed to boost the available Shetland workforce – had been brought in to build the necessary mooring jetties, pipelines and a temporary village to house the workers. Airline companies invaded the airport and built hangers to house the helicopters that ferried oil men out to the rigs. Engineers came to service the planes and many brought wives and families with them. Housing was at a premium, for the influx of so many people had doubled the population of Shetland.

In the Co-op, where she shopped, Catherine met her friend, Rose Sandison. 'Is there ever a day when there isn't a crowd on the street, Rose?' she said.

'Only when it's pouring with rain or there's a force ten blowing,' said Rose, with a laugh. 'Sooth-moothers aren't a hardy breed like us. They don't have the right clothes for a start. You can't look like a fashion plate in a gale of wind.'

'So what keeps them here? I suppose it must be the good money they're getting. Wait till they've had to soldier through a winter or two. Will you have time for a cup of tea?'

'It would be fine to sit down for a catch up,' said Rose. 'I want to hear all about what's happening in your valley. I'll meet you at the Noost.'

Pushing open the door to the Noost Café was easy, but queuing for a cup of tea and finding somewhere to sit was not. The place was filled with bearded and booted men; big men whose oilskin coats made them look even bigger. Clothes damp from the falling snow steamed visibly and filled the air with moisture, which condensed on the walls, there to form fat teardrops that trickled down in little streams.

The two friends did not sit long over their tea and cake; other customers' search for somewhere to sit made them feel obliged to get up and leave. They buckled their coats, pulled on gloves and, heads bent against the weather, walked out and along the street.

'It wasn't that long ago we could have stayed there for an hour or more and had a good gossip,' said Catherine.

'You're right,' said Rose. 'I suppose we shouldn't be surprised that so many outwith people have been brought in. We might well grumble, but at least the oil has made a lot of work and our men have well-paid jobs. Goodness knows how long it will last.'

'They say twenty years,' said Catherine, 'but that might be just a guess. If it does last that long I hope it quietens down a bit. All these incomers have turned the place upside down. It's the old folk I feel sorry for; things are changing too fast for them.'

'They managed all right during the war,' said Rose. 'There were enough changes then, what with soldiers and airmen and ration-ing, though *we* weren't short of food, so that didn't make much difference.'

'But *this* is different,' said Catherine. 'There's good money to be earned, far better than you'd get from running a croft. They say the council's got its fingers in the pie and we'll all be better off, if not rich. But it will be the bosses who get the cream, it always is.' Catherine gave a mirthless chuckle. 'Mark my words; there will be a price to pay. In fact Davy Jones has already started to collect.'

'Whatever do you mean?'

'Oh come on, Rose.' Catherine stopped walking and turned to her friend. 'You've heard of Davy Jones's locker, haven't you, where he keeps all his goodies under the sea bed? The oil companies are breaking into it and stealing the oil, so they'll have to pay. Think about the tanker spills and the oil that killed all those birds. It's going to take ages to clean up the damage that did. Remember the Torrey Canyon? Oil spread all along the Cornish coast and wind and tide took it to the Channel Islands as well. That's just the start. There'll be more to come; lives will be lost too, and we'll see that it's the working man who really pays.'

'You paint such a black picture. Do you really think it will be like that?' said Rose.

'I'm certain of it.'

'But my Bobby never brought home as much money as he does now, not even when the fishing was good.' Rose pushed a strand of wet hair out of her eyes. 'I'm not complaining.'

'It's not the wages I mean,' said Catherine. She looked at her friend, at the fresh countrywoman's face, and knew that Rose's prime concern was for the well-being of her man. Any thought of the way big business was conducted was not for her. 'Sorry, Rose,' she said, 'let's forget it and go home before this weather gets any worse. Come on, I'll race you to your car.'

They parted with promises to meet again soon and a short time later Catherine was driving home. The valley of Deepdale had been her home for the past thirty years and looking at it now she remembered the first time she saw it. A very new and travel-weary bride she had stood beside Robbie, her first husband – drowned long since – and recoiled in shock at the sight of the squat little croft house that was his parents' home, a far cry from the bungalow she had expected. It was a ruin now. Still piled against its walls was the rubble of the landslide, when great slabs of peat and turf, baked dry in an unusually hot summer had, due to the torrent of rain from a cloudburst, slid down off the rocky hillside to surround and consume whatever stood in its path. The thatched roof of the house had long since rotted, but between the stones of broken down walls, the thorny stems of Shetland roses claimed the right to grow. John Jameson, her father-in-law, had had a heart attack and died, and shock had tipped the balance for Jannie, his wife, who was already losing her mind.

But it was years since all that had happened and it was behind her now, for Norrie Williams, a kind and lightsome soul, had wooed and won her, brightened her days, married her and given her three more children to add to little Robbie, child of her first husband.

Time had brought many changes to the valley. The old folk were gone and she missed them, but the person she missed most of all, the one who had befriended her, had educated her in the ways, customs and traditional life of the islands, was Kay Burnett, Norrie's aunt, who, though she had died many years ago, was never far from Catherine's mind.

Her car parked outside her own house, Catherine carried in her shopping. Taking off her coat and hat she hung them up then changed her boots for indoor shoes. She saw to the fire, opened the dampers, and refuelled it. From her bags of groceries she took tins and jars and began to stack them on her cupboard shelves. She had almost finished when there was a knock on the door.

On the step outside a woman stood shivering.

'I believe there is a house for rent here,' said the woman. 'If it isn't already taken could you show it to me? I understand that you keep the key?' The voice was English and educated.

Catherine looked her visitor up and down. Cold pinched the woman's face and reddened her nose. The wind was tearing apart hair that had been swept up into a neat French pleat and snatched at the thin stuff of the coat the woman wore. Nylon-clad legs ended in high-heeled shoes. These were not the right clothes for a winter day in Shetland and the person who wore them was not one who would stay in Shetland long and not one that she would welcome to Deepdale. However, the house needed a tenant.

'Yes,' she said, 'I have the key. I'll put my coat on and come with you.'

Two

THE SNOW THAT had been falling when Catherine was in Lerwick had stopped, but the wind had gained strength. Clad in a padded anorak and a woolly hat, Catherine was warm and comfortable, but the woman who walked beside her was obviously not. The wind buffeted them both, but seemed intent on destroying the stranger. It tugged at her hair and slapped her coat against her legs; the poor woman, tottering along on impossibly high heels, was torn between holding on to her coat and trying to keep her hair out of her eyes.

As the two women approached the empty house, the passenger door of a car parked there opened, and a pair of legs in smart knee-high boots, topped by an incredible length of silk-clad legs, appeared. Speechless, Catherine stared as the girl to whom they belonged stood up. The legs ended in a minute pair of hot pants, but what was under the short furry jacket above them was anyone's guess. Long straight hair looked waist length; at least it might if the wind would leave it alone.

Catherine slotted the key into the lock and opened the door to the house.

'Ah, that's better,' said the woman as they stepped inside. 'What a frightful wind.' She reached up to take the pins out of her hair, 'There's no point trying to keep it up,' she said. Setting it free, she ran her fingers through it and released shoulder-length curls. 'Oh dear, what must you think of me, I haven't introduced myself. My name is Barrington and this is my daughter, Melody. Say how d'you do to Mrs Williams, darling.'

Melody, clutching her inadequate little coat, ignored Catherine.

Looking as though she had just bitten into a lemon she turned to her mother, 'Do we have to do this?' she said. 'You know you're not going to take the house, it's far too isolated.'

'But there's nothing else, darling, and we do need somewhere to live.'

'Well, you can live here if you like, but *I'm* not going to,' snapped Melody. 'It's the pits, it's the—'

'Don't say any more,' interrupted her mother and Melody, short of poking out her tongue, turned away. With an apologetic little smile and a shrug of her shoulders Mrs Barrington looked at Catherine. 'Shall we proceed?' she said.

Catherine led Mrs Barrington through the house. Melody, wearing a disgruntled look, followed them and grumbled about the lack of space as her mother mentally sized up rooms, looked into cupboards and asked questions.

'It is rather small,' said Mrs Barrington when they were back where they started. 'Not quite what I hoped for or what I have been used to. I'm not at all sure my furniture will fit.' She paused. 'Hmm,' she said at last. 'I'm afraid the smallness presents another problem. My husband is a senior helicopter pilot at British Airways. We are expected to entertain visiting officials and I need space for that.'

'Entertain? You can forget that,' said Melody. 'Unless you just have drinks parties where everyone has to stand up, but dinner parties, phoo . . . they're totally out of the question. And if you think I'll change my mind and agree to sleep in one of those poky little bedrooms you can think again. I'm going.'

As Melody slammed out of the house her mother gave a sigh of despair. 'I'm so sorry, Mrs Williams,' she said. 'Children are so difficult at that age, aren't they? I'll have to bring my husband to look at the house, so I will be in touch. Thank you so much, goodbye.'

Catherine watched them go. Mrs Barrington was a snob and her daughter a spoiled brat. They were *not* the sort of people she wanted in the valley. With a bit of luck the husband would agree with the daughter and would not want the house. She closed the door, turned the key and walked home.

Strangers might disrupt the lives of those who lived in the valley and she didn't want that. After all she had been through in the past few years, peace had been hard won. Her children, now adult, were no longer a responsibility. Soon it would be time for them to leave home and make their own way in the world. And when they did she would have more time for herself. But Shetland was buzzing. The tide was in; there was money to be made and saved against the day when the tide turned and ebbed away. And she had to go with that.

She was cooking the evening meal when Allen, one of her twin sons, came home. He was an accountant and his working hours were regular unlike his twin, Peter, who was a fireman at Sumburgh Airport and who worked shifts. Norrie and Robbie, both employed at the Sullom Voe terminal, would not be home till later.

'How's your day been, Mam?' said Allen.

'Much as usual,' said Catherine. 'I was on my way to Lerwick this morning and got run off the road by a truck. The driver was going too fast. I nearly ended up in the ditch. I was lucky not to damage the car.'

'You should make a complaint.'

'And what good would that do?'

'They'd know who was down this way and he'd get a telling off at least.'

Catherine dipped a spoon into a pan of minced beef, scooped up a portion, blew on it to cool it then tasted. 'Mmm, that'll do,' she murmured. She stabbed a fork into a pan of turnips, decided they needed a little longer. 'Well, I must say it shook me up a bit,' she said, 'but there was no harm done.' She lifted a pan of potatoes, set the lid at an angle and strained the water off them. 'I met Rose in town,' she went on. 'We went to the Noost for a cup of tea. I've never seen it so crowded. I don't know where all these people come from – it's an invasion. Are you going out tonight?'

'No, I've got to nail Peter down to get up to date with the croft accounts. Have you got any invoices lurking in your bag?'

All the houses in the valley came with a parcel of land. Catherine had inherited a flock of sheep from her first husband and it had grown in number. She had once been her own flock master, but looking after her growing family had swallowed more of her time and now the twins had taken on most of her work. Peter worked with the animals while Allen was the bookkeeper. The pair worked happily together.

'I'll have a look,' said Catherine. 'Oh, there was something else. A woman and her daughter came to look at Laura's house. They were

English. The mother's a snob and the daughter's a spoilt brat.'

'Not local then.'

'No. The husband's a helicopter pilot for British Airways. The wife was freezing, well, they both were. The girl wore little tiny trousers; I believe they're called hot pants. It's a wonder her legs hadn't turned blue. I ask you. You'd have thought they'd have had more sense.'

'Wow! Wish I'd been home, I'd like to have seen that.'

'You can forget it. You're already spoken for. Now get upstairs and change. I can hear Peter coming and your tea's ready.'

Catherine smiled as she set the table. It was hard to believe that her boys were now grown men. The twins, at twenty-five, were big and broad like Norrie, their father. Robbie, at thirty-two, was tall and lean. Judith, now a slim 26-year-old, lived and worked in Lerwick. She was still given to speaking her mind and still had her sights set on fame as a singer. Robbie had never given up on his ambition to go to sea again and Catherine despaired of him ever finding a girlfriend and settling down to marriage. He and the twins lived at home and Catherine remembered how Norrie said, as they sat at the table all those years ago, *'they're little now, but they'll grow and the house doesn't have elastic sides.'* How she wished it had for since Laura had died and Robbie had come home, with four large men and one small woman living together, space was at a premium. Surely it was time one of her boys thought about getting married and leaving, wasn't it?

'Something smells good, Mam,' said Peter as he opened the door and came in. 'I hope it's mince and tatties.'

'It is. I don't think you'd complain if I put it on the table every day.'

They sat down to eat and when they'd finished and the table had been cleared, Allen commandeered it. He began to spread invoices, bills and receipts on it as well as official papers from the Ministry of Agriculture, or Ag and Fish as it was more often referred to.

Peter groaned, 'Do we have to do that tonight? I wanted to go out.'

'You can ring your Rosie and tell her you'll see her tomorrow,' said Allen. 'If you want to expand the business you've got to pay attention to the accounts.'

'What's that you say?' Catherine had been about to refuel the fire.

Allen did not reply but looked down and began shuffling papers.

'I asked you a question,' said Catherine.

'Weeell,' Allen put up a hand and began to pull the lobe of his ear, 'we were going to tell you, but not just yet. We think . . .' he moved his hand to rub his chin. 'That is . . . Peter and I . . . .'

'Oh, for goodness' sake get on with it,' snapped Catherine.

Allen took a deep breath then plunged in with, 'We'd like to get a bigger place and there doesn't seem much prospect of doing that here. Even all four crofts combined still don't amount to much, and Peter wants to go into mixed farming.' He paused. Catherine sat down and waited for him to go on. 'We've talked about it and agreed to go into partnership provided we can get enough money together to buy a bigger place, but not here. Somewhere in Scotland, we think.'

Catherine turned her head and stared into the flames of the fire. Peter looked at his brother. Allen shrugged his shoulders and spread his hands. Neither spoke. At last their mother turned to look at them.

'And how long do you think it will be before you have enough money saved and you want to make the move?' she asked.

'That depends,' said Allen. 'We thought we might both look for better paid jobs, but if that takes us to Sullom it means that we won't be able to do so much for you here and you'll be left to look after everything. Of course, we'll do the lambing and clipping and no doubt Dad will help you. It's certainly not going to happen tomorrow. I expect it will take us a few years to get the capital together.'

'And what if you suddenly decide to get married and your wives don't want to leave Shetland? Norrie, Robbie, Judith and I each own one croft, but neither of you own anything. Of course your dad and I would help you get set up, but there are other things to think about.'

'Yes, we know. That's why we weren't ready to tell you yet.'

'You're saying nothing, Peter,' said Catherine. 'You're leaving it all to your brother, as usual.'

'Because he's better at that than I, but have you ever seen him clip a sheep?'

Allen chuckled and directed a playful punch at Peter. 'That's why we want to go into partnership. Neither of us can do what the other does so we need each other.'

'I had noticed,' said Catherine. 'Perhaps your father might have some ideas to add. We can ask him when he gets home. Now get to work so I can clear the table ready for when he and Robbie get here.'

It had not been long since Catherine had wondered if it wasn't time for her children to leave home and now two of them were making plans to do so. Even if everything went the way they wanted, though, it could not happen for some time. Plans could be made and dreams dreamed, but whether they came to fruition was another thing. In her experience dreams needed a lot of hard work to make them come true.

The shrill trilling of the telephone broke into her thoughts. She picked it up then held it away from her ear when the excited voice of Judith gabbled something she could not understand. 'Slow down,' she said. 'Say that again.'

'Mam, exciting news, I can't wait to tell you. I just wanted to make sure you were home. I'm on my way now.'

'Can't you. . . ?' But it was only the dialling tone that sounded in Catherine's ear. Judith had rung off.

'Judith's on her way, boys,' said Catherine.

Three

'THAT'LL BE JUDITH,' said Catherine when she heard the sound of screeching brakes and the clunk of a car door being slammed.

'Mam,' yelled Judith as she flew into the house and threw herself into her mother's arms. 'You'll never guess what's happened.'

Reeling from her daughter's onslaught Catherine gasped, 'Tell me, then.'

'I was singing at the Legion last night and there was a talent scout there. He wants me to go to Glasgow.'

'Glasgow? Whatever for?'

'Oh don't be dense, Mother. He said I should be in showbusiness. He works for a recording company and he wants me to go for a try out.'

'A try out – what does he mean by that?' Catherine sat down.

'Well, he wasn't going to hand me a contract on the spot, was he? He said I should have an agent and that I should be in a recording studio and not wasting my time up here. He's going to set it up for me.' The girl was bubbling with excitement. 'Oh, Mam, it's all happening. I told you it would, didn't I?'

'He sounds like a smooth operator to me,' said Allen. 'I can't believe you were that much of a sucker to believe him, Ju.'

Judith turned on her brother. 'You know nothing, Allen, you weren't there.'

'But how do you know he was telling the truth?'

'Allen's right,' said Catherine. 'I can't believe you let some smooth-tongued man get you to believe *that*. It's more likely he wants you for his own pleasure.'

'Oh Mam! How can you say that? He was genuine. He showed

me his papers, proof of who he was and who he works for.'

'Huh. And they could be fakes,' said Allen.

The excitement had gone from Judith's voice. 'You don't believe me, do you? You all think I've been taken in by a conman. Well, you can think what you like, but you'll see. Just you wait till I come home with a ticket for the plane and a date for a recording session.'

'Let's hope he *was* genuine,' said Catherine. 'But even if he was, Glasgow's a whole different kettle of fish to Shetland. You have to keep your wits about you. And not only that, I'm not happy about you going there on your own.'

'I'm not a kid, Mam, I'm twenty-six.'

'Yes, and it's about time you were married and settled down.'

'What? And be shackled to the kitchen sink, kids and cooking for the rest of my life? No thanks. I know I'm a good singer, every-body says so. I want a career and that's not going to happen while I stay here. I've a good mind to go south regardless if anything comes of this offer. Goodness knows this chance has been a long time coming. Glasgow just might be the door that leads to other things.'

'You might think you're old enough to know it all, Judith,' said her mother, 'but city folk aren't like us and men flatter and charm while they tell you lies.'

Judith laughed, put her arms round her mother and hugged her. 'All men are like that,' she said. 'I've lived long enough to have found that out. Tsk tsk. Are you afraid I'll bring home a little bundle? You don't have to worry about that because it's not going to happen.'

Allen and Peter still sat at the paper-strewn table.

'You've got it all mapped out, have you, Ju? Nothing's going to stop you from being famous. It might not be what you think, if you ever do get there,' said Allen.

'She might be a flop,' said Peter.

'I will *not* be a flop,' declared Judith. 'I shall go straight to the top.'

'It's all very well to be confident,' said her mother. 'But Peter could be right.'

'But Mam, why else would they ask me to sing at all the concerts and things and why do they stop to listen when I do? You've always told us that if we want something badly enough we have to believe in ourselves and make it happen. And that's what I'm going to do. If nothing comes of the trip to Glasgow I shall go to London, say what you like.'

'And there speaks the voice of authority,' said Allen. 'No point arguing with her; she's made up her mind.'

Later, when Norrie and Robbie walked in, the whole story had to be told again. 'Mam has already given me dire warnings,' said Judith. 'I think she's afraid I'll get into bad company. But you needn't worry. I can take care of myself.'

'I've no doubt you can,' said Norrie.

'Maybe,' said Catherine. 'But I wonder if you realize what you're letting yourself in for.'

'There you go again, Mam. Stop worrying.'

'I grew up in a city, my girl. I know it was a long time ago and things have changed since then, but . . . well, let's just say that if you won't listen to me, you've got a lot to learn.'

'I'm sure she'll cope,' said Norrie. 'You can't live her life for her.'

Robbie laughed. 'And if you make out all right,' he said, 'you'll be able to buy that luxury car.'

'That's my dream,' said Judith. There was a smile on her face as she went on, 'If you have one, make it a good one. I shall have that car, don't you worry.'

She stayed a while longer, listened dutifully to her mother warning of the evils of big city life. 'I'm not a child, Mam,' she said again.

'I know,' said Catherine. 'But you've grown up in a very safe environment. There's a vast difference between here and a city and I'd like you to remember that.'

'I'll be all right,' said Judith.

The Barringtons moved into Deepdale at the beginning of April. It was a Saturday and Norrie and Peter were at work. Allen had gone into Lerwick to be with Karen, his girlfriend, and Robbie was enjoying a day off. Catherine left Robbie luxuriating in a hot bath while she went out to feed the ewes. Lambing had started and the flock needed constant attention. Empty feed bags returned to the barn, she was taking one last look at the ewes before going indoors when she heard the sound of a lorry coming down into the valley. A removal van was slowly inching down the track. Catherine watched till it came to a stop. For a while nothing happened. Then the driver's door opened and a man got out. He walked towards Catherine.

'This is Deepdale, isn't it?' he said. 'And is that the house,' he pointed at Laura's house, 'that I have to deliver furniture to?'

'Probably,' said Catherine. 'Whose furniture is it?'

The man looked at the paper on his clipboard. 'Name of Barrington?'

'That would be it. I'll get a key for you.'

The Barringtons' car came down the track as Catherine came out of her house, key in hand. 'You'll get some help now,' she said as she handed it over.

'I wouldn't bet on it,' said the man. 'People are usually too busy worrying whether anything's going to get broken to be much help.'

'Well, give us a shout if you do need help, my oldest boy is home.'

'Thanks, I will.'

Robbie was standing by the open door as Catherine was about to go in. 'What's going on?' he asked.

'The new people are moving in.'

'Are they the ones you said you hoped wouldn't come?'

'Yes.'

'Why? What's wrong with them?'

'You'll find out. They'll probably find fault with anything and everything and be a pain in the neck.' She pushed past him. 'I want a cup of tea.'

'I'll make it. You sit down.'

'Oh, that's nice,' said Catherine as she took off her coat and boots. 'You can stay home more often if you're going to make a fuss of me.'

As Robbie poured tea she said, 'The boys say they want to get a bigger place and go into partnership. They'll be a good team; Allen will keep Peter on the right path. But they're thinking to go to Scotland.'

There was a knock on the door. 'When did they come up with this?' said Robbie as he went to answer it.

'Oh, hullo,' said a female voice. It was Melody Barrington. 'I've come to ask if you would give a hand with a heavy piece of furniture.'

For a moment Robbie said nothing and Catherine heard his indrawn breath, then his eager, 'Why, of course I will.' When she heard the silky sound of his voice her heart sank. Melody Barrington was going to be trouble. There were three virile young men under her roof and if Robbie, eldest, soberest and who, at thirty-two years of age, appeared to be set on a bachelor life, could react to Melody in that way, what were the others going to do? Oh well, they were old enough to fend for themselves, so it was up to them. She lifted her cup and drank the hot, dark liquid.

She had set up the ironing board and was halfway through a pile of shirts when Robbie came bursting in, Melody close behind him. 'Is that a clean shirt, Mam? Good. Talk to Melody while I get changed.' Robbie snatched up a shirt and ran upstairs. Catherine put down her iron and looked at the girl.

'I want to go shopping, and as I can't drive he said he'd take me,' said Melody.

'Oh.' What else was there to say?

'For God's sake, you don't iron shirts, do you? Haven't you heard of drip-dry?'

'Um, well. . . .'

Melody still wore the furry jacket, but the hot pants had been replaced by tight jeans that flared below her knees. Her hands were encased in gloves and a large bag hung from her shoulder. She turned her head and Catherine watched as the girl's eyes took in every aspect of the room. Eventually her gaze rested on Catherine. There was a smug look on her face as she twisted her lips into a pout. 'Very primitive, isn't it?' she said.

Catherine stood with her hand still on the iron. Speech had deserted her. Do not rise to the bait and do not even think of what you would like to do to this upstart, was going through her mind. From upstairs came the bumps and bangs of Robbie moving about. At last there was the clatter of feet on the stairs and he appeared. He smiled at his mother. 'I'm taking Melody into Lerwick,' he said. 'Don't wait tea. I don't know when I'll be back.'

'Just a minute,' said Catherine. 'Have you forgotten we're in the middle of lambing? You said you'd give me a hand.'

'Sorry, Mam, couldn't you call Allen if you need help?'

'He does his share.'

'Well, that's all right then.' Robbie put a proprietary hand on Melody's arm and ushered her out.

Catherine heard his car pull away and the sound fade as it left the valley. The same feeling she'd had when she'd taken him to school, that he was starting his own life and wasn't going to share everything with her, filled her now. But this time she *knew* that there would be secrets.

Four

CATHERINE WAS IN her kitchen when the postman walked in.
'It's a braaly cold wind,' he said as he handed her some letters.
'Likely all these new folk that are coming here'll no like our weather.'

Construction of the oil terminal at Sullom Voe was well underway, and the camps that had been built to accommodate the men who had been recruited to work there were full. As camps go they were really villages and the shop, the canteen and the entertainment area, not to mention all the dormitories, had to be stocked, run and kept clean, which made work for local people. Others that had come to fill onshore jobs had brought wives and children with them and there was hardly a house in the islands that was not occupied.

'They'll just have to get on with it, Alec.'

'I think we'll have more snow.' Alec set his bag of letters on the floor. He glanced at the kettle simmering on the hob. 'Might you be making tea?'

Catherine looked at him. Wisps of white hair escaped from under his cap and the face under it was deeply furrowed with wrinkles. His false teeth were so badly fitting that, when he talked, they clattered like castanets. He was stick-thin and his clothes hung on him. He looked old, and one who should not have to tramp the many miles he had to, to deliver letters. There was no bicycle or van for him; he walked his rounds come rain or shine.

'Yes,' she said. 'Sit you down while I do.'

Easing his bony body onto a chair Alec said, 'That oil they're pumping out of the sea is going to bring great changes to our islands and not all of it good. There will be much trouble. They've brought enough foreign people here already, but I'm hearing they're bringing more. There will be drunkenness and fights. The old folk are worried; they say it won't be safe to walk the streets at night.'

'Whoever told you that?' said Catherine as she spooned loose tea into a pot.

Alec shook his head, a grave expression on his face. 'It was bad enough with the soldiers here in the war. There was fornication, crime and deceit; wives lured from their husbands, children born who to this day do not know their fathers. There was every degree of wickedness. Our women will be in danger once again.' As he talked, to give emphasis to his words, he thumped the table with his fist. It reminded Catherine of the hell and damnation preachers at the meeting house.

'I think that's an exaggeration,' she said. 'Would you like a piece of cake?'

'I surely would. Du kens them folk from across the water,' Alec continued with his theme, 'are not like us. They are not God-fearing. They do not go to the church and they do not abide by the commandments. They have no morals and think of nothing but fighting and womanizing.'

'I'm sure their employers are aware of that and I rather think they'll keep the men working long hours just to keep them out of mischief,' said Catherine.

'Ay, but they'll bring the devil along wi' them. It was a bad day that they discovered the oil. It will be an abomination.'

'No, it won't,' said Catherine. 'It'll bring money into the islands. It already has, look at the jobs it's created. The council is getting a lot of money from the oil barons, which you can be sure will be spent for the good of us all. They're building a good new road north of Lerwick so it's already being put to good use.'

Tea made and the aluminium teapot resting on the side of the hob to keep warm, Catherine fetched cups and the cake tin. She cut a large slice of fruit cake, put it on a plate and handed it to Alec; eating it would keep him busy for a while. She watched as he reached out for it. The skin on his hands was thin and papery, and she wondered how old he really was; probably not as old as he looked. She poured the tea, a cup for him and one for her. She handed him his tea then sat down. The fire was hot and the room warm, and now she could smell him. It was not a bad smell, but that of damp clothes that had been dried to wear again, the smell of a man without a woman to look after him. She hesitated to speak to him as he struggled to manage cake and teeth at the same time. When he was almost finished she asked, 'How much farther do you have to go?'

He slurped his tea. 'I'm on to Norravoe then round the hill to Hayfield and then home.'

'It's a fair distance.'

'Ay, but it keeps me fit. Du only gets fat if du sits about.' He finished his tea with a noisy swallow, picked up his bag and stood up. 'That was a braaly fine piece of cake, thank you.'

When he had gone Catherine opened one of her letters. It was from her mother. *Your father's not been too good,* she read, *but he's well on the way to recovery. Nothing to worry about. I would have phoned if you needed to come.* She didn't stop to read any more but got up and reached for the phone. Before she had even begun to dial a number there was a knock on the door.

Mrs Barrington stood on the step. 'I'm so sorry to bother you, but I've come to ask a favour. I've run out of bread. I went to the town to shop this morning and the shelves in the Co-operative were almost empty. There was no bread and no milk and precious little else.'

'Come in, Mrs Barrington,' said Catherine. 'It's too cold to stand there.'

'But what has happened?' wailed the woman as she stepped in. 'Why was the shop so bare? Why were there no groceries?'

'We had a gale the other night, in case you hadn't noticed. It was bad and the boat didn't sail and it's the boat that brings us our supplies.'

'Really! Do you have to depend on food being brought here by boat?' said the astonished woman, her voice rising as she went on. 'Doesn't anyone grow vegetables? Aren't there farmers or bakers or butchers in Shetland?'

'Yes, of course there are,' said Catherine. 'But they can earn a lot more money on a job connected with the oil, so they leave what they're doing and there's no one left to grow veg, bake the bread or cut up meat.'

'Oh, but that's terrible.'

'I take it you're out of bread and you want to know if I have any to spare.'

'If you would be so kind,' said Mrs Barrington. 'I'm finding things so very different here. It's so confusing; it's a totally different way of life to what I have been used to. Are you busy, may I talk with you? There are so many questions I would like to ask.'

Catherine put a paper bag containing half a loaf on the table. 'I'm afraid that's all I can spare,' she said, 'but I expect you will be able to get some tomorrow.' Reluctantly inviting her visitor to sit down, Catherine pulled out a chair for herself and sat at the table. She drew a straw basket containing a pile of socks towards her, picked up her darning needle and began to darn. She wasn't going to waste time just talking. 'The boys buy these awful nylon socks now,' she said, 'but they still manage to get holes in them. What can I help you with?'

'I don't darn,' said the pilot's wife. 'I never have and don't intend to start. Socks are so cheap that when they get holes in them I just throw them away. But tell me, everything is so backward here; the shops are so small, and they don't have a very good selection of goods. The worst thing is that I can't understand a word people say. You're not a Shetland person, so how do you put up with it?'

'There's no point trying to fight it,' said Catherine. 'It's a case of "When in Rome do as the Romans". Shetland belongs to the Shetland people. We're the intruders so we're the ones who have to adapt.'

'But my dear, today was just an example. Yesterday I went to the local shop to order a Sunday paper and they told me that it would not be here until Tuesday. Obviously I didn't order it; the news would be quite stale by then. Why can't I have a paper on the day it's published?'

'Because there's that strip of sea between us and Scotland and it takes the boat fourteen hours to cross it. That means that it can take twenty-four hours, if not more, to get a newspaper from London to here. You won't get it any quicker, because that's another thing that has to come up on the boat.' Catherine, a sock draped over a wooden darning mushroom, wove a thread expertly back and forth.

'And is that why they sell milk in plastic bags? Is that something else that has to . . . come up on the boat?'

The pint of milk sealed in a square of plastic was a bugbear. It was clammy and cold and had to be handled carefully before popping it into a special jug then snipping off the corner to form a spout, but the cow on the back green saved Catherine from having to do that. 'Yes, Mrs Barrington, it is,' said Catherine. She smiled inwardly as she thought of the exodus of bakers, tradesmen and many others who left their jobs to go to oil-related occupations. It was a pity that it made hardship for others, but the oil boom would not go on forever, and the chance for them to have enough money to put some by was an opportunity not to be missed.

'Well, I suppose if that's the way of things I shall have to put up with it,' said Mrs Barrington. 'And by the way, my name is Anneka. Mrs Barrington is so formal, isn't it, and as I am to be your neighbour I would like you to call me Anneka. But please don't shorten it to Ann, will you. I think *that* is so common.'

'If you wish,' said Catherine. 'Now was there anything else? I have outside jobs to do before it gets dark.'

'Yes, there is something. Your house is so warm and mine so cold. Can you tell me how you keep your fire alight? I've not been used to solid fuel; I left a house that was all electric. I never had to dirty my hands with fires.'

'I'll come along later,' said Catherine.

Five

'GET A MOVE on, Robbie, or we're going to be late,' grumbled Norrie. 'What's the matter with you? You look as though you spent all night out on the hill.'

'All right, all right,' snapped Robbie. Bleary-eyed, hair uncombed and a blue stubble on his chin he picked up his cup of tea, slurped some, put the cup down and shrugged himself into his coat. 'Right, let's go.'

'You haven't eaten your breakfast,' cried Catherine.

'Don't want any,' said her son.

'You can't work on an empty stomach.'

But Robbie was already out of the door. Norrie shook his head. 'I think he's in love,' he said. 'With luck it'll pass.' Then he too was gone.

Catherine looked at Robbie's breakfast congealing on the plate. Norrie's plate was clean; he had even taken a piece of bread to wipe up the last of the egg.

For weeks now Robbie had been a stranger. He spent all his spare time with Melody and none, except to eat an occasional meal, with his mother or the family. He had become secretive. He was no longer willing to help at lambing time and had a ready excuse why he should not. His whole personality had changed and Catherine worried about him. 'He's in love,' Norrie had said. Well, in love or not the boy needed a good breakfast before he went to work. Why did the Barrington family have to come and live in Deepdale? Why did Tom Barrington have to agree to take the place and not say that it was unsuitable? And why did Robbie, of all people, have to fall for their daughter? The trouble was that he was too old to be given a good talking to or warned of impending trouble, for it was plain to see that trouble was looming. No, he'd have to suffer the consequences, whatever they turned out to be.

Catherine picked up the breakfast dishes and took them to the kitchen where she scraped Robbie's breakfast into the dog's dish. Noises from upstairs told her that the twins were getting up. Norrie and Robbie had a long drive to work, which meant they were up and away early, but the twins' journeys were much shorter. She was preparing breakfast for them as they entered the kitchen.

'Have you been round the ewes yet?' asked Peter.

'Yes,' said Catherine. 'There's nothing doing so you don't need to go out.'

'You can always ring me if you need a hand,' said Allen.

'I've been helping ewes to lamb since before you were born,' said Catherine. 'But it's nice to know somebody's willing. I wish Robbie was and I wish he'd never taken up with that girl. It's making him so bad tempered.'

'With a bit of luck he'll find out what she's like and dump her,' said Allen.

'Why, what do you know about her?'

'Only that it doesn't take much to see that she's a taker. She'll sponge off of him and make use of him until someone else catches her eye, and then he'll be yesterday's news. He should dump her before she dumps him.'

'Wish he would, but do you think he will?'

'I doubt it. He's hooked.' Allen put down his knife and fork with a clatter. 'Sorry, Mam, I've got to get off.'

'Me too,' said Peter.

Catherine was happy to clear away empty plates when they'd gone. Though both of the boys had girlfriends they did not, like Robbie, go out every night and stay away till dawn, and neither did they wake in foul moods in the morning.

Breakfast dishes washed and put away Catherine made beds and tidied the house, then she took her coat from where it hung and began to put it on. It was time to visit her sheep. The pedigree flock and the crossbreds had already dropped their lambs, now the Shetlands were about to start and, though they seldom needed any help, she liked to walk round them to see that all was well. But they could wait a while; she would have a cup of tea first. Taking off her coat, she hung it up again. She had just made tea when there was a knock on the door.

'I'm so sorry, but I've run out of milk, could you let me have some, please?' It was Anneka Barrington. 'I wouldn't bother you, but I know you have a cow.'

Hadn't the woman been married long enough to know how to cater for her family? First it was bread she'd run out of and now it was milk. 'All right,' said Catherine. 'Come in.'

In her kitchen Catherine took a pitcher of milk and poured some into a small jug the woman had brought with her. Anneka Barrington was sitting by the table when she came back to the living room. Regretfully, Catherine looked at the teapot and mug on the table, the teapot sitting snug and warm under a cosy. It looked as though her mid-morning break would have to be cancelled, because she was not about to invite the Barrington woman to join her.

'I do love your little cottage, it's very cosy.' said Anneka. 'Have you lived in Shetland long?'

'About thirty years,' said Catherine. She deliberately did not sit down; if she did it might be an invitation for the Barrington woman to stay.

'My goodness, then you must have seen a lot of change. But you're from England so what made you come here in the first place?'

'I married a Shetland man. Mrs Barrington—'

'Anneka.'

'All right – Anneka. I do not wish to discuss my personal life with you and if you don't mind I have work to do.'

'So you want me to go.'

'I'm sorry, but yes, I'm afraid I do.'

Anneka Barrington stood up. 'So kind of you,' she said as she took the jug from Catherine. She looked down at the milk, hesitated then said, 'But before I go there is something I must say.'

'Oh, what's that?'

'Your son is a very handsome young man. It is kind of him to take Melody out and entertain her, though I must say he brings her home at a very late hour, which my husband and I do not approve of.' The woman's expression had changed. It no longer appeared friendly and her voice had become stern. 'Melody has to continue her education and will soon have to go back to university. You must tell your son that he should *not* continue to have any hope of a relationship with her. My husband and I would not condone it.'

I don't believe it, thought Catherine. She's telling me that Robbie isn't good enough for her precious daughter. 'Robbie is old enough to make up his own mind who he takes out and who he wants to have – as you put it – a relationship with,' she said. 'I have no intention of interfering with what he does, and he's an adult so if there's anything you want to say, you should say it to him.'

'Well, if you won't speak to him I shall have to get my husband to do it, but I thought you might like to have a word with him first. You see, Melody is of a very impressionable age. I would not want her to get hurt.'

'And what do you think he's going to do to her?'

Anneka Barrington put out a hand to touch Catherine's arm. 'We know what young men are like, don't we?' she simpered. 'They flatter and cajole to get what they want and then won't accept responsibility for the havoc they cause. But that's not all that bothers me. Your boy is really too old for Melody, she needs someone younger.'

Anneka Barrington's attitude made Catherine angry. 'How dare you stand there and suggest that my Robbie is likely to put Melody in the family way?' she said. 'Because that's what you're implying, isn't it?'

'Oh, no, no,' interrupted Melody's mother. 'I didn't mean that at all, though of course that is a possibility. It's just that he's not *right* for her.'

'Right for her or not,' said Catherine, 'you have cast a slur on my son and I won't accept that. He has been brought up to respect women. If he should forget that, he would have me and his father to answer to. So take back your words.'

'I'm not sure I can do that,' said Anneka Barrington. 'Melody's father has a very responsible, well paid job and I have a private income. Put together, what Melody, as an only child, will inherit, will make her a very good catch for an island boy.'

Catherine took a deep breath. She was really angry now. 'What do you mean – *an island boy*?' she shouted. 'Do you think we're all stupid?'

Anneka Barrington backed away a little. 'No, of course not, but you don't understand, do you? My little girl has had a sheltered life.'

At this Catherine laughed out loud. 'You're joking. She goes to university, doesn't she? You can't shelter her there. She'll have been taught more in a couple of months than you could cram into her in a couple of years. It's Melody you should be talking to, not me or Robbie.'

But Anneka Barrington was not about to give up. 'No, my dear, of course I don't need to talk to Melody, she knows the facts of life. I made sure she knew all about things like that from a very young age. No, what she *needs* is a respectable young man, someone of her own class.'

The woman was insufferable and Catherine was fuming. 'Class! What do you know about class? How you can stand there and imply that my son is not respectable or good enough for your daughter I *really* would like to know. *What* makes you think that you're doing us a favour by coming here? You've done nothing but interrupt our lives and I for one will be only too glad to see the back of you. I don't want to hear another word. *Get out.*' She walked to the door, opened it and held it open. 'Goodbye, *Missus* Barrington.'

Anneka Barrington glared at Catherine and looked as though she was about to say something else, but then thought better of it and stepped out. Catherine slammed the door behind her. Never again would that woman cross her threshold, she could run out of bread and milk and everything else and starve for all she cared. She put her hand on the teapot. It was cold. Not only had she been denied her mid-morning break, but she and her family had been insulted into the bargain. Venting her anger Catherine roared through clenched teeth and hammered the table with her fists. Damn the woman. Who did she think she was? If nothing else she was blind as far as her daughter was concerned.

Catherine took the teapot to the kitchen and emptied it into the slop bucket then stuffed some dirty clothes into the washing machine and set it going. Taking her coat of its hook she put it on then spoke to her dog. 'Come on, Moss, let's go.'

Six

'JOE'S BEEN AT me again about the Broonieswick croft,' said Norrie as he and Catherine sat at supper. 'I've half a mind to sell it to him. When I retire the crofts here will be enough to keep me occupied.'

'Would you really think about selling it to him?' said Catherine.

'Ay, he's never given up on wanting to be a crofter and he asks me about it every time I see him, he deserves a chance. And the boys don't want to be bothered with that little parcel of land. They know what they want and it's not that.' Norrie chuckled. 'At least it would get him out of my hair. The man never stops talking. Where's Robbie?'

'He's gone to the Hayfield croft to give Rose's man a hand.' Catherine picked up their empty plates. 'I'm surprised he has, he hasn't got any time for us these days so I don't know what's persuaded him to help Bobby.'

'I wouldn't worry about it . . . What the hell's that?' From outside came the sound of car doors being slammed, then an excited voice and running feet on the flagstones. The door flew open, Judith burst in and, not a moment too soon, Catherine put down the dishes.

'Mam, oh Mam, I've had such a wonderful time.' Clasped tight in Judith's arms Catherine gasped, 'What *are* you talking about?'

'I'm going to be famous, Mam. They said I was a star. I told you, didn't I?'

'But . . . oh, Judith, you've been to Glasgow and you didn't tell me.'

'No, because I knew you'd worry. Can't you be a little bit glad for me?'

'Of course I can, but slow down,' Catherine, looking over Judith's shoulder, nodded her head towards a man standing just inside the door, 'and introduce us.'

'Oh, that's Dominic,' said Judith. Detaching herself from her mother she went to the stranger, linked her arm in his and turned to face her parents.

Catherine stared open-mouthed, stood for a moment saying nothing, then, snapping her mouth shut, said, 'Oh, Judith.'

Judith spread her arms and looked down at herself. 'It's what everybody's wearing.' Tight knee-high boots, a skirt that just skimmed the top of her thighs and a tiny halter top and a cardigan that reached almost to the floor. Catherine could accept that Melody Barrington would dress that way because she was a tart, but not Judith. 'Don't be a prude, Mam,' said Judith, 'and anyway, this is Dom, my minder.'

Dominic held out his hand and smiled as he said, 'I'm very pleased to meet you.' He spoke with a slightly foreign accent. 'I've heard a lot about you.'

Catherine took his hand. 'Hello Dominic,' she said. 'It's very nice to meet you, but please don't believe all that Judith tells you.'

A head of sleek black hair crowned a face that had been tanned by a Mediterranean sun, and Dominic de Angelo's brown eyes returned Catherine's scrutiny of him. The hint of a smile played about his mouth.

'I hope you're looking out for our girl,' said Norrie as he shook Dominic's hand. 'But knowing her you'll have a job.'

'Tell me something I don't know,' said Dominic.

'Where are the boys?' asked Judith.

'They've gone to a dance somewhere; it's the last of the season. Melody's gone with them,' said Catherine. 'She came looking for Robbie and when she heard the boys talking about the dance, she insisted that they took her with them. I don't know what Robbie's going to say.'

'What do you mean? What's it to do with him?'

'Do you really want to know? He's acting like a total idiot over the girl. You'd think she'd cast a spell on him or something.'

'Oh, like that, is it. More fool him, he's old enough to know better.'

'Try telling him that.'

'Well, never mind him. I've got lots to tell you, so why don't you make a cup of tea, Da. On second thoughts, let's open that bottle of wine we brought. Where is it, Dom? Get some glasses, Mam, and have you got any shortbread?'

Sitting round the table, shortbread and bannocks to go with the wine, Judith told her parents of the exciting things she'd done and witnessed. 'Dom looked after me,' she said. 'He took me sightseeing. The shops are fabulous, they've got everything and the city's so *big* and so *crowded* and everyone's in such a *hurry*.'

'But what did they say at the studio, did they like your voice?' asked her mother. 'Do they want you to make records, or didn't they say?'

'Um, well. Yes they do like me, Mam,' said Judith. A hesitant note had crept into her voice.

'What is it? What's happened? I hope you're not going to be disappointed.'

'You have nothing to worry about,' said Dominic. 'I have seen lots of would-be stars, but none come anywhere near this one. This girl is going places. But it might take a little while. The recording has to get into the right hands.'

A smile of relief crossed Judith's face. 'Dom's going to get me fixed up with an agent. I have to have an agent because I need someone to get the gigs.'

'And what about you, Dom?' asked Norrie. 'What's your place in all this?'

It was a question that was not about to be answered for the door opened and Robbie, his expression sullen, walked in. Ignoring the other occupants of the room he said, 'Where have the boys gone, Mam?'

'I'm not sure. I think it might be Tingwall.'

'I've got to find them.'

He was about to leave the room when his mother said, 'Stop right there, Robbie. We're used to your bad moods, but before you go *any*-where you can apologize to your sister and her friend for being so rude and ignoring them.'

'Oh, hullo Ju,' said Robbie. 'You will be stopping a while, won't you?' He merely nodded his head at Dominic. 'Excuse me, won't you, I have to find the boys, but I have to get cleaned up first.'

'Well!' said Catherine when Robbie had gone. 'How rude of him.

Big as he is, I've a good mind to go and give him a talking to.'

'Don't waste your time,' said Norrie. 'You know what they say – the harder the storm the sooner it's over – it'll blow itself out and then you'll be left with, well, not tears, but as good as.'

'Da's right,' said Judith. 'How old is Robbie, – twenty-nine? Thirty? No, he must be thirty-two. Oh, gosh, no wonder he's got it bad. I'm surprised this hasn't happened before.'

'His mind was always set on fishing,' said Catherine. 'Perhaps Melody's long hair made him think he'd caught a mermaid.' In spite of the laughter that ensued Catherine was angry at her son's behaviour. 'It's no good,' she said. 'I'm going to drag him downstairs and make him apologize.'

'You can't—' Norrie began but was interrupted when the door opened and Allen and Peter were there.

'I'm never going to get sucked in like that again,' Peter was saying.

'Nor me. Hey, look who's here,' said Allen. 'Hi Ju, why are you home? Didn't they want you down in Glasgow?'

'Mam said you'd gone to a dance,' said Judith. 'It'll hardly have started yet; it's only just gone ten. Why are you home?'

'Ha,' scoffed Allen. 'Ask the madam up the road. She insisted on coming with us. We tried to put her off, but she hung on like a leech.' Putting on an exaggerated female voice he minced across the room and said, 'Why do you do those silly dances and why are all the boys drinking out of beer cans, isn't there a bar? I don't like it, I'm not going to stay here, take me home.'

Allen had turned to face his audience and had his back to the door leading to the stairs. He didn't hear Robbie coming and was unprepared when he was grabbed by the shoulders, spun around and punched with a straight left. He staggered back. Peter caught and held him.

Norrie jumped up and laid hold of Robbie. 'You can stop that,' he said. 'I'll have no fighting here. Now, apologize to your brother.'

'No, I won't. He and Peter took my girl out. They had no right. Now he thinks it's all right to poke fun at her and I won't have it.'

'You want to ditch that one, Rob. She's already got you running round in circles. She'll have the shirt off your back before she's finished,' said Allen.

'Let go of me, Dad, and let me get at him,' snarled Robbie.

A restraining hand still on Robbie's shoulder, Norrie said, 'Not a chance.'

'You can think what you like, Allen,' said Robbie, 'but you'd better not let me hear you insult Melody again.'

'Look, Rob, you shouldn't be getting mad with Peter and me, we didn't ask her to come with us, she just demanded that we take her and said that if we didn't she'd get you to sort us out. We had to pay for her to go in and buy her drinks, and all she did was complain about the music and the dances, and then she made us bring her home. She's a sponger. She'll bleed you dry. Get rid of her.'

If Norrie hadn't anticipated the move, Robbie would have sprung at Allen again. 'Get out, boys, make yourselves scarce for a while,' he said. 'And you, Robbie, calm down. You should be ashamed of behaving like this while your sister and a visitor are in the house.'

With a reluctance that was obvious, Robbie apologized. 'I'll see you later, Judith. Sorry, but I've got to go.' When he had and the door had closed behind him, Catherine said, 'I'm so sorry, Dominic, I've never known the boys behave like that before.'

'They're young, and there's a woman involved,' said Dominic.

'Poor Robbie's got it bad,' said Judith. 'The boys haven't got anything good to say about her, it seems, but she can't be all bad for Robbie to fall for her. I know she's pretty, but what's she really like?'

'I wish she and her mother had never set foot in Deepdale,' said Catherine. 'If I could wind the clock back, I would. Her mother stood in this room and told me that her precious daughter needed someone of her own class. She made it plain that she didn't think Robbie was good enough, that he was an *island boy*, and that all he was after was money. I could have wrung her neck.'

Judith laughed at her mother's obvious dislike of the Barringtons. 'Have another glass of wine, Mam,' she said. 'It'll all come out in the wash.'

'If it were only that easy,' said Catherine.

Seven

'WOULD YOU EVER get out of my hair, boys?' June Thompson, no longer the slim, slip of a girl she had been, but a plump mother of two, pushed her sons out of the house. 'Go and play somewhere else and let me get on,' she said, 'but don't go too far and don't get into mischief.'

June was packing. Norrie had given in to Joe's persistence and sold him the Broonieswick croft. Peter and Allen had repeatedly said that going there to tend a handful of sheep wasted more time than they were worth, so, to Joe's delight, the little house and croft had become his.

Into a plethora of empty boxes June packed clothes, china, books and ornaments. As she sealed each one she wrote on it what it contained. She was in her bedroom folding and packing sheets and blankets when she heard Catherine calling her. 'I'm here,' she called back.

'Is there anything I can do to help?' said Catherine. 'Oh yes,' she said, as she walked into June's bedroom, 'let me help you fold the blankets.'

'I think I'm almost ready,' said June. 'Joe should be here soon with the truck. I'll have to come back later to finish clearing up; I'm afraid I won't be able to do it all before we go. You won't mind, will you?'

'Come back any time you like, there's no hurry. Have you time for a cuppa? If you haven't already packed the teapot, I'll make it.'

'The teapot is the last thing I put in a box,' said June. 'I haven't stopped since morning and my tongue's hanging out, so I'll find the mugs.'

Surrounded by bulging boxes and bags, the two women sat with mugs of tea and reminisced over the years they had known each other.

'I'll never forget the first time the kids saw Joe,' said Catherine. 'Do you remember? The twins were hiding under the table. But they loved him when they got to know him.'

'And he loved them. But then, Joe loves kids, full stop.'

'Did you know they called him "the chocolate man"? I shall miss him, but I shall miss you too. After me, you were the first young person to come into the valley. When I came everyone was fifty to sixty plus, and I did long for someone my own age to talk to. I would have got a job but with Robbie so little there wasn't much chance of that, though the old aunts offered to look after him and I did get some part-time work. It's hard to believe that my kids are grown up now.'

'Joe is thrilled to bits that Judith has made it,' said June. 'He always said she'd go far. She's set her sights on a career as a singer, hasn't she?'

'Yes, but she's not there yet. Going to Glasgow is only the beginning.'

At that June laughed. 'You've got to be joking. Have you ever heard her sing in public? No? Well, Joe has. He said everything stops while folk listen. You should look happy, why don't you?'

'It's all very well, this fame, but where is it going to lead? She was brought up in Shetland and you know how laid back everything is here. It won't be like that in Glasgow and if she's lucky enough to get picked up, well, I worry for her.'

'You don't need to. You're the one who would be lost in the outside world these days; you've been cloistered in this valley too long. Sheep are not the most intelligent companions, you know. Your children have left you standing. You've nothing to worry about over any of them.'

'I don't know about that, June. The twins are all right. They've both got sensible girlfriends and as for Judith, well, there's not much I can do about her. But when it comes to Robbie, I always thought he would marry some nice Shetland lass, one who would put up with his fixation on going to sea, but he's still besotted with that Barrington girl. She's totally wrong for him. The last couple of months have been awful. It's the middle of June now, the sun's shining and he ought to be smiling, so why isn't he? All he does is scowl and snap if he's spoken to. I dread to think where it's all going to end.'

'But he's an adult, Catherine. You'll be wasting your time to worry about him. All you can do is to be there to help him pick up the pieces if it falls apart.'

'But I do worry,' said Catherine. 'I think he's being very foolish and I thought better of him. Anyway, we'd better not sit here any longer. Joe will be back and you'll not be ready.'

June put her hand on the teapot. 'You're right, I had thought about having another cup, but better not.'

'Norrie's got to repair the roof of the barn, Robbie, and he needs some help,' said Catherine. 'Peter can't do it as he's on shift, and Allen will be away. Norrie says I'm not to do it, but you'll be here on Sunday, so will you give your da a hand?'

'No.'

'That was rather blunt, wasn't it? Why can't you do it?'

'I just can't. Melody wants to go to Aberdeen. She says the shops here are rubbish and she isn't going to be seen dead in an anorak and jeans, which is what everybody else seems to be wearing. I don't blame her so I said I'd go with her.'

'But—'

'We're going for the weekend, Mam.'

'You're going for the weekend? You don't need a whole weekend to go shopping. Why can't you go down on the boat and just spend a day there? That ought to be enough.' Robbie was fiddling with a biro that someone had left on the table. He was not looking at her; in fact he seemed to be deliberately avoiding her. Catherine's heart sank. He was planning something and she knew that whatever it was it wasn't going to please her. 'You never do anything to help your da these days; don't you think it's about time you did?'

'I don't see why I should. He's not my father anyway. You know that.'

'Robbie! How can you say such a thing?'

'Well, it's true.'

'So it might be, but he loves you as if you were his own. How can you turn on him now? You have much to thank him for. You could at least show some gratitude.'

'And should I be grateful for the times when he drank too much and bullied both of us? He didn't show me much love then, did he?'

'They were hard times, Robbie, and people do and say bitter things when life treats them bad. It doesn't mean they no longer care for you, but it's in the past, forget it. It would cost you nothing to give some help for an hour or two. Couldn't you go another time?'

'No, everything's arranged. I'm taking the car and I've already booked the boat.' Robbie got up from his chair.

'Why are you taking the car? For heaven's sake, you can't be going to buy *that* many clothes. No, don't go, Robbie,' said Catherine as her son turned away from her. 'You're not going to Aberdeen just to buy clothes, are you?'

'What I'm going for is none of your business, Mam. I don't ask you where you're going when you go out, do I? Where's Norrie?'

'I think he's in the barn.'

With indecent haste Robbie was out of the door and gone. Stunned at his attitude towards her, Catherine stayed where she was. What on earth had happened to him? Did she really need to ask? He had never been like this before, so it would be something to do with Melody. Catherine gasped and her hand flew to her mouth; surely he hadn't made the girl pregnant. That would be just too awful. If it were true, Melody's mother would boil with fury and tear her own defence of Robbie to shreds.

'Halloo,' called a voice. The door opened and June Thompson, followed by Joe, walked in. 'We've just come to say goodbye,' said June. 'Well, not a real goodbye, just to tell you that we're off. You can't get rid of us that easy, we will be back to see you again.'

'I would hope so,' said Catherine as she clasped her friend in her arms. 'Now, don't you go working too hard, take some time for pleasure.' She looked at the grinning black man standing behind his wife, 'And that goes for you too, Joe.'

'Work never hurt anyone,' said Joe. He was a tall man and, laughing as he did, he put his arms round Catherine, swept her off her feet and held her tight. She yelled for him to let her go. 'You've been so good to us,' he said as he put her down, 'and we're grateful. Don't hesitate to call if you ever need us for we'll always be willing to help out.'

'I'm sure you will,' said Catherine. 'I'm really going to miss you. Now you'd better go before I cry.' She shooed them out of the door then watched as they drove away. A family was leaving the valley. Another house left empty. Who would be coming to live there now? She was just turning to go back indoors when Norrie came in through the back door.

'Did Robbie come to see you?' said Catherine.

'Yes, he did,' said Norrie.

'What did he want?'

'He wants me to make excuses for him if he doesn't get back in time to go to work on Monday.'

'I knew it. He's not just taking Melody to do some shopping. They've got something else planned. I'm fed up with him, Norrie, and I'm beginning to wish he'd pack his bags and leave.'

'You don't really mean that.'

'Yes I do. It would be a lot more peaceful here if he did.'

'Well it might be, but if I know you, the minute he left you'd start worrying about him. Forget it. He's a grown man.' Norrie picked up the kettle, and putting it under the tap, began to fill it. 'Where have you put the bannocks?

Eight

CATHERINE LOOKED OUT of the kitchen window. Cloud shadows chased one another across the hill at the back of the house. It was a fine day and the weather was ideal for the work on the barn roof that Norrie had planned to do. It would have to be put off to another day now; there was no way it would be safe for him to work up there on his own. She would call him, he wouldn't be far away.

'No matter what I do I just can't get Robbie out of my mind,' she said when she and Norrie were sitting down with mugs of coffee. 'It's no good trying to talk to him because he won't listen. What would you do?'

'I'd leave things the way they are.'

'And are we to let him go on treating us like idiots, then? Let him use home like a hotel, a place to eat and sleep? I can't do that. He should do his share of the work the same as the others. How often do we get the ideal day for outside work? Just going to Aberdeen to shop doesn't depend on the weather.'

'You can't run his life for him. He's made up his mind and he won't thank you for trying to protect him.' He smiled at her and chucked her under the chin. 'Now that we've got the day to ourselves, why don't we go out?'

'Out...? Where?'

'One of these days I'm going to retire and I thought we might build us a house somewhere, so how about we go and look for a likely place?'

'Retire? You? And leave the valley?'

'Why not? I'm not getting any younger and neither are you. How long do you think you can go on chasing sheep?'

'As long as I'm able. I'm not ready to retire yet and neither are you. Men like you never do. They keep toddling on and get the rest of the family to do the work. You'll be just the same.'

'I admit I shall still want to keep a few animals and I can't see you sitting down with a piece of knitting. You know you'll want a few sheep, even if they are only for the freezer.'

Catherine did not reply. He was right, but she wasn't going to admit it. What would she do if she didn't have her sheep to look after? Other women would sit down to knit, but she had flatly refused to learn how. In any case, retirement was a long way off. Norrie would keep on working for as long as he could. She would humour him. She smiled at him.

'All right, shall I pack a picnic or are you going to buy me a meal?'

'We'll eat out. You don't have to cook today.'

'But I'll take a flask of tea.'

With the flask of tea and a packet of biscuits in a bag on the floor at her feet, Catherine sat beside Norrie. 'Where are we going?' she asked as he drove.

'I don't know,' he said. 'I'm going to go where the road takes us. We can explore some of the side roads, if you like, because I don't suppose you want to live in the town and we might find somewhere close to the sea.'

'I wouldn't want to go too far north,' said Catherine. 'And neither do I want to go too far from Lerwick.'

'Why?

'I wouldn't want to be too far from the kids.'

'But dammit, in that case we'd just as well stay where we are. If Allen and Peter get what they want they'll be in Scotland and if Judith's lucky she'll be gone south. And I can't see Robbie sticking around for long. You've got to think of yourself now.' When Catherine didn't reply, Norrie stole a glance at her. She was staring out of the window. Her hands were in her lap, thumbs rolling over one another. He took one of his hands off the steering wheel and patted her knee. 'It's just you and me now. The kids are leaving home and that's as it should be.'

'You're right,' said Catherine. 'I've got to let them go, haven't I?'

'I'm afraid so, darlin'.'

They had travelled north and west and at a point where the road widened Norrie parked the car. 'Let's have that cup of tea,' he said.

'Do you really want to leave Deepdale?' asked Catherine.

'Yes and no,' said Norrie. 'If we stayed there and I couldn't look after the place I'd hate to see someone else doing what I should, so it would be better to leave. But if Peter took over the crofts . . . well . . . then I think I'd want to stay.'

'That's exactly how I feel. But we came out to see if there's anywhere we would like to move to. That is, of course, *if* we decide to move, and I don't know that I want to. But whether we find somewhere or not, it's a day out and it's not raining so let's enjoy it.'

Biscuits, flask and cups stowed away, Norrie started the car and drove on. 'It's time we got off the main road,' he said and at the next junction turned the car onto a much narrower road.

'Are you sure this isn't a peat road?' asked Catherine. 'It doesn't look to me as if it's going anywhere else.'

'You'd be surprised,' said Norrie.

The road rose and fell and twisted right and left. When they'd travelled out of sight of the main road, they passed a small group of houses that were dotted along beside it. The road climbed now and the car crested a hill, and as it did Catherine leaned forwards to look at the panorama before her. The road bisected a wide sweep of hillside, then ran down it to end in the rough surface of a turning place beside the ruin of what had once been a house. Beyond the ruin, a pasture of rough grass ended in a grassy bank that fringed a small pebble beach and from then on there was nothing but the sea.

'What do you think of this?' asked Norrie.

'It's beautiful. But it's a lovely day; I wonder what it's like in winter.'

'Like everywhere else in Shetland. It won't be any different.'

'I've often wondered where the little roads led; it's nice to find out.' Catherine opened the car door and got out. 'I'm going to have a look around.'

The stones of a broken down wall marked the outline of what had once been a kale yard. A few scrawny sheep cropped the grass there. They scampered away as Catherine approached. She walked round the ruin of the house, shielded her eyes and peered in through the murky glass of the windows. The door was barred and padlocked. A garden at the front of the house was enclosed by a stone wall. The green haulms of potatoes, thin and poor, that struggled to compete with wild grass for existence showed that it had not been long since the garden had been cultivated. In a corner, taking advantage of shelter from the wall, a few stunted willows and Shetland roses grew.

'Look, Norrie,' said Catherine, 'there're raspberry canes here and there's some rhubarb, gone to seed, of course. I wonder who lived here.'

'Would you like to live here? Shall we buy it?'

'You're joking.'

'No I'm not. I could find out who it belongs to. But there're lots of places like this, we're only looking, aren't we?'

'Yes. It's a lovely spot, open to all weathers, but where is there a place that's not?' She smiled at him. 'Let's go.'

Norrie turned the car round and drove back the way they had come. Catherine turned to look over her shoulder as they climbed the hill, gave a sigh as they crested it then as they began to descend the view was lost to sight.

'I'm enjoying this,' said Catherine as Norrie drove along small side roads, many of which ended in a turning place by a cluster of houses. In some gardens willow trees or sycamores grew. When she said that what she'd really like to see were some *real* trees, twice as high as the ones they'd seen, and he said he'd take her to where there was a plantation, she'd scoffed and said he was kidding.

But he wasn't. He drove to Weisdale, bought ice creams in the Weisdale shop and parked by the side of the road while they ate them.

'There was a book written about Weisdale,' said Norrie, 'about life in the eighteen hundreds. They were hard times. The young men had to hide from the press gangs that were looking to capture them and take them off to serve in the navy. The youngsters today don't know they're born.'

Ice cream finished Catherine said, 'Where's this plantation then?'

'Not far.'

Taking his time so that Catherine could enjoy her first sight of the trees as they came into view, Norrie drove slowly past the Weisdale Mill. 'Stop the car,' she said when they were amongst them. She got out and stood to look up into the spread of branches. The trees were in full leaf. She breathed deeply. 'Oh, smell that, Norrie. Isn't it wonderful?'

Over the years, the annual fall of leaves had decomposed into compost at the base of the trees, dead branches, lichens and other mosses had added to it and the aroma it gave off was sweet and nutty.

Norrie Williams looked at his wife and at the delight on her face. How much did she miss her home in the south? And what had made her stay in this land that, apart from this plantation, was devoid of such trees? One day he would take her home, not to stay, but to gather memories to carry to her grave.

'Why aren't there more trees like this?' said Catherine.

'I think the soil is too acid and they don't like it. The fir trees do well. Other folk have planted them for shelter belts.'

But Catherine wasn't listening. She was leaning over the fence that divided the trees from the road. A blackbird was searching for food, tossing leaves aside with his beak then cocking his head to one side to listen for anything that moved.

'Are you done, then?' said Norrie, 'because I'm hungry and I could do with something to eat.'

Nine

İT WAS MONDAY. It was raining and not the sort of weather Catherine wanted; she had a basketful of washing to put out. It was now July; the sun should be shining and a soft wind blowing. Her laundry needed to dance in the wind and absorb the fresh clean smell that the wind's boisterous cavorting brought with it. All winter she had spread her washing over the pulley in the living room to dry and now, once again, she unhooked the rope that kept the pulley close to the ceiling and let it down. Piece by piece she spread the clean items over it and when it was full, hauled it and its extra weight back up. When that was done she put on her water-proofs and set out on her first trip of the day to look at the ewes.

Work with the sheep took up less of her time now. The twins helped, but Robbie made no bones about letting her know he wasn't keen. Where was he now? He had taken Melody to Aberdeen and they should be home. They were not and she wondered what had happened.

As she worked she thought about the first time her small flock produced their lambs. The ewes had lambed in the open, a far cry from today and the lambing pens in the barn that Norrie and the boys had built. She loved being there when the ewes were giving birth, loved the warm woolly smell of the sheep and the fragrance of summer that filled the air when she teased out the hay to put in the cribs. There was no more going on her knees in a wet field to deliver a lamb; they came into the world in an airy barn, to drop on and be bedded in dry straw. To ensure that lambs and mothers bonded well they were kept inside for a few days before being let out to join the flock.

So many things had changed since those early days and were changing still. Hadn't Judith dropped a bomb on Saturday night when she said that she wanted to move to Glasgow with Dominic? Not just yet, though, she had said, she wanted to be certain that it was Glasgow she wanted and not London. It should not have been a surprise for all the signs had been there; Judith's ambition to make a career as a singer, the way she was with Dominic and the looks she exchanged with him. Catherine gave a wry chuckle. The first of her brood was flexing her wings and planning to fly away. Who would be next?

Back in the warmth of her kitchen she let down the pulley. None of the clothes on it were dry enough to remove, so she would not be able to put her coat on it as she had hoped. Instead, she draped it over the back of a chair and stood it in front of the fire. She went into the kitchen to boil a kettle and make a hot drink. She spooned instant coffee into a mug, added milk, then, when the kettle had boiled, topped it up with hot water. As she did, she heard the slam of a car door, voices, and then her door being opened. She turned to see who her visitor was.

Robbie stood there, Melody's arm linked in his. Catherine, mug in one hand and spoon in the other, stared at them. This was not right. Why had Robbie brought Melody here? She should have gone to her mother's house.

'Hi Mam,' said Robbie. 'We're home.'

'So I see. Did you manage to get everything you wanted?'

'Yes.' A smile blossomed on Robbie's face then faded as quickly as it came. 'We have something to tell you,' he said.

A terrible foreboding filled Catherine. Oh, God, what has he done? Is Melody pregnant? Are they planning to get married? Time suddenly took on another dimension. Her body refused to accept that she was in control. She dropped the spoon with a clatter, reached for the table to put her mug down, watched as her arm moved so, so slowly, had nearly reached its destination when her hand let go of the mug and it began to fall.

Robbie jumped and caught it, spilled hot coffee over his hand and swore. 'Are you all right, Mam?' he said as he put the mug on the table. He took hold of her arm and led her to a chair. 'I'll get you some water.' He was drying his hand with his handkerchief.

'No, Robbie. Just give me a moment to get myself together.'

Catherine closed her eyes, gripped the arms of the chair and breathed deeply until she felt her body come back to normal. Then she looked at Robbie. 'I have a feeling that Norrie ought to hear what you have to say, but he's not here.'

'He is,' said Robbie. 'He was going into the barn as we drove up.'

'I thought he was working on the hill. Go and give him a shout, then.' The latch on the back door rattled, the door opened and was closed again as Norrie shut it behind him. 'No, there's no need, he's here.' Catherine turned her head and listened to the grunts of a man bending to take off his boots and the clunk, clunk, as he dropped them on the floor. Then Norrie was in the room with them.

'So you're home, then, Robbie,' he said.

'Yes, Da, we are.'

The room seemed the same as it always had. The old clock that Norrie had inherited from his Aunt Kay still ticked the hours away. A kettle, despite the fact that Catherine had an electric one, still simmered on the hob and the smell of burning peat, of dog, her wet coat and of human habitation filled every corner of the room.

'I'm glad you're here, Norrie,' said Catherine. 'Robbie and Melody have something to tell us.'

Robbie stood with his arm round Melody's shoulders. He looked down at her, then at his mother and Norrie and Catherine knew that any peace and harmony in the house was about to be shattered.

'What is it you have to say to us, Robbie?' asked Norrie. 'Is it so important it couldn't have waited till later?'

'No, it couldn't. Melody is now my wife. We were married in Aberdeen.' He looked from his mother to Norrie and when they did nothing but stare at him in shocked silence he said, 'I thought you'd be pleased.'

'You . . . bloody . . . stupid . . . idiot,' said Norrie. 'You've only known the girl five minutes. Have you lost your senses?'

'No, of course I haven't. I love her. I have since the first day I saw her.'

Melody glued herself tight into Robbie's side, her arms round his waist. 'I told you, Robbie, didn't I?' she whined. 'I knew they'd be against us.'

The first shock of Robbie's announcement drained from Catherine's body and left her filled with cold, calm anger. 'So, you ran off to marry in secret,' she said. Her voice, level and controlled, did nothing to give away the tumult of emotions that raged within her. 'When is it due?'

'What do you mean?' asked Robbie.

'Don't be stupid. She thinks I'm pregnant. I am *not*,' shouted Melody.

'Do not shout at me,' said Catherine.

'I'll shout at who I like,' Melody bawled again. 'You are not my mother.'

'Thank God for small mercies,' said Catherine. 'I would not want to have a fish wife for a daughter.' To Robbie she said, 'Either control that woman or take her out of my house.' Upset and hurt at the underhand way he had gone about things Catherine's anger got the better of her and as she spoke her voice rose. 'How could you have done this? The first of my children to marry and you deny me the pleasure of being at your wedding. You could at least have told me what you were going to do. I am your mother, not your jailer.' She put her hands up to cover her face, swallowed and choked back the emotions that threatened to erupt in tears. She stood up and Norrie put a protective arm round her shoulders. 'Have you any idea what you've done?' she went on. 'Where are you going to live?' She was on the verge of shouting now. 'There's not enough room here. And what are Melody's parents going to say? Do they know?'

'Not yet.'

'Well *they* won't be pleased that their precious daughter has married an . . . *island boy*. So I hope you're ready for the fall out.'

'What do you mean . . . island boy?'

'Melody's mother was very pleased to tell me that that one . . .' Catherine pointed her finger at the girl, 'would stand to inherit – well, we don't know quite what – but that she would be a very good catch for an *island boy*. Lovely choice of words isn't it?'

Robbie looked down at Melody. 'Did you know about this?'

'I don't take any notice of what my mother says. It's my life and I'll do as I like.'

Yes, thought Catherine, and everyone else has to suffer the consequences.

'How could you do this to your mother, Robbie?' said Norrie. 'Surely you realize that you're very special to her, you could have told her what you were planning to do.'

'She would have stopped him,' said Melody.

Robbie looked at her. 'No, Melody, I make my own decisions and when they're made and I'm set on them no one can make me change my mind. I was wrong. I *should* have talked to her.' He looked at his mother. 'I'm sorry, Mam. But I'd made up my mind and you wouldn't have changed it.'

'You don't have to worry about where we're going to live. We're not staying here. I hate this place, it's a dump.' There was a triumphant smile on Melody's face as she said, 'We've got a flat in Aberdeen.'

'No,' cried Catherine, 'Robbie, tell me that's not true.'

'Yes, it is,' he said. 'That's why we needed to go for the weekend. I'm going to work on an oil rig.'

'No, nooo.' Catherine put a hand to her mouth as the tears began to run down her face. 'Oh, Robbie.'

'See what you've done now?' said Norrie as he gathered his weeping wife into his arms. 'Did you have to break your mother's heart? Get out of the house and take that one with you.'

Ten

'THERE WAS NO need to talk to my mother like that,' said Robbie. He and Melody were on their way to her parents'. 'Don't let me hear anything like that again.'

In a sad, little girl voice, Melody said, 'But you know if you'd told her we were getting married she would have tried to stop us.'

'She probably would have, but it would have been better to have her on our side than against us. I'm wondering what your mother's going to say.'

'She'll read the riot act, but who cares? Stupid cow.' The girl's whine had changed to belligerence. 'She and Dad have had their turn; it's mine now and I'm going to make the most of it.'

'Wait.' Robbie stopped walking and Melody, a few paces ahead, stopped to look at him. 'Come here.'

'What is it now?'

'What's got into you? I've never heard you talk like this before. Whatever you think of your parents you should not speak of them like that. Your mother thinks the world of you and it seems that she gives you everything you want.'

Robbie's new wife hung her head and twisted her fingers together, then, with an apology for a smile said, 'I'm sorry, Robbie. It must be the stress of the wedding, then getting the flat. Please forgive me.' Creeping up to him she twined her arms round his neck and kissed him gently, oh so gently, on the lips.

Despite his annoyance, Robbie looked down at her and thought how beautiful she was. How could he resist her? She had curled and coiled up her hair to frame her face. A tendril or two had been left loose to kiss her cheeks. He slid his arms round her and pulled her close. 'You know I do,' he whispered. 'When you look the way you do and do the things you do, I could forgive you anything. But we've got to tell your mother, so come on, but, and you'd better remember this, I'm not going to let you get away with everything; you're going to have to show a little more respect for your parents or you'll have me to deal with.'

'Oh all right, if you say so.'

Anneka Barrington greeted her daughter warmly. 'Did you have a lovely time, darling? What did you buy?'

'Oh, lots,' said Melody. 'Are you going to make us some coffee?'

'You *both* want coffee? Doesn't your young man have to go home?'

'Well . . .' Melody put her arm through Robbie's, 'he's not my young man any more . . . he's my husband.'

'Your . . . *husband*?' Anneka reached blindly for a chair. 'For God's sake, tell me you're joking.'

'No joke, Mother. We went to Aberdeen to get married.' The wail that Melody's mother set up was loud enough to be heard all through the valley and halfway to Lerwick. 'Oh, *do* shut up,' said Melody. 'Anyone would think I'd been *murdered* with the noise you're making.' But this made Anneka wail louder and, raising her hand, Melody slapped her mother's face . . . hard.

Tears filled Anneka's eyes. She put up a hand to cool the sting in her cheek.

'Melody,' shouted Robbie, 'you didn't have to do that.'

'Oh but I did,' said Melody. 'She'd have gone on and on. I've heard it before. She's queen of all the dramas.'

Robbie took his new wife by the arm. 'You'd better remember what I said to you. Apologize to your mother . . . now.'

'Don't be daft.'

'Do as I say.'

Melody hesitated, but when she felt the increasing pressure Robbie was putting on her arm, she did as she was told. 'I'm sorry, Mother,' she said.

'I forgive you, darling,' said Anneka.

'But you *were* making the most awful racket and I had to do something,' muttered Melody.

Robbie turned away from them and reached for the door handle, 'I think I'd better leave you to talk,' he said. 'I'll come back later.'

'Where do you think *you're* going?' spat Melody. 'You can't run away.'

'I'm not, but you've got a lot of explaining to do, which I think your mother needs to hear, and so does mine so I'm going to talk to her.' Robbie kissed his wife. 'We've given our parents a big shock, so be kind to your mam.'

Ignoring her mother, who had risen from her chair, Melody snapped, 'No, you stay here. Your place is with me, your lot can wait. I want you here.'

'I don't have to tell you that my mother was very upset, because you were there and added to it. Now I have to—'

'No.' Melody grabbed Robbie by the arm. 'Stay . . . here.'

Anneka Barrington picked up her phone and while Melody was busy telling Robbie he had no option other than to stay with her, made a call. She laid the phone back on its cradle, sniffed back her tears and said, 'Melody, listen to me.'

'What now? Are you going to read me the riot act or something, or are you going to call the police and have me clapped in goal?'

'No, I've called your father. He's on his way home.'

Melody threw her hands in the air. 'Oh, that's all we need. And what's he going to do? He can't undo what's done.'

Anneka Barrington pulled a handkerchief from her pocket and blew her nose. Then she said, 'I would like to think he could knock some sense into your silly head.' She looked at Robbie. 'Not just you, Melody, but the pair of you.'

'Mother,' said Melody, 'you're pathetic. Come on, Robbie, I'm starving. Let's see what's in the fridge.'

Catherine had been about to make tea but Norrie said, 'I need something with a bit more kick in it than that.' He went to the cupboard and took out the whisky bottle. 'You'll join me in a dram now, won't you?'

'I won't refuse,' said Catherine. The first slug Norrie poured out she drank quickly. Now she sat with a refilled glass in her hand. 'Well, I don't know what you think, Norrie, but I wasn't expecting that.'

'I know Robbie's not my son,' said Norrie, 'but he's as good as and all I feel like doing at the moment is wringing the stupid idiot's neck. Not that it would do any good, but it would make me feel better. Are you going to drink that?' He pointed at the glass of whisky she was nursing.

'Not yet. I can't understand why Robbie planned all that without telling me.'

'It would be Melody who would have made him keep it secret. She'd have been afraid you would tell her mother.'

'Tell her mother? Ha! I'd have brought the roof down on their heads before I'd have done that.' Catherine laughed out loud. 'I wonder what Anneka Barrington's making of it? I was angry, *still* am, but she took such pains to tell me that Robbie was "not right" for her innocent little girl. Not so innocent now, is she? And if I know anything about it, that girl never was.'

'How do you think her father's going to react?'

'No idea. I've hardly spoken to him. I daresay we'll find out soon enough.'

'I could do with something to eat,' said Norrie. 'Is there any cake?'

'You want cake? Why don't we have our dinner? It's near enough that time. What would you like, soup and a sandwich?'

'That'll do.'

They got the soup, but the sandwich had to wait, for Anneka Barrington and her husband, Tom, were knocking on the door.

'I told you, didn't I? I told you he wasn't right for her; now look what's happened,' blustered Anneka. 'We have to put a stop to it. I won't have my daughter married to a . . . a. . . .' She stopped and her eyes switched from Catherine to her husband.

'Yes?' said Catherine, 'what were you going to say – an island boy, a peasant?'

'Certainly not, Mrs Williams,' said Tom Barrington. 'She wouldn't dare. She married one. Not an island boy, I admit, but a peasant, certainly. I come from farming stock.' Then he laughed a rich, rounded, belly laugh. 'I'm sure there's nothing wrong with your boy. They're just silly idiots. Melody thinks she's an adult, let her find out what being an adult's really like.'

'Oh Tom, how can you say that?' cried Anneka. 'Melody has to go back to university; she has to continue her studies.'

'Well I'm not going to pay for it if she does,' said Tom. 'She's a married woman now, not my responsibility.'

'But you're her father and you said you would back me up,' wailed Anneka.

'Yes, I did, but I didn't say I was going to agree with everything you said.'

A grin that started with a tweak at the corner of his mouth crept slowly across Norrie's face and culminated in a laugh to match Tom Barrington's. He slapped his chest and said, 'I like it. You're dead right.'

'Oh, but *Norrie*,' said Catherine. 'Fools they might be and like it or not, we have to accept what's happened, but we *ought* to be able to help them. They should be living somewhere near and they *won't*, they'll be too far away.'

'What do you mean, too far away?' demanded Anneka.

'Oh, haven't they told you? They've got a flat in Aberdeen and Robbie's going to work on an oil rig.'

Anneka waved her hands in the air and cried, 'Oh, my baby, my baby. She'll be left on her own for weeks at a time. The men on the rigs work shifts, don't they? Tom, we have to stop her. We can't let her go to that wicked town. She'll be raped or murdered or something.'

Tom took his wife by the shoulders, steered her towards a chair and sat her down. 'Shut up, Ann,' he said. Anneka promptly burst into tears. Above the noise Tom turned his attention to Catherine and Norrie. 'I don't know what you make of this,' he said. 'Melody's always been headstrong. Her mother gives in to her, you see, and I'm away too much to have any influence. What do you think about it?'

'I could have wished they'd talked to us about it,' said Catherine. 'At least we could have pointed out the problems and tried to make them wait a bit longer, but it's too late now.'

'I doubt very much if Melody will stay the course,' said the girl's father. 'But on the other hand if your boy is strong enough it could be the making of her.'

'It might be the making of both of them,' said Norrie.

Anneka's fit of crying had subsided into a series of sniffs and nose blowing. 'I'd like to go home, Tom,' she said.

'All right, I suppose we'd better. We've got to see what the two love birds are up to before they flit off somewhere else.'

'You'll let us know, won't you?' said Catherine.

'I'll make them tell you themselves,' said Tom. 'Sorry we had to meet under such difficult circumstances, but nice to know you anyway.'

When Tom Barrington had taken his wife's arm and led her away Norrie said, 'Can I have that sandwich now?'

Eleven

THERE WAS AN empty place at the breakfast table, a bed not slept in and one less man to send off to work. Catherine had always known that her children would leave home one day, but that day should have been joyful and she should be happy. She feared that no good would come of Robbie's partnership with Melody; with a spoiled child for a wife, how could there be?

She made beds, cleaned rooms, loaded the washing machine and switched it on. When she had done her work in the house she put on a jacket and went out to walk round her flock. There was nothing better than being out in the fresh air, and no better way to get out of the house than to use the sheep as an excuse. Sheep, in her opinion, were not particularly well endowed with intelligence and they sometimes did some very stupid things, which was why she kept a watchful eye on them. But all was well and at home again she boiled the kettle and made herself some coffee. She carried it through to the living room and sat down at the table.

The rain of the last couple of days had cleared away and the day was fine. The door to her house stood open and from outside came the busy twittering of sparrows searching for the last of the crumbs she had thrown out for them. As she drank her coffee her mind went again to Robbie. She had begun to think that he was destined to become a lifelong bachelor. Girls never seemed to interest him, and she had accepted the fact that one day he would achieve his ambition to have his own fishing boat, and from then on would love only the sea. So why on earth did he lose his senses over Melody? The girl would not be satisfied with life as the wife of a fisherman. And Robbie would want to go back to it, she was sure, for hadn't he said that he was saving up to buy a boat? Coffee going cold in the cup Catherine stared out of her window. Conscious of a warm weight being placed on her thigh, she looked down into the eyes of her dog; she put out a hand and stroked his silky head. 'It's all right, boy,' she said. 'I'm okay.' She got up, took her cup to the kitchen, rinsed it and turned it up to dry, then, as she turned to go she said, 'Come on, Moss, I have to hoe the neeps. You can come and watch.'

She stood on her doorstep and turned her head to look towards the bay. The wind was southerly and carried the smell of the sea. She looked out beyond the headlands at the mass of water that was never still, at the water that had reached up and taken Robbie's father and drowned him so that he could never come back to her. She tried so hard to persuade young Robbie not to become a fisherman and had only partly succeeded. Would Melody do better or would she drive him to it?

She turned her attention to the hill. It was the place she went in troubled times, the place that enveloped her in its timeless serenity, shrank her worries to manageable proportions and restored her sense of peace. It was what she needed right now, for troubled times had come upon her again. There was no one at home to make demands on her, the Barrington house appeared shuttered and barred, and goodness only knew where Robbie and Melody were. Catherine put her hoe back in the barn then pulled the door of her house to and closed it.

Time had dealt kindly with Catherine. Her hair was still a mass of short dark curls, her complexion fresh and unlined, her figure, though perhaps fuller, was still trim. Life, she thought, after all she'd been through, was still good and to be savoured, even though it had a sour taste at the moment. She was now in her mid-fifties and as she climbed the hill she moved slower, took her time and stopped now and then to look back. Deepdale was still mostly out of sight but as she climbed higher she could see the township of Broonieswick and how its boundaries had spread. New houses had been built and more were going up, many of them of the new timber construction and all painted in different colours. How would they stand up to the extremes of weather that Shetland was liable to throw at them? How long would they last? Probably not as long as the squat croft houses with their three foot thick walls.

She was on the moor and glad she had picked up her staff from where she had laid it by her door. Skuas and terns were nesting and the great skua, a skilful flyer, would think nothing of attacking an intruder. Catherine held her staff above her head as she walked, if she didn't there would be a rush of wings and possibly the dig of talons. There were other birds that would attack and from which she had to defend herself. Little black-headed terns screamed their defiance, their graceful bodies at odds with their aggression. Catherine chose a path well away from their nesting sites.

Not all of the birds that nested on the moor were aggressive. The little plover, a tiny handful of a bird, ran before her, leading her away from his nest. The lapwing, or peewit, with its long legs and crested head was a handsome bird on the ground, but when it flew it became a blunt-winged fool, and tumbled and fell through the air as though out of control. Then there were the skylarks, and these were Catherine's favourites. They would rise up out of the heather almost at her feet and climb the sky in a series of runs; up a bit then pause, up again, and again, until all that was to be seen was a dark spot up there in the blue, singing all the way up and all the way down. When it touched down it ran through heather and grass to where its nest was hidden. Catherine had previously searched hoping to find one, but had had no success.

She was walking through the peat banks now, past the ranks of peat slabs stacked in pyramids to dry. She looked at the bank that belonged to her and Norrie, thought that maybe while she was here she ought to turn the peats and then decided not to; this was her time and not for work. She wanted to sit down and looked around for a dry patch. A wooden pallet lay by a peat bank. It was just what she wanted, for though the ground was not visibly wet a warm body would draw moisture up from it. The pallet might not be a soft seat, but at least it would be dry.

Sitting down she stretched out her legs, clasped her hands in her lap and gazed at the ocean. Shining on the water the sun sent sharp needle points of light flashing from the tops of waves as they rose and broke. Semaphore, thought Catherine, but what was the message and who was it for? Far away in the distance a fishing boat rode the waves, rose, fell, and rose again. It was so far off that it appeared very small, but small or big, the ocean was far bigger, and every vessel that sailed on it was minute when compared to it. How she hated it when gale force winds whipped the sea into a fury, how she prayed for the fishermen whose living depended on it. Not far away from her now, waves were breaking at the foot of the cliffs; a rumble, a pause before they broke, and then a hiss as they exploded into a shower of spray. Above her head skylarks sang and the wind tempered its strength to breathe on her face and play with her hair.

Gradually she relaxed and let the slow and steady beat of the moor's heart calm the restlessness of her own. Nothing changes here, she thought, even though everything else does. Even though winter makes this a desolate place, when spring comes again it makes wild flowers push up through the tangle of heather and dead grass bloom again, birds come back to mate, nest and rear their young, rabbits breed, like rabbits do, and life go on the same as it had through centuries. The things men do to each other, declare war, fight, set off explosions and take life, meant nothing here. She smiled as a butterfly drifted down to settle on the edge of the pallet. For a moment or two it stayed to flex its wings as if asking her to admire them. It didn't stay long, but lifted up and floated away on the breeze.

The way of life here on the moor seemed to be so simple, but of course it wasn't. There was rivalry between the birds, gulls that came to steal eggs and even chicks, and men who came with guns to shoot the rabbits. Life for the inhabitants of the moor was just as fraught with trouble as hers. So why am I worrying about Robbie? she thought. He's chosen his path, and whether it's right or wrong only he can walk it. I can do nothing but be there for him if he needs me.

Once again the peace that she sought and always found on the hill had put her worries into perspective. Feeling refreshed, she stood up, and started on her way home. As she crossed the main road and began the descent into Deepdale there was still no sign of life around the houses other than the hens, but there was a car parked outside her house and she knew that Peter was home.

'I've just made some tea, Mam. I'll pour one for you.' He poured tea and brought her a little cake on a plate. 'What an unsociable way it was that Robbie chose to go and get married. I bet it wasn't his idea. I tell you, Mam, that piece of stuff he's landed himself with—'

'Don't say any more, Peter. He'll find out what he's done soon enough.'

'Well, I'll tell you now, *I'm* not going to have a wedding like that. Um . . . Mam, I've been thinking . . . your little house . . . it's empty. Can I have it?'

'You want to buy it?'

'No, I just want to live in it, well, me and Rosie.'

'Oh, you do, do you? Tell me more.'

Twelve

'WHAT'S THE MATTER with you, boy?' said Catherine when Peter looked down at his hands and started to pick at his finger-nails. 'Why do I have the feeling that there's a confession coming on?'

'Oh, Mam, I don't know how to say this.' Peter chewed his top lip. 'Rosie's expecting. We want to get married and we'll need some-where to live. They don't have enough room for us at her mother's and even if they had, we'd rather have a place of our own, but you know what it's like now with all yon soothmoothers coming in, there's nowhere.'

Catherine looked at him and didn't answer. She put down her tea cup. 'I don't know,' she muttered, then spat, 'First Robbie and now *you*. What's the matter with you? Have you no more respect for your girl than to do that to her?'

'Mam, everybody sleeps together these days.'

'More's the pity, because look what happens – illegitimate chil-dren. I thought you had better sense.' Catherine sighed. 'How far gone is she?'

'She's just missed a couple of . . . um . . . you know.'

Poor Rosie, thought Catherine. Yes, I know only too well how she feels, but she's luckier than I was; her seducer is able to marry her. 'Has she been to the doctor?' she said. 'Is she certain that she's pregnant?'

'Can't do that, Mam, her cousin works at the surgery. Everybody would know, and what they didn't know they'd invent.'

'Well, there are such things as pregnancy test kits; she could get one from the chemist,' said Catherine. Peter sat, shaking his head.

'What is it now?'

'Her auntie works there.'

'Damn and blast this place,' said Catherine as she sprang up from her chair. 'You can't say or do a thing without the whole island knowing. What about her parents, have you told them?'

'Rosie hasn't said anything, so no, not unless they've guessed.'

Catherine reached for the teapot, decided that what it contained was hot enough to drink, so put milk into her cup and filled it. Peter watched and waited for his mother to speak.

'Well,' she said at last, 'you might have jumped the gun and I could wish you hadn't, but Rosie's a nice girl. You'd better bring her out to see us and we'll discuss what's to be done.'

'So can we have the house then?'

'I don't see why not. But you're going to have to tell her parents about her condition first, you can't let them find out from someone else. And when you've done that I guess we'd better see about getting you married.'

'We don't want a big fuss.'

Catherine laughed. 'Ha, that's what I said when I married your father. So do you know what happened? Everybody clubbed together, even my mother and father were involved. They put on a great feast and a dance and they kept it so quiet I didn't suspect a thing.' A happy smile lit Catherine's face and for a while she was lost in her memories. But then she turned to her son. 'Nobody has a quiet wedding in Shetland. You've been to enough to know that, and this one won't be.'

'I thought you'd be really mad at me. I know you like Rosie but—'

'Peter – it's done and can't be undone – get on with it.'

'I wonder what Robbie's wedding was like?' said Peter.

'Half an hour in a registry office in front of strangers, I would think, when it could have been here with all his family and friends. What a fool he was.'

'He never seemed to have any interest in girls so what did that one do to him?' said Peter. 'She must have trapped him somehow. You'd think he was old enough to know better.'

'That's as may be,' said Catherine. 'Now, while I start to get something ready for tea would you fill up my peat bucket? It may be July but it's none too warm and I do like a fire to sit by in the evenings.'

Peat bucket filled and fire made up, Catherine was in the kitchen peeling potatoes while Peter had gone to shower and change, when Robbie walked in.

'Why aren't you at work?' said his mother.

'I don't work at Sullom anymore. I gave in my notice ages ago.'

'So what are you going to do now? Why are you here and what have you done with Melody?'

'She's gone to see her mother and to pack some of the gear she wants. I'd just like to collect some of my things and then we're away on tonight's boat.'

For a moment or two Catherine, potato in one hand, knife in the other, stared at her son, then, throwing potato and knife back in the bowl she dried her hands and said, 'Come and sit down, you've got some explaining to do.'

'Now, Robbie,' she said when he was sitting opposite her. 'I want to know what possessed you to rush into getting married and to throw away all your dreams of owning a boat. Start talking.'

'What do you want me to say?'

'It would be nice if you could tell me why you couldn't see fit to talk to me. I tried, didn't I; to get you to do anything but go to sea, but you had your mind set on it. You let nothing get in your way, you never played football, you never went dancing, you never had a girlfriend and all you ever thought about was saving enough money to buy a boat. And *now* look what you've done.'

'But, Mam . . .' interrupted Robbie. It did no good, for Catherine went on.

'Now you've got the expense of running a house, providing for your wife as well as yourself and possibly, in the not too distant future, children. You've blown it, haven't you? I want to know what made you sneak away to get married. It was such an underhand thing to do and so unlike you. Couldn't you have told me what you were planning? Couldn't you have let me help? Surely you could not have thought I would not want to be there to see my son get married? Am I an ogre? Did you think I would forbid you?'

Robbie hung his head. 'I'm sorry, Mam. I knew you didn't like Melody, neither did the boys or Da, and I thought you'd make me wait. But I couldn't, because I loved her from the first time I saw her and I had to make her mine.'

'But you could have told us that,' said Catherine. 'And you could have had a proper wedding here, something to remember, a good send off. We might not have thought you'd made a good choice, but if it was what you wanted we would have been happy for you. It's too late now, though.'

Catherine stood up and walked across to the window. She stood there looking out and for a while neither she nor Robbie spoke. Then she said, 'Are you really going to work on the rigs? I wish you wouldn't.'

'Yes, I am. I know you think I've given up on the idea of a boat, but I haven't. I can earn good money on the rig and it's not the same as being at sea on a fishing boat, and I know you don't like that. The rigs are huge and they fly us out to them so I won't actually be on the sea at all.'

'And does Melody know you want to own a boat and fish for a living?'

'No, I haven't told her.'

'I think you ought to. It's not a good idea to start married life with secrets. What's she going to do while you're away on shift? Two weeks is a long time for a young woman to be alone. Is she going to get a job?'

'I don't know. Anyway when I come off shift I'll be home for two weeks so it hardly seems worthwhile. Look, I'm sorry I've upset everybody, but it had to be done. Melody's mother would have locked her in her room if *she'd* known.'

'Ah,' said Catherine. 'Anneka Barrington is endowed with some sense after all, and now I understand that it was Melody who made you keep it all secret. I might have guessed.'

Robbie turned his head away and would not look his mother in the eye. 'Um . . . it was me as well,' he said. 'I was afraid there would have been an almighty row if I'd told you, especially knowing what the twins thought of Melody, and I just couldn't face that.'

'If you say so, Robbie, but it's all over and done with so we'd best forget about it. Now, if you've got a boat to catch, hadn't you better go and get the things you want?'

'Yes . . . Mam?'

'Just go, there's no need to say anything else,' said Catherine. She turned her head to watch him as he left the room, heard him run up the stairs, the murmur of his voice as he spoke to Peter and the sounds of their movements, their conversation. And she knew that it would be a long time before he would be in her house again. Then there they both were, Robbie with a suitcase in his hand, and Peter, his hair still damp from the shower, smelling of aftershave.

'You will be back to see us from time to time, won't you, Rob?' said Peter.

'Of course I will.'

'And you'll let us know how you get on, I mean on the rig, won't you?'

'Why, are you thinking you might like to join me?'

'No way, well, at least not until they grow grass and keep sheep there. I've got to go to work so I'm off, take care, Rob. I'll see you later, Mam.' And Peter was gone.

'My dear boy,' said Catherine as she held out her arms to Robbie. 'Come and give your old lady a hug.' Robbie put down his case and hugged her. He was tall and Catherine buried her face in his chest. There was a catch in her voice as she said. 'I shall miss you. Take care of yourself.' Swallowing back tears she smiled as she looked up at him. 'Keep in touch, phone me. Promise me you will.'

'I will, Mam, every week.' He put a kiss upon her cheek, picked up his case, went to the door and opened it. Catherine followed and watched as he put the case in the car.

'Don't forget that I'll always be here if you need me,' she said. She watched as he turned the car to drive away, but didn't stay to watch him pick up Melody. Instead she turned, went inside, sat down again and promptly burst into tears. Her family was unravelling and she was powerless to stop it.

Thirteen

WHEN TOM BARRINGTON rattled on the door, opened it, and, with a six-pack of beer in his hand, asked if he could come in, Norrie laughed and said of course he could.

'Ann's gone down to Aberdeen,' said Tom, 'and drinking on your own is no fun. In fact it can lead to some very bad habits.' He pulled a can out of the pack and handed it to Norrie. 'You'll have a beer with me, won't you?'

'I will,' said Norrie.

'And what about you, Mrs Williams, are you going to join us?'

'We've not long had our tea.'

'That's all the better,' said Tom, 'you won't be drinking on an empty stomach.' He smiled at her. 'Will you have one, then?'

'Why not,' said Catherine, 'but I'll have mine in a glass.'

'You've not heard from the children, have you?' asked Tom as Catherine poured the contents of her can of beer into a glass. 'We've heard nothing.'

'Robbie rang to say they were settled in, but that was all,' said Catherine. 'Has Anneka gone down to see them?'

'That's what she said she was going for, but I think it was an excuse. Why do women have to shop all the time? They call it retail therapy, and say it's good for them, but it's just another way to spend money. Ann's got a wardrobe full of clothes already, but I guarantee she'll come back with a lot more.'

'She told me that you're expected to entertain other pilots and their wives, as well as visiting officials so I suppose she does need the right clothes for that.'

'Only because the other women make catty remarks if she wears the same thing twice. I have to hear all about it after they've gone home. You'll excuse my language, Mrs Williams, but they're a lot of bitches. Not like you, you don't strike me as that sort.'

'I wouldn't want to be thought a bitch,' said Catherine, 'but I know what you mean, I've met people like that. And my name is Catherine.'

'All right – Catherine,' said Tom. He laughed as he said her name with the long West Country a – Caaa-therine. 'No, you're not a bitch, far from it.'

'We have to keep our women happy, Tom,' said Norrie, 'and as long as retail therapy, or whatever they call it, keeps them that way, does it matter?'

'Ah, but that's the problem. Keeping them happy takes a lot of doing. Ann's certainly not very happy at the moment. She can't get used to the isolation here. She was born and bred in a town and wants pavements and shops, big department stores, cinemas and theatres, you know, that sort of rubbish, and she ain't going to get that here, so I'm afraid we may be leaving you before too long.' Tom leaned back in his chair and stretched his long legs out in front of him. 'Shan't be going too far, though, I've put our name down for a house near the airport.'

'What made you come here, then, if that's what she wants?' asked Norrie.

'When you land a good job with good money and concession-ary flights to anywhere in the world, what more can you ask? One thing's for sure, you don't turn it down. Surely that's worth putting up with a few disadvantages, isn't it? I thought it might make her appreciate what she's had and what she'll get again when we leave, because this oil boom won't go on forever.'

'You're right there,' said Norrie. 'I don't see how it can last. When they've got the terminal up and running and the oil flowing they'll be cutting the workforce. All the construction workers will leave and go to some other place.'

'Even the airport will suffer,' said Tom, 'because there won't be anything like as many people flying in and out. Eventually, even people like me will have to leave. But I hope that won't be for some time because I like it here.'

'Why's that?' asked Norrie, 'I went south during the war and I know that things there are far in advance of what they are here. You probably think we're very backward and behind the times. Doesn't that get to you?'

Tom threw back his head and laughed. 'You have to work with what you've got, Norrie. I hate town; I grew up on a farm. Father had seven hundred acres of the chalk downs in Wiltshire. The place was a bit bigger than yours. We grew corn mostly and ran sheep and some beef. There were big skies and wide horizons, the same as here. I loved it and I love it here. There's that same sense of peace. You're away from the rat race, because that's what it is in the city, everyone's trying to go one better than their neighbour and nobody's happy.'

'So what made you give up working on the farm and become a pilot?'

'I had to do something,' said Tom. 'My older brother was next in line to take on the farm from Father. Farm machinery got bigger and one man could do what two did before; my position was looking shaky and I was about to be made redundant. We were close to a small airport and I used to see the Cessnas and Pipers flying over. I got the itch to get up there too, so I trained for my pilot's licence. Little planes were fun, but I wanted something else, and I thought I'd try choppers. As soon as I got into a helicopter I knew that was it.'

The men sat either side of the fire. Tom, sitting back in his chair, looked relaxed and at home. Norrie obviously liked him, for as Tom talked about his life, he smiled and nodded and paid close attention to what was being said. Catherine, sitting a little apart from them, drank her beer and listened to their conversation. Tom was not a snob, so how was it that he had a daughter like Melody?

'I can't imagine what it must be like to farm the sort of acreage you mention,' Norrie was saying. 'I take it you didn't have any close neighbours.'

'No,' said Tom. 'The nearest were a couple of miles away.'

'It must be hard on the women,' said Catherine. 'Isn't it lonely for them?'

'It's not the sort of life for a city girl; well you must know that, I believe you came here from a city. With your men at work all day you must spend a lot of time on your own, so it must be the same for you. '

Catherine smiled. 'I *was* a city girl as you say, but when I came to

Shetland I got hooked on sheep. I inherited a flock so I learned how to look after them and I never looked back. I've been here more than thirty years now and I wouldn't want to live anywhere else. But you say you might be moving?'

'Yes, Ann's not a country girl. I was hoping she'd settle down, but it's not going to happen, I'm afraid.' Catherine smiled. Tom called his wife 'Ann,' where was the posh 'Anneka'? 'She wants to go to Aberdeen, but I won't let her,' went on Tom. 'She'd only interfere with the kids, and they have to sort out their own mess.'

Norrie laughed. 'You're absolutely right, Tom.'

It wasn't long before talk between the two men went back to the pros and cons of farming in such diverse situations as the rolling chalk hills of Wiltshire and the unforgiving terrain of Shetland. Tom found it hard to understand what drove men to think they could wrest a living from such poor land as appeared to cover most of Shetland, what it was that kept them battling on. Didn't they know that as soon as they laid aside their tools nature would come creeping back to reclaim the territory they had won? Of course they did, so what held them?

And then Norrie said that he'd be bored out of his skull if he had to sit on a tractor and work alone, all day and every day, criss-crossing, what was it, twenty-, thirty-acre fields? Shetland may look like a barren place, but that was far from what it was. Though wildlife might be restricted to rabbits, hares, polecats, stoats and hedgehogs, said Norrie, the fields and ditches overflowed with wild flowers. Then there were the migrating birds that passed through in spring and autumn bringing birdwatchers from great distances. Not only that, the pattern of croft life through the year meant that there was no time to sit and dream or to be bored. Summer, wet or fine, with its many hours of daylight, was the time to do all the jobs that could not be left to the dark days of winter. Winter was the time to socialize, to catch up with friends. It was also the time to take down the fiddle and play. Norrie looked at Tom and smiled when he finished speaking. 'Does that answer your question?' he said.

'I have to admit, when you put it like that, there's more to Shetland than meets the eye,' said Tom.

'And then of course, when you go into the history of the islands . . .' said Catherine as she set some bannocks and a plate with slices of cold meat on the table.

Tom held up his hands. 'Enough, enough,' he said. 'Please let me take it in one step at a time.'

'Come and help yourself to some food then,' said Catherine.

Fourteen

Try as she might, Catherine could not get Robbie and Melody out of her mind. True to his word Robbie phoned every week, but she always had the feeling that he wasn't telling her everything. Yes, he had got a job on one of the oil rigs and the money was good. She didn't have to worry that he'd be anywhere near a boat because he and the other men on his shift were flown out to the rig in a chopper. He didn't know if he would be able to come home for Peter's wedding but he would let her know. No, Melody wasn't working yet, but she was looking for a job, and, yes, Melody's mother had been to see them, but she and Melody didn't get on so she wasn't staying. With variations, that was the gist of his conversation week after week. He isn't going to tell me if things aren't going well, thought Catherine. Tom Barrington was right, Robbie and Melody would have to sort out their own mess and, with that, she did her best to push thoughts of her errant son to the back of her mind.

Uppermost now was Peter's wedding, and that would surely not be a quiet affair, but as most of the preparation would be undertaken by Rosie's parents, Myleen and John Inkster, there would be little for Catherine to do. The Inksters were crofters and Rosie, their eldest child, had dogged her father's footsteps from an early age and, from a stream of constant questions, had learned all she could about running a croft. Her father often boasted that her stockman's eye was better than many a man twice her age. Any suggestion that Rosie was in any way more butch than a girl should be, was belied by the fact that behind it all was a softly spoken young woman, not given to hysterics or outbursts of rage, quite the opposite, in fact.

Rosie Inkster was serene and loving, competent and capable, and the ideal wife for Peter.

Catherine had gone to her old house, opened windows, swept and dusted and looked it over to see if anything needed to be repaired. The original stove, its name, Modern Mistress, now far from apt, was still there. It was the one she had lost her temper with so many times and shed tears over until she had learned how to control it. She would ask Norrie if they couldn't have an electric cooker put in. Rosie deserved better.

In the weeks running up to the wedding, she and Rosie went shopping. They bought material for curtains, which Rosie made up using Catherine's sewing machine. Catherine bought rugs for the bedroom and living room. Furniture was delivered and it was agreed that it would be better to wait to see what was given for wedding presents before they bought anything more.

'Make a list,' said Catherine, 'and let me know if there's anything else you want that I can get for you.'

'Haven't you done enough already?' said Rosie.

'My dear, I'm happy to help. Your mam and da are going to bear the brunt of the cost for your wedding, so I'm happy to help here.'

'Fine that,' said Rosie. 'Now I'd better go or I'll miss the bus.'

When Rosie had gone Catherine walked along to the house again. Rosie had said the stove would do for now. Catherine had lit it that morning to keep the house aired and it was still warm. The new furniture, curtains and rugs, filled the place with a different smell. It was not a lived-in smell, not of cooking, people or a dog, but the aroma of a showroom and newness. That would change, though, for soon there would be people and later on, a baby, talcum powder and nappies, and all the other smells that went with life and the living of it. There would surely be a dog here, if not two, for Peter loved them.

It should be Robbie, the eldest of her children, starting his married life here, not Peter, the youngest. Why did he have to fall in love with Melody? He should have chosen someone who would know what it would be like to be married to a fisherman, for one way or another Robbie would find his way back to the fishing fleet. My God, I'm turning into Jannie, the disapproving mother-in-law, I'll have to watch that, thought Catherine. Of one thing she was sure, though, and that was that Peter had chosen wisely. When it came to Karen, Allen's girlfriend, she was not so sure. Allen had trained as an accountant, Karen was a bookkeeper, and they had much in common; but Karen's family were business people and the girl carried an air of superiority about her. But perhaps that was imagination, thought Catherine, perhaps she had spent so long messing about with sheep and working with the land that she had developed an inferiority complex. When it came to Judith there was no telling what sort of man she would choose. But this was not the time to start worrying about it, and, with a last look round, Catherine went home.

Much to her surprise, Robbie did come to Peter's wedding. As luck would have it he was off shift. 'The best part of it is being here with you,' said Robbie when she met him at the airport.

'All my family will be together,' she said. 'What more could I want?'

She didn't ask him why Melody wasn't with him and Robbie didn't offer an explanation as to why she was not. Melody was a subject best left alone. When Peter saw Robbie his first words were to ask him to be his best man. Robbie protested that he'd surely already asked Allen. 'He's your twin, I can't take his place,' he said.

'Allen won't mind,' said Peter. 'I can see him any time, but you're away from us now.' And it was settled.

Flowers decorated the church and brought a splash of colour to its grey interior. Catherine, hands in her lap, fingers laced, sat beside Norrie. Judith, Allen and Karen were in the pew behind her. The shuffle of feet and sibilant conversations filled the little church as guests took their places. Catherine looked at Peter, sitting in front of her, at his broad shoulders and at the way the tuft of hair on the crown of his head still defied all attempts to tame it and make it lie flat. She looked at Robbie, at his dark head, and caught her breath when he turned to speak to his brother and she saw in him the mirrored likeness to his dead father.

Norrie turned to her, reached out and covered her hands with his. 'Are you all right?' he asked.

She smiled. 'Yes. It was just a memory that grabbed me.'

The organ, which was being played softly in the background, suddenly sprang to life to fill the church with the chords of the *Wedding March* and the vicar, his white surplice billowing out around him, walked down the aisle towards the entrance. The congregation got to their feet and turned to watch as he returned with Rosie, beautiful in a white dress, on the arm of her father. Slowly they proceeded up the aisle to where Peter stood waiting for her. When they met it was plain for all to see that this was a marriage that would be founded on love.

Catherine took a handkerchief out of her handbag and blew her nose. People often cried at weddings but she would not, though what else was she expected to do? Vaguely she became aware that the vicar was saying the words of greeting, but there was a dream-like quality about it, about everything, about the church, about the fact that she was standing there to witness her youngest child – born twenty minutes after Allen – get married. The dream went on. She stood or sat when required. She sang and made her responses. The service went on and before she knew it the vicar was declaring Peter and Rosie man and wife. The register was signed and then the pair with beaming faces were walking, hand in hand, down the aisle and outside to where a photographer was waiting.

With his hand on the small of her back as he walked with Catherine out of the church, Norrie said, 'You're not really with it, are you? Buck up, you'll have to go through it all again when Allen and Karen are ready to tie the knot.'

'Do you think it will get any easier to let them go?' she asked.

'That's up to you; you know you can't hang on to them.' They watched as Peter and Rosie posed for the photographer, and when they were called to join in a family group, Norrie, taking her arm, said, 'It's a happy occasion, don't forget to smile.' He grinned at her then slid his arm round her waist.

There was no 'make do' for this wedding, no joining together of resources or of neighbours providing this and that, as there had been when Catherine and Norrie married. Times had changed and this was a time of plenty. Rosie's wedding was an occasion to celebrate and her parents had surpassed themselves in providing the wherewithal for that. Norrie had been asked to bring his fiddle and join in with the band to play for the dancing. He had been delighted to do so. Catherine watched him when he played and saw the joy on his face as he tucked his beloved fiddle under his chin and drew the bow across the strings. Judith stepped up on to the stage and sang. Her voice was strong and true. Rosie, plump and pink-cheeked, showed no sign of being pregnant. Peter, much to his embarrassment, turned shy and was teased unmercifully. Robbie sat beside his mother to watch and listen as the hall filled with the whooping and hollering of dancers rendering a boisterous eight-some reel.

'I'm glad I came, Mam,' he said. 'It's been nice to be with the family. Not sure about Allen's girl, though. She seems a bit of a snob to me.'

'It takes all sorts, Robbie. What suits one doesn't suit another.'

'Is that a dig at me?'

'No, darlin', you made your choice and, for better or worse, we've all done that. Now, aren't you going to ask me to dance?'

The dancing went on well into the small hours and at last Norrie was there. He'd put down his fiddle and told the band he wanted to dance with his wife. 'Come now,' he said to her, 'it's time to dance with me,' and as he slid an arm round her waist said, 'Does du remember how we danced at our wedding?'

'Could I ever forget?'

The band was playing a waltz. Norrie bent his head close to hers and whispered in her ear, 'Du was the bonniest bride as I ever saw.'

'Norrie, you're an old fool.'

'I am no. When I saw you lying on the peat bank I knew I had to make you mine. Boy, did du make me wait?'

'That was a long time ago, Norrie.'

'Ay, but du was worth waiting for.'

Fifteen

BREAKFAST HAD BEEN eaten and plates cleared, dishes washed, beds made and the house tidied. Sheep had been inspected. The first round of jobs for the day over and done with, Catherine boiled the kettle and made coffee. While she sat to drink it she began to make out her shopping list. It would not be a long one. It was a wet day, not the best weather to go shopping; perhaps she should wait for a fine one, or she could phone Rose Sandison, and suggest that they meet in Lerwick for tea and a gossip. Yes, that would be nice.

She reached for the phone, but before she could pick it up there was a knock on the door. It opened and Anneka Barrington looked in. She held an umbrella. 'We're moving today,' she said. 'I'm expecting the men with the removal van to be here soon. What do you want me to do with the key?'

Tom Barrington had found them a house near the airport. 'Perhaps Ann will be happy if she's amongst her own kind,' he said when he came to tell Catherine they were leaving. 'I hope Shetland's not prone to power cuts; the house is all electric.' He laughed when he said that if the power went off perhaps she wouldn't be so fussy about a solid fuel fire in future.

'You are heartless,' said Catherine.

But Tom only laughed again. 'It's been really nice knowing you and your husband,' he said. 'I may drop by now and then, if you don't mind.'

Catherine hadn't seen him again since then and it was his wife who now stood on her doorstep. 'You've chosen a good day for moving,' she said.

'I know, isn't it awful,' said Anneka. 'I hope the men have

something to cover the furniture with. I wouldn't want it to be spoiled with the rain.'

'I'm sure they will, in fact they'd have to, wouldn't they? People move at any time of year. Did you see Melody when you went down to Aberdeen?'

'I did. And I have to apologize to you.'

'Whatever for?'

'I'm afraid I underestimated your son, I called him a. . . .'

When Anneka hesitated Catherine said, 'An island boy?'

'I should never have said that. He's a gentleman. He found a flat and furnished it and made a lovely home for my daughter. He made me most welcome, unlike Melody. I hope she realizes how lucky she is.'

'Thank you, Anneka. It's nice to hear you say that.'

The door stood open and from outside came the patter of rain on the flagstones and from farther off the sound of lazy waves dropping on the shore. There was another sound, that of a motor. It grew louder.

'I can hear the lorry coming,' said Anneka. 'What will I do with the key?'

'Just leave it in the door. I doubt if anyone is going to come and steal it. I'll pick it up later. Good luck; I hope you'll be happy in your new home.'

Barely a couple of minutes after Anneka Barrington had gone the door opened again and a postman, a young man and not Alec, came in.

'Where's Alec?' asked Catherine. 'He's not ill, is he?'

'Ill? That old man is so dried up that any germ that landed on him would die a death in a nanosecond. No, he's gone to a funeral.'

'I don't know what it is with you lot, you can't stay away from them, can you?'

The young man grinned at Catherine. 'You should know by now that we're all related, so we take time off work when there's a funeral because we all have to go. It would be disrespectful not to.'

'Yes, all right, I know. Anyway, what have you got for me?'

The young man riffled through a handful of letters. 'There's one from your mother, a couple of bills and – ooh – this one looks official.' He gave Catherine her letters, then, with a cheeky grin, said, 'I'll come to your funeral if you like. Just let me know when it's going to be.'

'Get away with you,' laughed Catherine. 'I'm not planning on popping my clogs just yet; you'll have a long wait.' She looked at the letters in her hand, at the spidery scrawl of her mother's handwriting in particular. How did that young man know who the letter was from? The postmark, of course, but then everyone knew everything about everybody else here, didn't they? The logos on two of the envelopes made it easy to guess that they probably held bills.

But the last one was different. The envelope was of good quality paper, was addressed to Mr & Mrs N. Williams and was office franked. Should she wait till Norrie was home before she opened it? No, it was addressed to them both. She slit the envelope open and pulled out the single sheet of paper it contained. It was the heading on that paper that made Catherine gasp. Across the head of the page in glossy green script was the name and address of a firm of land agents. Quickly she scanned the page: *Would Mr Norman Williams please get in touch with the Acorn Development Group at the above address when he may hear something to his advantage.* Whatever was that all about? Why would land agents be writing to them? She studied the paper the letter was written on. It was expensive and not the sort that someone might have used to write on for a joke. But surely someone was playing a trick on them so it was a good job it was July and not the first of April or she would have thrown the letter straight in the fire. As it was she put it back in its envelope and tucked it behind the clock. Norrie would know what to do with it.

It was still raining and as it showed no sign of letting up Catherine abandoned the thought of shopping. It could wait until tomorrow. A basketful of clean clothes was waiting to be ironed and there would surely be something amongst it that was short of a button or had a rip that needed to be repaired. Ironing was one of her favourite tasks. She loved the smell that rose up from freshly ironed cotton, loved the smooth action of the iron and the feel of the clothes as she folded them ready to put away.

When the ironing was done and a couple of shirt buttons replaced, she went into the kitchen and switched on the cooker. She made bannocks, then got out baking trays and tins and made cakes to replenish her store. That done, she put on a pot of stew to cook for the evening meal.

She was putting cutlery and condiments on the table when Allen came home. Norrie was working late and wouldn't be home for some time.

'Do you want your meal now or will you wait till your da comes home, Allen?' she asked.

'I'll wait. I want to have a shower first anyway.'

Catherine was reading the local paper when he came downstairs. 'Did you have a good day?' she asked.

'A good day will be when people learn to keep legible accounts and not hand me a box of invoices and bills and tell me to sort it all out.' It was said all in one breath. Allen breathed in again and went on, 'It's so easy to enter up once a week when it would only take a few minutes, but will they do that? No. They stuff everything in a box and then can't face it and I get landed with it.'

'And that's why you have a job that pays you good money,' said his mother. 'So don't knock it, boy.'

'What time do you think Da will be here?'

'He shouldn't be long now.'

'Good,' said Allen. 'Mam, have you got anyone lined up for Laura's house?'

'Not yet. Why do you ask?'

'I've asked Karen to marry me and I wondered if we could have it.'

Catherine put down the newspaper and looked at him. It wasn't long ago that she had been wondering which of her brood would be the first to leave home, and now they were behaving like fledglings leaving the nest. 'Is it catching,' she asked, 'this desire to be wed and away from home?'

'I've been thinking about it for some time.' He smiled at her. 'But with Robbie and Peter gone I thought it was time for me to go too. Surely it'll be nice for you and Da to have the place to yourselves, won't it?'

'Possibly. But the house will be empty without you all and I shall miss you. When do you think to have the wedding?'

'We thought September. And if Karen and I were in the valley it would be easier for me to go on helping Peter with the croft.'

'I know we call it Laura's, but it's Judith's really. You'll have to ask her.'

'That's if I can pin her down. I'll have to phone her, I suppose.'

'Not for a little while yet, but she does have to work.' Catherine got up from her chair and finished laying the table. 'She's been asked to sing at the opening of the new British Legion.'

'You will have to go to *that*, Mam.'

'Yes, she's made me promise I will but, oh dear, these special occasions are getting a bit much. I shall have to get a new outfit for your wedding; couldn't you have waited a year or two so I could wear the one I bought for Peter's?'

Allen laughed. 'Mam, you deserve as many new outfits as you like. You look lovely when you're dressed up. You're always working and all we ever see you in is an anorak and jeans.'

'Go away with you. I wouldn't know what to do with myself, I mean, wear a skirt in the day time? You must be joking. Anyway, I think I hear your father's car. Can you fetch me a bucket of peat while I put some dumplings in the stew? They'll be ready by the time you both are.'

Norrie had offered to have an electric fire put in to replace the old stove, but Catherine had refused. 'I'm not going to sit here and shiver if the electric goes off,' she said. So the stove stayed where it was and it was where the saucepan of stew was now happily burping and bubbling away. Catherine lifted the lid and dropped in a handful of dumplings.

Allen came back with the peat. 'Just going to the loo, Mam,' he said.

Catherine smiled as she heard him pounding up the stairs. Why did young people have to do everything at speed? Then she sighed. Soon it would only be the plod of hers or Norrie's feet she would hear.

Sixteen

CATHERINE LAY UNMOVING in the bed. She had been awake for some time. Her mind raced with thoughts of her children and their happiness, partners and new beginnings. What would it be like when they were all gone from home? If Allen and Peter realized their dream and went away to Scotland, how would she and Norrie cope? Robbie had already left the island and it wouldn't be long before Judith was gone too. Norrie was now in his mid-sixties and neither he nor she could stop the advancing years.

Jannie came to mind, the mother of her first husband and the woman who, with bitter words and actions, had done everything she could to undermine her. It was the evidence of the loss of a baby daughter that gave reason for Jannie's bitterness, which was then compounded when her son, in adult life, was taken from her too. That must have been the hardest blow and the knowledge of what Jannie had to bear had turned her forbearance for the old lady into sympathy. And then there was Daa, a kind man who had looked fondly on the girl from the city who had begged him to teach her how to run her croft. Catherine smiled remembering him, sighed to think of the way he had struggled to cope with Jannie's odd ways. Would she and Norrie finish up like that?

There was movement in the bed beside her. Norrie turned over then raised himself up to look at her. 'Are you awake?' he said. 'Would you like a cup of tea?'

'Does that mean you want me to make it?' asked Catherine.

'No, I will. No hurry to get up, I've got the day off and the boys are going to look round the flock.' With that Norrie threw back the bedclothes, sat up, pushed his feet into a pair of slippers and shuffled away down the stairs to the kitchen. Catherine heard the gurgle of water in the pipes as he filled the kettle, the clunk of the fridge door as he slammed it shut and the clink of china as he set mugs on a tray. A few minutes later she heard him climbing the stairs, and it *was* the plod of heavy, mature feet.

'What are you going to do today then?' she asked when she and Norrie were sitting up in bed drinking hot, sweet, tea.

'I thought we might take a run out in the car.'

'But it's raining.'

'It'll probably clear up by midday.'

'We'll go another time, perhaps. Why don't you take things easy for a change? Have a nice long hot bath and while you're at it, trim your beard; you're looking more like Father Christmas every day.'

'I can't help it if it grows and I can't do anything about it going white, that is, unless you want me to dye it.' He looked at her and from the twinkle in his eye she knew he meant mischief. 'Now what colour should it be? I fancy red. Would you like me in red, Catherine? Should it be a ginger red or the nice dark red of mahogany? Eh?'

'I know you're not going to dye it, Norrie Williams, but if you did I'd cut it all off while you slept. Just trim it, make it neat and tidy. I wouldn't want anyone to think I was married to a billy goat.'

'Getting fussy in your old age, aren't you?' laughed Norrie.

'Not so much of the old age,' quipped Catherine. 'You'll be drawing your pension before me.'

After a late breakfast, when Peter had gone home to Rosie, and Allen had laid claim to the bathroom, Catherine began to prepare the Sunday lunch. From time to time while she stood at the sink peeling potatoes she raised her head to look out of the window. Was it ever going to stop raining? There was very little wind and the rain kept falling, gently, but relentlessly, and she was glad she had persuaded Norrie not to go out.

His wet hair slicked back and smelling of aftershave, Allen emerged from the bathroom. He stood at the top of the stairs and shouted down to his mother. 'What time's dinner, Mam?'

'It'll be ready in about half an hour.'

When it was and they sat at the table, Catherine said, 'You cannot take Karen out in this weather. What are you going to do?'

'Mam, the whole afternoon will be taken up with talk about the wedding. Karen and her mam are as bad as one another. It's a good job I don't have to pay for it because the guest list is as long as your arm already, and when it comes to bridesmaids and how many and what they're going to wear, I don't have any say. I'm beginning to wonder if I've got anything to do with it at all.'

'You'll find out. If you aren't there, all their planning will have been for nothing. Your name will be mud and when they catch up with you you'll be drummed out of the country.'

'I shall be glad when it's all over.'

'But that's just it, it won't be,' said Norrie. 'That's when it all starts. Her mum will be there helping her choose curtains and colour schemes. She'll be planning the garden and telling you to put up a garden shed and . . . and . . . there'll be no end to it. That's when you realize what you've done.'

'Shut up, Norrie,' said Catherine. 'You'll put the boy off. Don't take any notice of your da, Allen, he's just teasing you.'

'I know,' said Allen. 'But you know what they say – there's many a true word spoken in jest. I won't have any pudding. I'd better get off, see you later.'

'Now look what you've done, Norrie,' said Catherine as Allen went out of the door. 'I think he was halfway to believing you. Let's hope it doesn't make him change his mind.'

'From what I've seen of Karen,' said Norrie, 'Allen's going to have to stand firm. I think she's the sort who'll take charge and if he lets her he'll regret it.'

'I have to admit she's not my favourite,' said Catherine. 'I always feel a bit uncomfortable when she's here. It's not that she . . . well . . . it's a job to put it into words. It's, well, she makes me feel inferior.'

'I know what you mean. Her old man's got money but that doesn't make him or his family any better than anyone else. I doubt if you'll see her that often so I wouldn't let it worry you.'

'I'm not going to. Do you want any pudding?'

'What is it?'

'Rhubarb pie and it's cold.'

'I won't then. I don't think it would sit well on what I've already eaten.'

Table cleared, dishes washed and put away, Catherine picked up a book and sat down with the intention of reading it. Norrie, never one to sit and do nothing, took himself to the barn where he said he was going to tidy his work bench, and Catherine was left alone. The room was warm and, replete after a good meal, it wasn't long before the words on the page began to blur as sleep tried to claim her. The book was one that had been loaned to her and she was determined to finish reading it so that she could give it back. But her eyes grew heavy and threatened to close. She struggled to keep them open, but the struggle was unequal and admitting defeat she closed them and slept. It was the snick of the latch on the back door that woke her. She yawned and stretched as Norrie came into the room.

'Ha,' he said. 'I caught you sleeping. Is that what you do when I'm away working to put a roof over your head?'

'You know it isn't,' she said.

'I'm glad we didn't go out, it's still raining. I thought it would have given up by now. I'll make us some tea.'

While Norrie put the kettle on and got out cups and milk and sugar, Catherine went to stand by the window. The water in the bay looked grey and sullen. Dark, rain-bearing clouds drifted slowly across the sky. There was no sign of life, neither man, animal nor bird. They might just as well be on a desert island as in this valley.

'Here you are,' said Norrie as he put a tray with two mugs of tea on it on the table. 'Come and have this.'

Catherine turned away from the window. 'Do you realize that in a few weeks, all our boys will be married men?'

'I had thought about it.'

'And all in one year. You'd think it was catching, wouldn't you?'

'Well, maybe it is.' Norrie laughed. 'When we slip the rams there's maybe one or two of the ewes ready, but then they all line up wanting to have a go.'

'Norrie that's rude.'

'But it's true.'

'Perhaps it is, but all this has happened so fast. It wasn't long since they were teenagers, and now they're grown up. I don't know where the time goes.'

'You slept some of it away today.'

Catherine glanced at the clock. 'Twenty minutes, perhaps,' she said. Was that really the time, had she slept that long? And then she saw the edge of the envelope she had tucked behind it. She got up and reached for it.

She handed it to Norrie and said. 'I forgot all about this. It came a day or two ago. I thought it was someone playing a joke on us – I'm still not sure they're not.'

'What's it about then?' he said as he took it from her.

'It's from some land agents. I don't know what they want with us. Read it.'

Norrie slid the sheet of paper out of the envelope, held it and began to read. 'Looks genuine enough to me,' he said. 'Wonder what it's all about. Let me see.'

He was not about to finish, for the door burst open and Allen came rushing in. Startled by the wild look on his face Catherine cried, 'My God, what's happened?'

Seventeen

'WHERE'S ME BOOTS, Mam? Where's me boots?'

'What do you want your boots for?'

'I've got to go to the airport, Peter'll need me. A Dan-Air's gone off the runway. Where's me boots?'

'Where you left them, by the back door.'

Allen snatched up his work boots and dashed out of the house leaving the door to slam shut behind him. Driver's door open and motor running, Allen threw his boots on to the passenger seat of his car, jumped in and, crashing the gears in his haste, raced away. There was not a minute to spare; people's lives were at stake. Regardless of the wet surface of the road, Allen drove fast. He set the windscreen wipers to go at full speed and cared not for oncoming drivers and whether, in trying to avoid him, he might cause them to go into the ditch. When he reached the top of Ward Hill, and the widespread view of the airport below him, his heart missed a beat.

The airport, built on a peninsula, had not been constructed with large aeroplanes in mind and the runway the plane had been taking off from was short and bounded by the sea at either end. Failing to take off and with nowhere else to go, the Dan-Air had plunged into the sea. More than half of its body was under water and nothing but a short length of its tail was to be seen. From behind him as Allen drove down the hill, came the wail of an ambulance siren. He pulled over and the vehicle screamed past. He followed and kept pace with it.

Shoes off and boots on Allen looked for Peter. Not there. Don't wait. Move on. He ran to the end of the runway, stopped, covered his mouth with his hand and whispered, 'Oh, my God.'

Now that he was closer to it, the tail of the plane reared up like the fin of some weird sea creature. There were people in the water. The plane's fuel tanks had ruptured and a rainbow-hued sheen of fuel oil covered the surface. A helicopter flew low, the roar of its engine almost drowning out shouted orders or survivors calling for help. A man close to Allen raised his fists at the chopper. 'See what it's doing?' he shouted as he pointed at the little boats and the rescuers. Downdraft from the rotors flattened the sea, compounding the difficulties for the small vessels. Then, realizing what was happening, the pilot turned his aircraft away.

The splashing of a man in the water brought Allen's attention back to why he was there. Huge rocks put there as sea defences at the end of the runway confronted the man and he needed help. Allen plunged forward, 'Get hold of me,' he cried as he reached out to him. Green algae, wet and slippery, had him slipping and sliding; the sea lapped between the rocks and filled his boots with water. The man was close now and the face that looked up at him was frozen in shock and disbelief, the eyes black and bottomless. It was a face Allen knew would haunt him for the rest of his life. He gripped the hand that was reaching out and held on to it till they reached level ground and the man was on his feet. Water poured from the man's clothes. He looked down at himself. 'They were new trews,' he said. 'First time I had them on. Cost me a lot of money. Now I shall have to buy some more.' The trousers clung to him like a second skin and water running from them made puddles round his feet.

'Never mind that,' said Allen. 'Let's go and find you some dry clothes.' As they walked to the terminal building Allen said, 'Is there anyone I can get in touch with to tell them you're safe? No doubt they'll hear about this on the radio or TV. You wouldn't want them to worry.'

'No, no, I'll call them myself. There'll be a pay phone in the terminal, won't there?' The man, who walked purposefully, spoke with confidence. 'We were going home, but we'll be a bit late. You don't know if they've got another plane, do you?'

'I wouldn't know about that, but I think there is a public phone you can use,' said Allen. The man had only just escaped death, how could he be so calm and composed?

Allen led his charge to the café in the terminal, pulled up a chair and said, 'Sit there, I'll get you a hot drink and—' He didn't finish what he was going to say for the man burst into tears. Deep, racking sobs shook his body. Then there were running feet and Allen was being pushed aside, the medics would take over. He stood back and a hand grabbed him.

'Allen, what are you doing here?' It was Peter.

'I came to help.'

'Then come with me.'

The fire station was Peter's workplace, and his task there that day was not one to savour. As dead bodies were pulled out of the plane, they were brought ashore and taken to the fire station to be laid out for identification.

'It's a bad business,' said Allen as they set down a dead body. 'He's no older than you or I.'

'No, that's the hell of it,' said Peter. 'I'm glad you came down, because I'm never going to forget this.'

They worked on till at last word went round that there was no more to be done that night. Allen looked at his brother, at the tired look on his face and his dull, sad eyes and, not knowing that he looked the same, said, 'They're dishing out tea over in the café. Come on, I don't know about you, but I could do with some.'

Catherine was banking up the fire and getting ready for bed when Allen came home. He stood and looked at her. She stared back at him and the look of him warned her not to start asking questions. The kettle, the one she wouldn't get rid of, stood on top of the stove. 'The kettle's hot,' she said, 'If you'd like a cup of something.'

'They put tea on for us.'

'What about something to eat?'

Allen shook his head. He sat down in one of the chairs next to the fire and began to take off his boots. He unlaced them, pulled them off, then his socks. 'They're wet,' he said. 'Sea water, you'll have to wash them.'

'We'll leave your boots by the fire to dry. I'll get you a towel for your feet.' She gave him a towel and while he dried his feet she stuffed newspaper inside the boots to absorb some of the moisture. 'Did you find Peter?'

'Yes . . . well . . . actually, he found me.'

'How was that?'

But Allen had bent his head and was weeping. She heard the dry sobs of a man who thought it unmanly to cry. He had covered his face with his hands and though he made little sound his shoulders shook as he tried to contain his grief. She put her arms round him and laid her head against his.

'Oh, Mam,' sobbed Allen. 'It was awful. I helped a man . . . he was in the water . . . he must have swum from the plane. It was his face, I'll never forget it. I said we'd go and get him some dry clothes and he seemed to be coping . . . . He was complaining that the trousers he had on were ruined, they were new, he said. And then he was saying they were on their way home but that they'd be late now. But then we were in the airport and he just broke down and cried, I mean . . . he broke his heart and I didn't know what to do.'

'Ssh,' said Catherine. 'It's all over now.'

'No, it isn't, there are still bodies in the plane. A lot of people died. Divers were going into the plane to get the bodies out. Peter and I had to help take them to the fire station. They had to have somewhere to lay them out so they could be identified. Some weren't any older than Peter or I—'

'Allen, shush, don't say any more.'

'But I have to, I have to tell somebody. Poor dead people, I didn't like seeing all their dead faces.' His voice broke as sobs welled up. 'They were young. They were oilies off the rigs, going home to Aberdeen on leave. Their families will be waiting for them and now they won't ever go home again.' Looking at him Catherine saw the pain of remembering written on his face. 'Why did they have to die like that?' he cried.

'I don't know,' said Catherine. She wrapped her arms round him, smoothed his hair and held him till he regained some of his composure. Then she went to the cupboard that housed the whisky bottle, took it out and poured some into a glass. She handed it to Allen. 'Drink that,' she said.

'I don't like whisky.'

'I don't care; you're going to drink it now.'

Allen dutifully took a sip then turned his head away and made a face. But as the fiery liquid ran down through his chest he drank more.

Catherine fetched a stool and sat beside him. 'It's no shame to show your grief. I can't begin to imagine what you've been through, but it must have been something that few people are ever called on to witness. Yes, you will talk about it, but later on when you've come to terms with it.' Allen was taking another small mouthful of whisky. She gave a little smile. 'How's the liquor?' she said.

He turned to her and gave a weak semblance of a smile. 'No bad.'

'No bad, eh? I thought you didn't like it.'

'I don't, but today's different.'

'Well that's for sure. There's one big thing that's made it different, though, and that is that you didn't hesitate to go and help. Not everyone would. It's something you will always be glad you did.'

'But I didn't do much; a lot of it was over before I got there.'

'The point is that you were there. Drink up the rest of that whisky then get to your bed. I'm ready for mine, and . . . I'm proud of you, Allen. '

'But I was thinking about Peter. I couldn't let him be there on his own.'

'I know. Go to bed.

Eighteen

GLOOM, DARKER THAN the dark days of winter, settled over the airport after the Dan-Air disaster. The laughter and banter of the workers in the terminal were replaced by sober words and soft voices. Young men, not much more than boys before the crash, matured rapidly. Work went on as usual, but in a quiet, sober, atmosphere, the last of the bodies were removed from the aeroplane, and gradually the day to day running of the airport returned to normal.

Catherine worried for Peter; he became very quiet and withdrawn, but it was Rosie he turned to, Rosie who cared for him now. Allen unburdened his soul to Norrie; their conversations going on well into the night. Gradually, Catherine thought that the boy's face started to relax and he did not seem so borne down by all that he had experienced. Time, that great healer, was doing its work.

Despite the disaster of the plane crash, and the emotional upheaval it caused her boys by being there to help and witness the aftermath, life on the croft went on as usual for Catherine. Sheep still had to be tended and fences looked at and mended if they had been broken. With all her men working away from home, much of the day to day work still fell on her shoulders. The heavy outdoor work was left to Norrie and the boys when they had time off, but there was still much to do in the house. She was standing at the ironing board tackling yet another basketful of shirts and sheets when Judith walked in.

'Hi, Mam,' she said. 'Long time no see. How are you?'

'I'm fine,' but then, looking at the girl's long face, 'what's wrong?'

'Nothing.'

'If that's the case, I'm a Dutchman. Don't try that with me – what is it?'

'It's Dom. He's dragging his feet. I still haven't heard from the recording company and I'm getting fed up with waiting for him to do something.'

'You never did have any patience, did you? You're lucky that he got you to Glasgow for a try out. I'm sure he's doing his best.'

'Well, I'd been hoping that he might have got me a recording contract by now, but he says I've got to wait.'

'Then that's what you've got to do.'

'There's a big do at the town hall next month and I've been asked to sing. Will you come?'

'I'd love to . . . oh, drat the ironing.' Catherine threw a half-ironed shirt back in the basket and switched off the iron.

Judith was standing by the fire place. 'Why don't you get an electric fire, Mam and get rid of this old stove? It must make a lot of work for you.' She ran a finger along the mantelpiece. 'When did you use the duster last? I could write my name here and what's this tucked behind the clock?' She took hold of the corner of an envelope and pulled it out. 'It's addressed to you and Dad.'

'Then it's none of your business, give it to me. And whether I dust the mantelpiece or not is none of your business either.' Judith handed the letter to her mother and when Catherine looked at it she gasped, 'Oh my goodness. I'd completely forgotten about this. Your dad said I had to ring them and I haven't done it yet. I must.'

'What's it about then?'

'I don't know. It's from a solicitor and I've got to ring him to find out.'

'A solicitor! What does he want? You aren't in any trouble are you?'

'I won't know till I ring him, will I?'

'Then you'd better do it. Have you made any bannocks?'

'Deepdale wouldn't run properly if I didn't make bannocks,' said Catherine. 'And as to this, I don't know what it's about and I won't till I've made that phone call, but I'm not doing that while you're here. I'll put the kettle on.' In the kitchen Catherine ran water into her kettle. In the living room the telephone rang. 'Answer that, will you, Judith? I'll be there in a minute.'

Judith picked up the phone. 'Hullo? Uh . . . hang on. Mam, it's for you.'

'Oh, drat, it always rings when you're in the middle of something. Who is it? Go and make the tea Judith, there's a dear, the kettle's just boiled.' She took the phone from her daughter and putting it to her ear said, 'Hi, I'm here, who's that? Janet. . . ? What the heck are you phoning for this time of day; don't you have a job to go to? *What*?' Shock at what she heard had Catherine reaching out for a chair. 'When? Oh, my God . . . how's Mum? Right away . . . I'll let you know.' Catherine set the phone back on its cradle, then looked at Judith. 'It's your granddad. He's had a stroke. He's in hospital and they say it doesn't look good. I have to go.' Stricken, she slumped in the chair and seemed visibly to shrink.

Judith, who had made the tea, poured it out. This was not like her mother, the one who battled the odds, who wasn't afraid to tackle jobs others would shirk. She ladled a couple of spoonfuls of sugar into one of the cups. 'Drink this, Mam. It'll do you good.'

'Why did I have to come and live so far away from them?' said Catherine as she drank her tea. 'I ought to be there to help.'

'Why? You've got two sisters and a brother, can't they do it?'

'I suppose they can. But they can see them any time they like; it's years since I was home last. I must be there so I have to go.'

'That's easily arranged,' said Judith. 'When do you want to go, today?'

'How can I?' said Catherine. 'Who's going to look after your dad and Allen? You know what men are like when they're left on their own.'

'I can look after them.'

'But you've got to work.'

'Don't argue. I'll ring up and see if I can book you a flight. When you've drunk your tea, go and pack a bag.'

'Who's giving orders now?'

'I am, but only because I need to and for once it's your turn to do as you're told, so we won't have any arguments.'

Peter was in the terminal buying a magazine to read in his lunch break. To his surprise he saw his mother standing by the check in desk, a suitcase at her feet.

'What are you doing here, Mam?' he said. 'Where are you going?'

'Your granddad's taken a stroke. I have to go home and be with my mother.'

'Can't Auntie Janet and the others look after him?'

'He's in hospital. It might be my last chance to see him and my mother will expect me to be there. But I'm very nervous about getting on a plane . . . especially after . . . you know.'

'You'll be all right, Mam, lightning doesn't strike twice, or so they say. Come and sit down. I can stay for a little while.'

'Thanks for trying to boost my confidence, but I don't think it's helped much.'

'Who's looking after Da? And when will you be back?'

'Judith's standing in for me. I'm not sure how good a cook she is so ask Rosie to look in now and then. I don't know when I'll be back but I'll ring you.'

Peter stayed till it was time for Catherine to go through to the check-in. As she went through the doorway, she turned to give a brief wave. Then she was walking in line with other passengers to where luggage was inspected. From there, in line again, she went to the departure lounge and sat down to wait. She clasped her hands together and twiddled her thumbs, then, in case anyone was watching, slid them under her thighs and sat on them. God, she was nervous. She could feel her heart pounding. She looked around. Was anyone else as nervous as she?

After what seemed an age it was time to board. She walked out towards the plane, climbed the metal steps, found her seat, sat down and buckled her safety belt. The pilot hadn't started the engines and the door to the plane was still open. It would only take a moment for her to get up and get out. She didn't *have* to go, but how could she not?

Then everything happened all at once. Boarding steps were rolled away and the door slammed shut. Engines came to life with a roar and the plane, like some waking animal, shook itself, the vibrations of its action rippling through its fabric. It's too late to change your mind now, Catherine. She sighed and gave herself up to looking out of the window as the aeroplane taxied out to the runway. She'd forgotten to look at the windsock. Which runway were they taking off from? Then she remembered; the wind was southerly, it would be up and over the lighthouse.

With the plane, ready for take-off, standing at the end of the runway, the pilot revved the engines to full throttle. Catherine pushed her hands, fingers crossed, down between her legs as suddenly, with a surge of power, they were off. The plane raced along the runway until, with a sigh, it lifted up and was airborne.

She was on her way.

Nineteen

'WHEN'S MAM COMING BACK?' Allen sat at the table and watched as his father helped himself to braised beef and vegetables.

'Tomorrow. Why?' said Norrie. 'Don't you like Judith's cooking?'

'It's okay. No, it's just that I asked Mam if Karen and I could have Laura's house, but Karen says that it wouldn't be very convenient. She said it would be better for us to stay in Lerwick. She could walk to work if we lived there.'

'And did you think your Mam would mind if you turned it down?'

'I don't know. She didn't like the Barringtons and I think she thought if we all lived here she wouldn't get people like them again. But it wouldn't work.'

'Why not?'

'Because she couldn't help herself, she'd have to keep an eye on us all and, to be honest, I don't think she gets on with Karen very well.'

Norrie was eating and didn't answer straight away. Then he said, 'I don't know why we keep on calling it Laura's house; it's Judith's now, though what she's going to do with it I don't know. I doubt if she'll ever come back here to stay.'

'But what do you think Mam will say?'

'I'm sure it won't matter one way or the other, but you won't have to wait long to find out.'

'Mmm.' Allen sat for a while and said nothing. Then he stood up. 'I'll leave you to do the washing up. I'm going to see Karen; you'd never believe what a lot of fuss she's making about getting married. It's all she ever talks about. I wonder sometimes if the wedding is more important than getting married.'

'That's women for you, boy.'

'There's no need for it. We could be married just the same without the fuss.'

'It's the most important day in their lives, son,' said Norrie. 'There's no way you're going to get out of a proper wedding, you can't deny your girl that pleasure. You can't do what Robbie did and have a hole and corner affair. It broke your mother's heart and we can't have that again. It's only one day in your life after all. I remember when I married your mother—'

'I've heard it before, Dad. Save it for the grandkids.' Allen got up and pushed his chair back under the table.

'You may mock,' said Norrie as he helped himself to more beef. 'When your kids are grown up and thinking of getting wed you'll be in the same boat yourself.'

'Ay ay, that's if we have any. See you later.' And Allen was gone.

The house was empty when Catherine got home. Norrie, Allen and Judith had left for work straight after breakfast, so there were dishes to wash and beds to make. But there was something else that had to be done first. She picked up the phone and dialled her mother's number. After a few rings Janet answered.

'I'm sorry I couldn't stay longer,' said Catherine. 'How's Mum coping?'

'She's at the hospital every day, can't keep her away. She'd sleep there if they gave her a bed. But you know how close they always were, talk about living in each other's pockets. You'd have needed a jemmy to prise them apart.'

'Are they going to let him come home?'

'I think so, but I don't know when. He's going to need a care assistant every day to wash and dress him. Mum can't do it. I suppose I shall have to learn how.'

'What's going to happen, and I hate to say this . . . but what if he dies?'

'Don't go there, Sis. Let's cope with that if and when it comes, eh?'

'Fair enough, but promise me you'll phone right away if you want me to come back. Don't do it all yourself; get the others to help.'

Standing there, the phone to her ear, Catherine nodded from time to time as Janet assured her that there had been nothing to keep her in Southampton, and that there were enough of them there to look after their mother. She would let her know if anything happened or if she was needed again. 'Promise me you will,' said Catherine, 'and I'll be on the next plane. Thanks for everything. Take care, bye now.'

She put down the phone. Was the thing a boon or a bugbear? Its ring often demanded attention when she was baking and her hands were floury or sticky, or interrupted her housework or the progress of a meal. It brought good news and bad and she wished there was some way bad news could be filtered out. The stark announcement of a death should be delivered by someone who could also comfort and not by a disembodied voice on the phone. But at least it sometimes gave a chance to say goodbye to a loved one when otherwise it would be too late.

She picked up her case and carried it up to her bedroom. She changed into jeans and a cotton shirt and pulled a jumper over her head. After warm days in the south the cooler temperature of Shetland was noticeable. She made beds, washed dishes and filled the washing machine and set it going. She tidied the sitting room, stoked the fire, then, looking at the clock to see how time was going, saw, with a shock, the edge of the envelope tucked behind it. Had Norrie seen it? If he had, he probably wouldn't have taken any notice of it, thinking that it was something of hers and nothing to do with him. But, so that it wouldn't be forgotten again, she took the envelope from its hiding place and put it on the table.

She changed her shoes for boots, then put on a jacket and went out. The wind was in her face as she climbed up to the lower slopes of the hill where the sheep grazed. It smelled fresh and clean, unlike the fume-laden air of the city she had visited so recently. The appearance of her father had shocked her. He had lost a lot of weight and his hair, once luxurious, was white and sparse. The stroke he had suffered had left him paralyzed down one side, and the wizened little man lying in the bed bore no resemblance to the cheery character he had once been. How could all this have happened to him since she had seen him last?

The same was true of her mother. Five years ago she had still been the capable domineering woman she always had been. But now she seemed to be quite happy for someone else to run her house. She sat and watched as Janet cooked and cleaned, ate what she was given and never, ever criticized or complained.

'How long has she been like this, Janet?' Catherine had asked.

'Job to tell,' said her sister. 'I think she's got dementia. She says some funny things and she often seems to be off in a world of her own.'

To Catherine's mind came memories of her mother-in-law, Jannie, and the odd way she had behaved and she needed no telling that the same thing was happening to her mother. It also explained why when they were at the hospital she sat beside her husband's bed and watched as the nurses tended him. Doris Marshall, who would once have pushed the nurses out of the way and nursed her husband herself, had made no move to help, but had watched and said nothing.

'This is not like her,' said Catherine. 'Where's the old fire gone?'

'The doctor said it's shock,' said Janet. 'Dad's stroke was very sudden. Mum's hardly spoken a word since it happened. Think about it, they were everything to one another and they've been together for nearly sixty years. I bet they were beginning to think they were immortal. She won't do anything, but she won't leave him, she just sits there and watches him.'

There was no telling how long Peter Marshall would live, so Catherine had come home, but it wasn't long before she was back in Southampton again.

'Father's sinking fast,' said Janet when she phoned. 'I don't know if you'll get here in time.'

But she did, and with her sister, one each side of their mother, she sat beside his bed. When Peter Marshall died, his wife, dry-eyed, said, 'Take me home.' There she sat in her chair, stared out of the window, accepted food and drink as it was brought to her, but said nothing, neither a please nor a thank you. She went with Catherine and Janet and other members of the family to the church and plodded between them as they followed the coffin. She sat between them and gazed round at the interior of the church, had to be prompted when to stand and to sit. She showed no emotion as the service proceeded and she walked between her daughters as the coffin was carried out. Then she looked into the grave and said, 'That's not my Peter. He wouldn't leave me.'

But he had, and when days went by with no change in her mother Catherine said, 'I'll have to go home, but I feel guilty about leaving you to look after her.'

'I'm the one with least commitments,' said her sister, 'so I can move in here for a while. We'll see how it goes.'

So Catherine had come home again and here she was now leaning over a gate looking at her sheep. 'You don't know,' she said to them, 'how simple life is for you. You're free to roam, you get fed in winter. You produce a lamb in spring and keep it till autumn and don't seem to care too much when it's taken away. You go on from year to year with no family to care for, to bother you or break your heart, no tears, no heartaches . . . .' She faltered and stopped, then went on. '. . . Unlike me. Is it ever going to end? It'll be my mother next, I suppose, another funeral and then it'll all be over and there'll never be a home to travel south to again.'

She sighed. A little way off a ewe lay down and huffed its breath as it settled its legs in a comfortable position. It began to chew the cud and Catherine heard the soft thud of its jaws as they came together, watched as its chin went from side to side to grind its food into a more digestible mass. It swallowed then held its head up. A moment or two later came the rattle of regurgitation and the whole process began again.

A chuckle rose up in Catherine's throat and set itself free. 'You're a silly old thing,' she said to the sheep, 'and it might look as though you have a carefree life, but whatever gets thrown at me, it could never be so bad that I would want to change places with you. What? Lose every child you produce? At least mine will come home again, unlike yours.'

Twenty

'WHAT'S THIS, CATHERINE?' Norrie had picked up the letter she had once again put next to his plate – knowing that he would do nothing about it while she was away she had put it back behind the clock.

'It's that letter from the solicitor,' she said. 'I forgot about it. I've never phoned them and I'm surprised that they haven't been in touch with us again.' She looked at Norrie as he scanned the page. 'What do you think we ought to do?'

'I don't understand it. Someone's interested in buying some land. What would make them think that we have any to sell, anyway? You'll have to ring up. Could you do that tomorrow? And don't forget this time.'

'It is odd, isn't it? I wonder if the boys have said anything about going into farming together and might move to Scotland. That might be it, and someone has got the wrong end of the stick. I shall ask them.'

'By the way,' said Norrie. 'Allen doesn't want Judith's house. Karen wants to stay in Lerwick.'

'Why doesn't that surprise me? I sometimes think that if we weren't Allen's parents she wouldn't have anything to do with us. I think we're too down to earth for her liking. Never mind, that's her loss. I doubt she would ever make a croft wife. We'll have to let the house to somebody else, then.'

'There's somebody after it already. They rang when Judith was here. She wrote their number on the pad. It's not late, why don't you ring them now?'

'I might as well.' Catherine picked up the message pad from

beside the phone, read the number and began to dial thinking, please, please don't let it be another Anneka. Holding the phone to her ear she listened as somewhere a telephone bell was ringing. On and on it went. She turned to Norrie. 'I don't think there's anyone at home,' she said, then jumped as a loud voice said, 'Hullo, hullo?'

'Hello,' said Catherine. 'I believe you might be interested in renting a house in Deepdale. If you—'

There was a gasp and a hasty, 'Yes. When I can come and look at it?'

Catherine held the phone away from her ear. The voice boomed and did not carry cultured tones, but accents that hailed from somewhere in the middle of England. 'Just let me know when it's convenient for you,' said Catherine.

'I'll be there mid-morning tomorrow. See you.'

There was a clunk and the phone went dead. Catherine held it and looked at it as if expecting it to come to life again. She put it down and turned to Norrie.

'Well, she never said who she was or where she was, so I've no idea what to expect, but she's coming here tomorrow. I suppose I'll find out then.'

'I can tell you now,' said Norrie. 'Their name's Finney. The husband's an aircraft engineer and works for Bristow's Helicopters.'

'And how do you know that?'

'Because she told Judith.'

'Then why didn't she come and look at the house when Judith was here? It's Ju's house and she's the one who should decide who to let live there.'

'Because Ju said that you and I would have to live next to them, so it was up to you to decide if they were suitable. I thought that was fair comment.'

Next morning, when Catherine was feeding the chickens, a car, one that had definitely seen better days, came rattling down the track. The driver, a young woman, saw Catherine, waved, drove up to her and brought the car to a halt. She got out and slammed the door. She beamed at Catherine and walked towards her, hand outstretched. 'You must be Mrs Williams,' she said. 'I'm Tracy Finney, but call me Tracy. How are you, me dook?'

This was no Anneka. Catherine took the proffered hand and

found it gripped firmly. 'I'm fine. I take it you've come to see the house?'

'That's right. Lead me to it.'

'Wait a moment, I'll get the key.'

To her surprise Tracy Finney did not wait, but followed her, talking non-stop as she did. 'It's not too much like a summer day, is it? I'm freezing cold so I've had to put on some extra layers. If this is summer, what's it like in winter? I can't imagine. Do you wear fur coats?'

'It's not that bad,' said Catherine as she opened the door of her house and walked in. 'Sometimes it's worse in England than it is here. We don't always get a lot of snow and when we do it rarely stays long. It's because we're surrounded by the sea, and something to do with the Gulf stream.' Tracy was right behind her.

Catherine had banked up the fire in preparation for leaving it while she worked outside. It was burning steadily and the room was warm. Above the stove, pulled up to the ceiling, was the pulley. It was draped with clothes to air.

'Wow!' exclaimed Tracy. 'I could be right back in me granny's kitchen. I love it. Where's your cat? You must have a cat. Do you make jam and chutney and bread? I love homemade bread. I hope the house you're going to show me is like this.' It seemed as though Tracy never expected her questions to be answered for her words flowed like wine.

'It'll not be as warm,' said Catherine. 'We don't keep the fire going when there's no one in it.'

The house had been empty for a while and, even though it was summer and the sun was shining, the rooms were chilly. 'Never mind, me dook,' said Tracy. 'A good fire will soon change that. I'll take it.'

'But you haven't looked all round it and I haven't told you what the rent is.'

'Tell me now then.'

Catherine did and Tracy smiled. 'I still want it,' she said.

'But oughtn't you to bring your husband to see it so that you can look at it together? He might not like it.'

'Yes he will. He'll agree with whatever I want. He says that a wife spends most of her time in the house so she's the one who has to decide where they're going to live. And if I like it so will he.'

'He sounds very agreeable,' said Catherine.

'Oh, he is.'

'I haven't asked if you have any children,' said Catherine.

'Sore subject,' said Tracy. 'No luck so far and not much hope. It breaks my heart. I love kids, but if that's the way it's got to be there's nowt I can do about it.'

I like this girl, thought Catherine as she turned the key in the door to relock the house. 'Are you in a hurry to be off or would you like to come and have a cup of coffee with me?'

'I'd love a cup,' said Tracy. 'You can tell me all about what it's like to live here. I've a hundred questions to ask.'

And a hundred questions there were. Tracy wanted to know everything about Shetland that Catherine could tell her. How long was it going to take her to understand what people were saying? Was she going to be accepted or would she be treated as a foreigner? Was there a Women's Institute she could join? She couldn't sit and twiddle her thumbs because it wouldn't take her all day to clean the house, so would she be able to get a job?

She had grown up in a terraced house in Stoke-on-Trent. When she married, she and her husband had moved to Manchester to be closer to the airport, where he'd got work. Their accommodation there was a house on a street like any other, and everywhere there was noise and pollution of traffic. It had left her unprepared for the quiet roads and wild wastelands of Shetland.

'This place reminds me of the Yorkshire moors; they're desolate places too. How on earth do people make a living here?' she asked.

'It's better than it was. There's plenty of work now – oil has seen to that,' said Catherine. 'That's why you're here, isn't it? The oilies have to be flown out to the rigs and helicopters are needed for that.'

'Do you have a job?'

Catherine laughed. 'You could say that. I have a flock of sheep, a cow to milk, chickens to feed and a husband and son to keep house and cook for. It's enough to keep me busy.'

Tracy jumped up. 'And here I am blethering away and hindering you.'

'No you aren't.'

'I should be going anyway,' said Tracy. 'You won't let anyone else have the house, will you? I'll pay a deposit if you like.'

Catherine stood on the flags outside the house. 'Drive carefully now,' she said as Tracy got in her car. And then she smiled. The girl was a breath of fresh air. It would be good to have her as her neighbour. She chuckled as she turned and went indoors.

Twenty-One

Recognizing the sound of Norrie's car Catherine rushed out to meet him. 'Someone wants to buy Deepdale, all of it,' she shouted. 'You can't let them have it.'

Norrie, hand on the door of his car stood and looked at his distraught wife. 'For goodness' sake, woman, slow down, you aren't making any sense.'

'But, Norrie—'

Norrie slammed the car door shut. 'Hold on and let me get indoors.' While his agitated wife fussed around him he took off his jacket, hung it up and sat down. 'Do you have tea made?'

'Of course I do,' snapped Catherine.

'Well, get it on the table then, and then tell me what's bothering you.' Impatient to tell her news Catherine put the meal she had been keeping hot in front of her husband. 'Now,' said Norrie. 'What the devil's happened that's got you all het up?'

'I rang the solicitor. He said a developer wants to buy our land.' Her words came out in a rush. 'I asked them what made him think we would sell and he said when we knew how much money was involved he was sure we would. What do they want it for?'

'How would I know?' said Norrie, between mouthfuls of food, 'Perhaps they want to build something.' Norrie stopped eating and was silent. Then he said, 'That would mean a lot of money. Remember what Magnie said, "Land will go up in value".' He shook his head. 'No, we're too far away from Sullom so it can't be anything to do with oil and I'd have thought if they were looking for land for offices they'd want something in the town. Perhaps it's houses.'

'No, Norrie, we can't let them fill Deepdale with houses. They can't make us sell, can they? What would happen to us? You can't

110

move house with three hundred sheep to think about. What would we do with them? And what about all the other stuff – and then there's the kids and . . . Where would we go?'

'I don't know. We don't know who wants to buy us out yet, do we? Well, we'll find that out later. Didn't they want to come and see us?'

'Yes. I've got to ring back and let them know if we're interested. They want the names and addresses of everyone who owns land in Deepdale.'

'So we're all going to get a separate offer, then. I wonder if Smith's told them that it's croft land, and that it'll have to be decrofted if they want to build on it.' Norrie gave a chuckle. 'I reckon that'll be a fight; Crofters' Commission won't want to decroft four crofts all in the same place. I can see this dragging on for months.'

Catherine gave a sigh. 'I've lived here nearly forty years. I wept for Kay and for Mina when they died and for Laura when she left. I wept for Daa and even Jannie, though she did treat me bad. I've seen the valley change and I've watched Shetland change. Now it's gaining speed and I wonder where it's going to stop.' She looked at Norrie and said, 'This valley is my home, it's where I belong. I don't want to sell, I don't want to leave it and I'm not going to.'

'You're jumping the gun,' said Norrie. 'At the moment all we know is that someone is interested in buying land. If it wasn't ours it would be someone else's. We don't know what they might offer or even if the land is suitable for what they want. We have to take it one step at a time and as for moving, we'll cross that bridge when we come to it.'

Tracy and Paul Finney moved into Deepdale on a fine sunny morning.

'We haven't got much,' said Tracy when Catherine took them a tray of tea and some bannocks, 'but what we've got is paid for. I can't stand debt.' She turned to her husband. 'Paul, say hello to Mrs Williams.'

Paul Finney, unlike his buxom, bouncing wife, was thin and wiry. When he shook Catherine's hand the firmness of his grip ruled out any thought of hers that he was also weak, and, as he smiled and greeted her, she noted the penetrating look he gave her. This was not a man who would suffer fools gladly. While Tracy's conversation bubbled it seemed that he was quite happy to stand back and leave it all to her, but Catherine had no doubt that any decisions they had to make would be made jointly.

'When I'm straightened out you'll have to come and have a meal with us,' said Tracy. 'We'll have a house warming. And you can teach me how to make these things.' She held up a bannock. 'What do you call them?'

'They're bannocks,' said Catherine.

'Well, they're awful nice, but maybe that's something to do with the butter. You make it yourself, don't you? If you show me how to make bannocks I'll show you how to make Stafford oatcakes. Mrs Williams has got a cow, Paul, and a lot of sheep.' Tracy switched her attention back to Catherine. 'I don't know anything about the country, or cows, or sheep, but I'd like to learn. Can I come and give you a hand some time? Perhaps you'd teach me.'

'I'd enjoy your company,' said Catherine and knew that she meant it.

Tracy beamed a smile at her. 'Thank you. I shall look forward to that, but are you sure you can spare the time? I wouldn't want to be a hindrance. This lady is a very busy woman, Paul.'

'We'd better not hinder her then,' said Paul. 'And we'd better get on; I've got to be on shift in a couple of hours. Nice to meet you, Mrs Williams.'

'Okay,' said Tracy and to Catherine, 'Come along any time, there'll always be a cup of coffee and a welcome for you.'

'Thank you, I'll take you up on that.'

'They're late, Norrie. They said ten o'clock and it's now nearly eleven.'

Norrie chuckled. 'Calm down, you're making more fuss than a wet hen; you can't make time go any faster. They'll be here . . . in fact I think they're here now.' He got up from his chair and went to the door. Catherine followed him.

The two men who got out of the BMW were clearly business men. The suit worn by one was tailored and crisp, certainly not off the peg. His shoes were black and highly polished. The other, who, from the letter sent to Norrie and Catherine they knew to be the man from the agency, was similarly, though not so expensively, dressed. They both carried fat leather briefcases. Catherine looked at them and at the broad smiles on their faces, and cringed, afraid that she and Norrie would be no match for them.

'Good morning, Mr Williams,' said one as Norrie's hand was clasped and shaken. 'I'm Peter Blackhall, I'm from the Acorn Land Agency and this,' he turned his head and nodded to indicate the other, 'is Andrew Patterson. He's the man who's interested in your land.'

Patterson reached out to shake Norrie's hand. 'I'm very pleased to meet you,' he said. Peter Blackhall's voice had been brisk and business-like; this man's was smooth and patronizing. Catherine bit her lip.

Norrie turned to her. 'This is Catherine, my wife,' he said. 'She is partner in everything to do with this valley.'

'But of course.' Patterson gripped Catherine's hand. He appeared to be on the point of bowing. 'So nice to meet you, Mrs Williams,' he said. Wrong move, Mr Patterson, thought Catherine as she took back her hand.

Seated round the table the men made small talk while Catherine made coffee. She would not give them bannocks; they would probably think them 'quaint'; they could make do with plain biscuits. Coffee served, the talk turned to business and Catherine, a pad and pencil in front of her, began to take notes.

'Excuse me, Mrs Williams,' said Blackhall, 'we can give you print-offs with all the information you'll need. You don't need to do that.'

'That's very kind of you,' said Catherine, 'but I still want to take notes.'

'Clever girl,' said Patterson. Ignoring her he turned to Norrie. 'Now, Mr Williams,' he said, 'let's get down to business. I have no doubt that you are aware that the oil industry has renewed interest in the islands and, with new money flooding in, opportunities are opening up for entrepreneurs to start up new businesses. I'm looking for development land for that very purpose and the Deepdale Valley and its surrounding area is just what I want. If you are interested and prepared to discuss it, after we have walked the land, of course, I'm sure you will like the terms I am prepared to offer.'

'We're not going to sell.' All eyes turned to Catherine. She looked at their shocked faces. 'I am the owner of one croft, a quarter of the valley, and I have decided that I do not want to sell,' she said.

'I know croft land doesn't make a very good price,' said Blackhall. 'But this is development land we're talking about and when you hear what Drew Patterson is going to offer . . . well . . . that is a very different matter.'

'That's as may be, I don't care,' said Catherine. 'I don't want to sell and if I don't sell the rest is no good to you.'

'You could at least hear what they have to say, Catherine,' said Norrie. 'And remember it's going to affect the boys and Judith as much as us. Don't forget they would have to have their say as well.'

Catherine sat back in her chair and threw her pencil on the table. 'I'm aware of that,' she said. 'But the impression I'm getting here is that because I'm a *woman*, I can't be expected to know anything about business. Gentlemen, I am not merely a croft wife, the woman who milks the cow, hoes the rigs and cooks the supper. Norrie and I work all the land in the valley and my share in it is fifty per cent, and that means fifty per cent of responsibility, work, pleasure and monetary returns.' She clasped her hands in her lap and turned stony eyes on Patterson. 'I knew nothing about land or animals when I came here first, but I built a business breeding pedigree sheep. No doubt you saw the sign by the entrance at the top of the track. The business is thriving. Need I say more?'

The man had the grace to look guilty. 'I do apologize most humbly, Mrs Williams,' he said, 'if I have offended you. But it is very rare for our clients' wives to be involved. In this case I was mistaken. Please accept my apology.'

'Apology accepted,' said Catherine.

'So, can we get back to business now?' said Norrie.

'You can talk till the cows come home,' said Catherine. 'Whatever conclusion you come to, remember that I am not going to sell my land. You can take these men round and show them what a wonderful place a croft is. But leave me out of it. All I'm going to say to you, Norrie, is to keep your head and don't get carried away with sweet talk.' She stood up. 'Good day to you, gentlemen, enjoy your walk.' She pushed back her chair, left the room and closed the door.

Twenty-Two

TRACY FINNEY, RED hair tied in a bunch on top of her head, opened the door of Catherine's house and called out, 'Hi, cooee, where are you?'

Catherine, upstairs making beds, smiled as she heard her neighbour's cheery voice. 'I'll be down in a minute,' she called back. 'Come in and wait.'

In the kitchen Tracy put the kettle on. 'I hope you don't mind,' she said, when Catherine came down. 'I thought it was about time for coffee so I brought you a couple of Eccles cakes. I made them myself. I was wondering if I could help you today, I've got time on my hands.'

Catherine laughed. 'How much do you know about sheep?'

'Not a thing. There aren't many in Stoke.'

'I don't suppose there are,' said Catherine. 'I've got to look over the lambs today; you can come with me if you like.'

'Lambs, ooh, how lovely.' Tracy's face lit up.

'These are not lambs to get excited about,' said Catherine. 'They're not little.' And as they drank coffee and ate the cakes she explained the lifecycle of a sheep and that the lambs she was going to sort out that day would be those that were fit to kill. 'People have to eat,' she said, 'and if they want to put meat on their plates the farmer of crofter has to provide it.'

'I can get along with that,' said Tracy. 'And I am partial to a juicy lamb chop wi' mint sauce. How many sheep have you got?'

'About three hundred give or take a few.'

'Really! And you look after all of them?'

'These days I do little more than keep an eye on them. They need watching. Sometimes when they've got a full coat of wool a sheep will get on her back and if she can't get up she'll just lay there and die. In fact, I'd say that sheep do seem to have an inbuilt death wish; you can nurse them when they're sick, stay up at night, do every-thing you can to make them well again and when you think they're getting better they'll turn up their toes and die just to spite you.' Catherine gave a hearty laugh. 'Bloody sheep.'

'Why do you keep them, then?'

'Because you can keep sheep where you can't keep cows, they're the right sort of animals for the grazing we've got here. If I had my time over again I'd still go for sheep. If you treat them right they trust you, and believe me, it makes handling them a whole lot easier. Take my dog for instance. All he wants is bed and breakfast and he'll work his heart out for me. Would you get that from another human?'

'I see what you mean.'

'Right then,' said Catherine. 'If you've finished your coffee we'll be off.'

With Catherine's dog running at their heels the two women climbed the hill to where the sheep grazed. When Catherine sent the dog away to round them up Tracy was fascinated. She watched as it circled wide to come up behind the flock then, dodging back and forth, kept them in a bunch and brought them to the mouth of the pen. With a little cajoling they were all in and the pen closed.

'You only have to shut the gate on them, don't you?' said Tracy.

'They're not always as easy to pen,' said Catherine. 'It's just that the old ones have done it several times before. Just try penning a bunch of young ones. You'd be tearing your hair out if they were Shetlands.'

'Shetlands, what do you mean?'

'The Shetland hill sheep can jump a five-barred gate if pushed.'

'Never.'

'Would I lie?'

For the next hour Tracy did as Catherine asked and opened and shut the gate to the pen as Catherine pushed out the animals she did not want. At the end of that time twenty prime animals were left.

'What are you going to do with them?' said Tracy.

'We'll take them down to the valley and put them in a park there. It will be easier to load them into the trailer when they have to go to market.'

'I take it a park is a field and not a place with swings and roundabouts.'

'That would be right,' said Catherine. 'If you stand back there with the dog, I'll let them out this end of the crö. That's what we call the pen.'

Lambs running ahead of them and the dog trotting at their heels, Catherine and Tracy drove the animals back down the hill. The gate to one of the small parks in the valley bottom was already open and after coaxing, cajoling and some heated words when a lamb broke away and tried to escape, they were at last all in. Once through the gate all thought of flight forgotten, heads went down and small teeth cropped the grass.

'Thank you, Tracy,' said Catherine.

'Why? I did nothing but open and shut the gate.'

'That's why,' said Catherine.

It had taken a week to get the family together to discuss the offer Andrew Patterson, the developer, had made for Deepdale Valley. Robbie's shift pattern on the rig was two weeks on and two weeks off, so the meeting had to wait till he was ashore. Catherine had been surprised when he said he would stay for the weekend. She had hesitated to ask if Melody would be with him and was relieved when he said she would not.

She stood in the airport terminal, stared out of the window and waited for the plane from Aberdeen to touch down. It would be landing on the north–south runway and there it was, a big graceful bird winging in over the lighthouse, putting down its undercarriage and slowly descending to meet the land. There was a puff of smoke as its rubber-shod wheels briefly kissed the runway before making continuous contact. When it had slowed down the pilot taxied it close to the terminal building and brought it to a stop. Catherine watched as doors opened and exit steps were put into position. She saw luggage being offloaded and passengers begin to disembark. And then there was Robbie.

Head and shoulders above the other passengers, travel bag slung on his shoulder, he came walking towards her. He took her in his arms.

'Ay, Mam,' he said. 'It's good to see you.'

'How are you, Robbie?' she asked. 'You look tired.'

'I am a bit, we work long hours.'

'You'll have to tell me what it's like to work on an oil rig, though I wish you didn't, I hate the things.'

'They're not the best of places, but the money's good.'

As she drove, Robbie asked her what was so important that he had to come home. 'I guess everybody's had a letter from the developer and they would all have said the same, so you surely could have talked to me about it on the phone.'

'That's not the same at all. We thought it would be best if we were all together to discuss what's been happening,' said Catherine. 'It involves all of us so it's only right we should all have the chance to say what we think.'

'Nothing seems to change here,' said Robbie as Catherine turned off the main road and on to the road into the valley.

'Oh, it does,' she said. 'Things are changing all the time; it happens gradually so we tend not to notice as long as we're here. It's when we go away and then come back. We remember things as we last saw them and it's then we notice the changes. You haven't been away long enough yet to see it.'

Tracy, carrying a bundle of dry clothes she had just gathered from her clothes line, waved as Catherine drove by.

'Who's that?' asked Robbie.

'That's Tracy Finney, the new tenant in Judith's house. She and her husband come from the Midlands, he works at the airport.' Catherine chuckled. 'I like her; she's quite a live wire and she's brightened the place up.'

'That's good then.'

'Allen spends most of his time in Lerwick with Karen these days,' said Catherine as she parked the car in front of her house. 'They're planning their wedding. He'll be here later. Peter's on shift and Norrie too, but they'll be home tonight. Judith will be here tomorrow. Are you hungry?'

'Cup of tea and a piece of cake will do fine.'

'Tell me what it's like to work on an oil rig then,' said Catherine as she made tea. *What I really want to know is what's going on in your life, what Melody is up to and if you are making a go of your marriage.* 'What are the conditions like? Do you get time to yourself and do they feed you well?'

'We work long hours,' said Robbie. 'But I don't mind that. It would be very boring if we had time off with nothing to do. There is a library and we have television. And we can play pool – there're lots of things to do.'

'And what do you do with yourself when you're on shore? Um . . .'

Robbie gave a wry smile. 'It's all right, Mam. I know you want to ask about Melody.' He looked down at the cup of tea his mother had put in front of him, picked up a spoon, put a couple of spoonfuls of sugar in and began to stir. 'You were right. I should have talked to you, though I doubt if I would have taken much notice. But, marry in haste, as they say, and repent at leisure.' He stopped stirring and looked at his mother. 'I think she's having an affair.'

'Oh, no. What. . . ?'

'Little things I can't put a name to. I just know.'

'What are you going to do about it?'

'Nothing. It might fizzle out or she might just up and leave. I've told her she has to earn her own money. I'm not going to subsidize her little games.'

'And has she got a job?'

'Huh, do you really think Melody would get a job? Pigs might fly. I don't know what she does, she'll be there one minute and then she's gone. Norrie was right, wasn't he? I was a stupid idiot. But I intend to stay on the rig because the pay is good. I can pick up a few odd jobs when I'm ashore and what I earn from them goes into the kitty. I've got plans for the future and when they happen you'll be the first to know.'

'I've been so worried for you, Robbie.'

'Well you don't have to worry any more. I've seen the light, as they say.'

Twenty-Three

IN CATHERINE AND Norrie's living room Allen and Peter sat side by side at the table with Robbie at the end while Judith lounged in an armchair. Catherine was in the kitchen making coffee, Norrie putting out a plate of biscuits.

'What's this all about then?' said Allen. 'Do you know, Judith?'

'Robbie, you know, don't you?'

'Yes, of course I do.'

Catherine put a tray of coffee cups on the table.

'Haven't you told the twins why we're here, Mam?'

'No. Your dad and I decided it would be better to wait till we were all together. Now we are, so come to the table, Judith, and let's get started.'

Norrie, a plate of biscuits in one hand and a fruit cake, which he had sliced, in the other, set them down on the table and sat at its head.

'I guess you'll all remember,' he began, 'when my cousin Magnie appeared out of the blue and came home from Australia.'

'I do,' said Allen with a laugh. 'You socked him good and proper.'

'Yes, well, he deserved it. But that's not the point. He said something then that I thought was ridiculous, but it wasn't, and now something's happened that you two,' Norrie indicated Allen and Peter, 'have to know about.'

'What's anything he said got to do with us?' asked Peter.

Judith was examining her fingernails. The mention of Magnie stirred memories of creeping behind one of the fireside chairs to hide and listen to the conversation between him and her father.

'He said there were plans to drill for oil under the sea,' Norrie went on. 'I thought he was talking out of the back of his head, but he said that it would come ashore on Shetland and make a lot of work for people, that it would bring in new money and that land would go up in value. He said Uncle Callum had left my house and croft to him and he was claiming it. He was wrong, of course.'

'What? He never did. Is that why you gave him a hiding?'

'That was then,' said Peter as he picked up a slice of cake. 'What's happened now?'

'I was just coming to that. We've been approached by a developer. He wants to buy Deepdale . . . all of it.'

Peter, with his mouth full of cake, coughed and choked and spat cake crumbs. Allen slapped him on the back. Judith laughed. 'They can't,' she said. 'Well, they could . . . ' she paused, then said, 'but only if we all agree.'

'What do you mean?' said Allen.

'We all own little bits of it, don't we?' said Judith. 'Mam's got her croft, she and Dad own this one, Robbie's got Granddad's and I've now got Laura's. And if we don't all agree to sell there's nothing they can do about it. The place is useless to them if someone – like me, for instance – is sitting in the middle of it refusing to move.'

'Couldn't they make you?'

'No. I think only the council or should I say, the government, can do that. If I did sit tight it would take a lot of money to shift me.'

'Well that's all right for you,' said Allen. 'You might be in line to make a lot of money, but Peter and I don't own anything at all.'

'You don't need to worry, Allen,' said Catherine. 'I might as well tell you now that I do not intend to sell. What about you, Robbie?'

'My little bit's not worth much, especially with that ruin on it.'

'They're not interested in the land to work it like we do,' said Norrie. 'It's not croft prices they're talking about. They're developers. We're told that what they've got in mind is a sort of holiday place with a clubhouse and some chalets.'

'That's ridiculous. Who's going to want to come here for a holiday?'

'You're forgetting the birdwatchers,' said Catherine. 'They'd be here in spring and autumn and be only too glad of a place where they could come and go as they please. They'd love a clubhouse where they could get together in the evenings and chat over a pint and a pie and talk about whatever new bird they'd spotted that day.

And when they were gone the place would be available for summer visitors, so it would be a six- to eight-month season.'

'It sounds as though you're sold on it, Mam,' said Allen.

'I do think it's a good idea and one that would be good for Shetland, but they can have another think because they're not going to build it in Deepdale.'

'What sort of money were they talking about, Da?' asked Judith.

'They haven't exactly told us yet, but I've no doubt it runs into many thousands. I'm sure it's negotiable, though, but we'd need to get advice on that.'

For a while no one spoke then Robbie said, 'I don't want to sell. I might want to come back here and build myself a house.'

'A house? You?' said Allen.

'I would like to sell,' said Judith. 'But I wouldn't want to be a pushover so the offer had better be good.'

'I'm in favour of selling,' said Norrie.

'No,' shouted Catherine. 'You can't.'

Allen jumped to his feet. He thumped the table with his fist. 'It's all very well for you lot to quibble about whether you're going to sell or not, but what about Peter and me? We do a lot of the work here now Dad works at Sullom. I don't know why you asked us to come to this meeting. We've got nothing, and we're going to get nothing, but doesn't anyone think we ought to?'

'Your mother and I appreciate what you do and we'd see you all right,' said Norrie.

'What with? The money you'd get off *our* land?' said Judith.

'Of course not, there'd be enough for us all.'

'You don't know that.'

'I know that whatever they offer, if we hold out, the offer will go up.'

Catherine stood up. 'In case you hadn't noticed, Norrie, nothing's going to get sold because we have a stalemate, two for and two against.'

'Oh, heavens.' Norrie put his elbows on the table and cupped his face in his hands. 'We've hardly got going on this discussion; this is not the time to give up. Why can't you all agree? No developer is going to offer peanuts, whatever it is it'll be money that would take us forever to earn. Can't you see that? We'd all be set up. But no, you don't. Well, I've had enough, that's an end to it.'

'No it isn't,' snapped Judith. 'Robbie's not going to come back. He could build a house anywhere with the money he'd get. He never was one to dip his hand into his pocket, so he's probably saved enough already.'

'You can get lost, Judith. Just because I don't splash it around, what I do with my money is none of your business. I've had enough of being told what I can and can't do.'

'Oh dear.' Judith shook her head. 'Hm-mm-mm. Melody got you wrapped round her little finger, has she? Has she been raiding the piggy bank or have you locked it up and thrown away the key? '

Robbie gripped the arms of his chair and jumped forward. 'You can quit that. Say what you like; my life is no more of a mix up than yours and that foreigner you call Dom,' he hissed. 'Where is he, by the way? Haven't seen much sign of him lately, have you. I thought he was going to make you a star?'

'I *will* be a star,' shouted Judith. 'And I don't splash my money about, but I haven't got enough yet to go to London.' Through clenched teeth Judith snarled at Robbie. Mention of Dom had touched a raw nerve. 'You, you selfish pig,' she spat. 'You want to hang on to that bit of land to spite the rest of us. You're the one holding things up. Da could make Mam change her mind. But you—'

'You heard what Mam said, she doesn't want to sell.'

'That's all very well, if she wants to live and die in Deepdale that's up to her, but she shouldn't expect us to do the same.'

'You can stop right there, Judith,' said Norrie. 'In fact you can all stop. We're not going to reach an agreement, that's quite clear, so the meeting's over.'

Allen said, 'But Judith's right. I mean, can you see Robbie coming back?' He turned to his step-brother. 'Mam and Da might not want to stay here and if they moved out and if the rest of us moved away, there'd be no family to come back to. There'd be strangers here and it wouldn't be the same. In that case, would you really want to?'

'When you put it like that . . . hmm . . . I'd have to think about it.'

'What's there to think about?'

'I'll tell you,' said Peter. All eyes turned to the one member of the family who had listened to all that had been said and who had hardly said a word. 'Not everyone can be a winner,' he said. 'You're all right, Robbie. You've got a good job, good money and good prospects. You're all right too, Judith. You've already got an income with the rent off Laura's house. I'm sure you're salting it away the same as Robbie, so it won't matter if you get to be famous as a singer or not. And you, Allen, you and Karen have both got good jobs. You won't ever have to scrabble in the dirt to make a living. Now, as for me,' he sat back and smiled round at his family, 'well, I've got Rosie, the best wife a man like me could have. She knows that all I want to do is work with animals and she's capable and willing to work beside me. I know I could get a job as a shepherd anywhere in Scotland. There's not much anyone can teach me about sheep. So you can squabble over money or the lack of it if you like. I couldn't care less.' He stood up. 'I'm going home.'

Twenty-Four

'WHAT TIME IS your plane, Robbie?'
'I'll have to check, but I think it's about three. There's no hurry.'

'Shouldn't you let Melody know what flight you're on? Won't she be expecting you?'

'Now come on, Mam, you should know better than that. She probably hasn't even noticed I'm away.'

'Are things *really* that bad between you?'

'I told you what's going on, didn't I? There's nothing I can do about it at the moment. Give a man enough rope, as they say. I'm certainly not going to pay someone to find out what she's up to, so I'm not going to talk about it. Shall I come with you while we take the dog and walk round the sheep?'

When she was on her own Catherine could walk at her own pace, but Robbie, a fit young man, was with her now and trying to keep up with him made her out of breath. She asked him to slow down. He stood and waited for her.

'You're going too fast for me,' said Catherine. 'I'm not as young as I was and it's hard to keep up with you.'

'Might that not be telling you something? I've never known you do anything but work so isn't it time now to take things easy? I mean, how much longer are you going to go on doing this? Or do you intend to die chasing sheep?'

'Don't be silly, Robbie. I don't want to retire and anyway, I'm not old enough to do that yet.'

'What about Dad then? How old is he, sixty-five? I think you ought to sell; the money you would get would make your pensions

125

no more than pocket money. You could buy yourself a place with a few acres so you can keep a few animals just for the fun of it. I know you wouldn't want to be without a few sheep.'

Would it be nice not to have to put on a coat and hat and go out of a warm house into the rain, just to look at a few sheep and see that they were all right? It would be, thought Catherine, but she'd already had days like that and had stayed in and been bored. 'I must admit there are times when I've been tempted,' she said, 'but I've not given in yet and I don't intend to. I shall keep going until my body tells me it's time to give up.' She smiled at her son and felt like saying 'So there.' But instead she said, 'I've got my breath back, so come on, let's go.'

They walked on. Sheep were counted and fences followed and all found to be in good order. As mother and son turned for home Robbie took his mother by the arm and, spreading his arm to indicate the area of more or less level ground in front of them, said, 'You've got to hand it to them, this could be turned into a grand little golf course. And think about the valley, Mam. It's a lovely sheltered spot, just right for holiday-makers.'

'You're getting at me now,' said Catherine. 'But don't think you're going to get me to change my mind. I might be getting old, but old folk don't like being pulled up by the roots and transplanted. So you can give over.'

'I was awake half the night thinking about it,' said Robbie. 'Judith was right. I could build a house anywhere. It wouldn't be fair of me to insist on not selling. I'd be denying the others their share. So I say sell.'

'That's not fair. If you sell everybody's going to hate me because I'm *not* going to. So, *no* . . . I will not be pushed into a corner, not by you or anyone else. My mind is made up so don't say another word. End of conversation.'

End of conversation it was, for though Robbie tried to broach the subject again, Catherine would have none of it. The journey home was completed with only the briefest of exchanges between them. Before it was time for him to go back to Aberdeen, Catherine fed her son and saw to it that he gathered up all his belongings. She drove him to the airport. There she hugged him, made him promise to keep in touch and to come home for a visit whenever he could. She watched him board the plane, waited till it took off then walked to her car.

The hope that Robbie was going to stand by her in her deter-
mination not to sell her share of the valley was gone. He had
capitulated and had tried to persuade her that it would be best for
her to sell too. Now she was alone in wanting to stay, but she wasn't
going to tell Norrie that. Let him think that Robbie stood shoulder
to shoulder with her. Otherwise her whole family were against her,
even Norrie. Would he put pressure on her to change her mind,
and if he did could she continue to hold out against him?

Unhappy at the way her family had behaved over the developer's offer she was filled with unrest. As she drove the car down
into the valley, reluctant to go back to the day to day routine, she
looked for Tracy. The windows of the young woman's house were
open and there was washing on the line. Catherine stopped the car,
got out and slammed the door.

'Tracy,' she called as she opened the door of the house. 'Are you
there?'

'In the kitchen, come on in.' Tracy was baking and the little
kitchen was filled with the aroma of spicy buns. A dozen of them
were cooling on a wire rack. 'How've you been? I saw you had
family home at the weekend.'

'Oh don't talk about it,' said Catherine. 'I love my kids and I love
to see them but I'm glad that get together is over.'

'Oh dear, didn't things go well, then?'

'We've had better times. There was something that the whole
family had to discuss and we were all at loggerheads. Nobody
could agree so nothing got resolved. I might as well admit it. I'm
totally fed up.'

'Sounds like you need to get away and have time to yourself.'

'I had thought about it. I'd really like to spend a week or two
lying in the sun on a beach somewhere. But that isn't going to
happen. I did have a half-baked notion of going down to Aberdeen
for a day shopping. But that's no fun on your own.' Catherine
watched as her neighbour lifted the kettle and poured boiling
water into a teapot. 'Tracy, you wouldn't like to come with me,
would you?'

A grin spread across Tracy's face. 'Nothing I'd like better. The
shops here aren't quite up to Marks and Sparks or Debenhams, are
they? And a dose of retail therapy is a brilliant idea, just what you

need, and me too. When shall we go?'

'Whenever you like,' said Catherine. 'But it won't change any-thing, will it? The problem will still be there. I don't know what I'm going to do. Something came up that I'm against and all the family are for.' There was a hint of tears in her eyes as she looked at Tracy.

'You'll drink this cup of tea,' said Tracy. 'Then, if you like, you can tell me all about it. A trouble shared is a trouble halved, as they say, and you can rest assured that anything you say to me will go no further. I won't even tell my Paul. You'd better put a couple of spoonfuls of sugar in that,' she said as she poured out a mug of tea and put it in front of her friend. 'Now, what's bothering you?'

As Catherine stirred her tea she began to talk about the land agent, the developer and the arguments and disagreements of the family. 'I came here as a bride in 1946,' she said. 'I hated it at first and everything seemed to be going wrong, but this place gets a hold on you. I want to stay, but the kids don't and I'm the only one that's stopping anything happening. I'm afraid Norrie is going to want me to change my mind.'

'Big problem,' said Tracy. 'Not something to decide in a hurry. But, surely something like that takes a long time to put together and until you've actually signed on the dotted line, you could always change your mind, couldn't you?'

'I think you've got something there. Norrie said there're a lot of hurdles to jump, planning for instance and environment. So it might not happen at all.'

'I'd be very sorry if you did sell. I love the valley. It's so peaceful. It's a little world on its own and of course Paul and I would have to find another place.' There was a sad expression on Tracy's face as she looked at Catherine, but the irrepressible young woman could not be sad for long. 'Hey,' she said, as her face broke into a smile, 'a day in Aberdeen will do us both good. Forget about the family, let's go and trawl through the shops and have a slap-up lunch. We'll go on the boat and make it a real away day. Are you up for that?'

It was hard to hold on to sadness in the light of Tracy's enthusi-asm and a smile crept across Catherine's face. 'I am. With you for company it'll be fun. The question now is when?'

'Just as soon as you like, talk to your man and let me know. Now then, I think them buns have cooled enough and are just about ready to eat.' Taking a plate from her dresser Tracy filled it with the buns that had been cooling on a rack. 'Help yourself,' she said as she put the plate on the table. And knowing how good a cook Tracy was, Catherine did.

Twenty-Five

THE LETTER CAME while Catherine was in Aberdeen. Norrie opened it, read it, put it back in its envelope and put the envelope in his pocket. It could wait until he was ready to discuss its contents, but not until he had time to think about it.

He had tried to persuade Catherine to change her mind about selling her croft, but without success. She still flatly refused and he had written to the solicitor and told him that there would be no sale. And, just as he had thought, the developer had come back with a higher offer. It was very tempting. There would be enough money to do all the things they wanted. He and Catherine could buy land big enough for a house as well as the few animals both he and she would want. He was ready to retire. A life of hard work was taking its toll. It showed in the increasing amount of effort it took him to do jobs he had thought nothing of a few short years ago. Although Catherine never complained, he thought it must be the same for her, and it was high time they both began to take life easy, but he knew she would not admit to that. He didn't really *want* to retire, but knew it was time that he should. Whether he could persuade Catherine to do the same was another story.

He would say it was Catherine he was thinking of. Robbie was very fond of his mother and it might be enough to tip the balance. He had no worries about Judith. With money from the land that was hers, she would be all right. There should be enough to give to Allen and Peter to enable them to make a start on the farm they'd talked about, though when Peter had said that whatever they decided meant nothing to him because he already had all he needed, Norrie knew that that might not be an option for them.

All this was just surmise, though; everything depended on whether Catherine could be made to change her mind. He wondered how she was getting on in Aberdeen and was glad that Tracy had gone with her; the girl's outgoing personality was just the tonic Catherine needed. And then he thought that if they did sell and move away that friendship was something else Catherine would lose. She had had no room or time for friends when he had first known her, Robbie's grandmother had seen to that. And then when he had married her and the care of three small children was added to her already busy day, friends were again lacking. June and Joe Thomson had come to the valley then and he cringed mentally as he remembered how, with a foolish, drink-fuelled act he had nearly put paid to the friendship that had grown up between Catherine and June. And then he laughed as he remembered Catherine's fierce treatment of him. She had not let him off the hook, and he had retaliated by ignoring her until she had begged to make amends. How foolish they had been.

But enough of memories; when it came to the sale of land there were so many things to be considered. Applications would have to be made for decrofting, and men from the planning office would surely quote the rule book and cause delay. No doubt the Department of the Environment would poke its nose in too. Negotiations alone could take months. They were still going to be in for the long haul. Would they all still be speaking to one another at the end of it?

The trip to Aberdeen was a great success. When Catherine said she might try to find something that she could wear to Allen's wedding, Tracy had dragged her into shop after shop and encouraged her to try on several outfits.

'You have to look the cat's whiskers,' she said, as, one after another, she rejected what Catherine took off the rack. The colour was wrong, the style was wrong or the material was no better than a dish rag. This was too long, that was too short, and, no, no, no, that one made her look a frump. But at last there was something that pleased her and when Catherine emerged from the fitting room Tracy said, 'Wow, for a woman your age you've got a great figure. When your husband sees you in that he'll fall in love with you all over again.'

And she had been right, for now as she stood in front of Norrie and asked him if she looked all right there was no mistaking the look of admiration in his eyes. 'My peerie yarta,' he said, 'my little darling, you're beautiful.'

She smiled and said, 'Isn't it a case of fine feathers making fine birds?'

'Darlin', when you're ninety you'll still be beautiful to me.'

'I wouldn't bank on it if I were you,' said Catherine.

'Mam,' called Allen as he came clattering down the stairs. 'Can you give me a brush down? Where's Peter? He should be here by now.'

'Stop panicking, boy, there's plenty of time,' said Norrie.

'But I've got to be there first and you know what Karen's like, fretting and fuming in case she's going to be late. If I was, I'd never hear the last of it.'

'Stand still while I brush you or I'm liable to poke you in the eye and that won't do,' said Catherine. 'There, that's done. Here's Peter now. Allen's afraid that the bride will get to the church before he does, Peter. Remind him that it is traditional for the bride to be late, will you?'

'That's right, bro. Rosie kept me waiting ten minutes, don't you remember? It'll be the same for you, Karen's Mam will see to that. You sure you want to do this?' asked Peter. 'This is the last chance to change your mind.'

'Stop your nonsense, Peter, come on, get me to the church.'

'You're in an awful hurry,' said Peter as Allen put a hand on his shoulder and almost pushed him out of the door. 'Karen will be late, brides always are.'

'I don't care. *I'm* not going to be.'

The drive into Lerwick and the church that Karen and Allen were to be married in was a short one. Guests were drifting in to fill the pews. As Catherine and Norrie walked up the aisle heads turned to look and smiles were exchanged. Catherine knelt to say a prayer, looked at the flowers and up at the stained glass window. Then she looked at her sons, no longer boys, but men as they sat side by side, heads close as they talked. Against the muted strains of a piece of music being played was the hiss of the congregation's whispered conversations. Then the vicar was walking down the aisle. Karen would soon be there. And then she was, for the resounding chords of the *Wedding March* filled the little church. With a rustle of clothes and a clatter of feet the congregation stood and turned to watch as the bride, on the arm of her father, walked up the aisle.

Catherine listened as the wedding service progressed, stood to sing the hymns, bent her head in prayer and wished she could hear what the vicar was saying. Then Allen and Karen were exchanging rings and declared a married couple and the last of her boys would no longer be at home for her to care for. It was then that unbidden tears flooded her eyes. 'Norrie,' she whispered as she gave him a nudge. 'Do you have a hanky?'

He looked down at her. 'Why do you cry? This is the time to be joyful.' Karen and Allen followed the vicar to the vestry and Norrie said, 'Come on, they're going to sign the register. We have to go too.'

And then it was all a blur. The press of people, congratulations and photographs, the reception, food, wine and speeches then dancing, until Catherine said the rest of the night was for the young and couldn't she go home.

At home she sat down and kicked off her shoes. 'It's awful quiet here,' she said. 'Our children have flown the nest and it's empty. I don't know if I like it.'

'You've forgotten Peter and Rosie. There'll soon be a little one there and I don't suppose they'll stop at one. You'll soon have a brood around you again.'

'How could I forget? It was just the thought that I wouldn't wake and hear footsteps going up the stairs and know that one of the boys had come home.'

'Just be glad that you won't be worrying about them and you'll be able to get a good night's sleep.'

Norrie fuelled the stove. 'That's done then,' he said as he straightened his back. 'Time for bed, ah wait a minute. There's a message on the answerphone.'

'Leave it,' said Catherine. 'It'll still be there in the morning.'

But Norrie was lifting the phone and pressing the play button. He put the phone down and looked at Catherine.

'What is it?' she asked.

'It's your mam. She died, slipped away quietly this afternoon. Janet said she'd ring again tomorrow. There's nothing you can do now, darling.'

'I knew it wouldn't be long,' said Catherine. 'I shall have to go down.'

'Of course you will. Will you have a dram now?'

'No. Take me to bed and hold me.'

Twenty-Six

THE END OF September brought rain and when the wind moved westerly, more and yet more. Catherine put on her boots and a waterproof jacket and went out to milk her cow and feed her hens. She looked at the hill where her sheep grazed but did not go and check them. Peter would do that when he came off shift.

With Judith in Lerwick and all three of her boys married, the house echoed with emptiness. Her father had died and now her mother. Rosie, five months pregnant still worked so, other than Tracy – if she was at home – there was no one else in the valley. It had all happened so quickly, and loneliness, something Catherine had never known before, settled on her and she found it hard.

Confronted with a long face when he came home night after night, Norrie told her she should get in the car and take herself out. 'You need company and folk aren't going to come to find you.' But she said no, she didn't want to and stayed at home. She was sorting invoices, bills and statements, ready to enter in her accounts book when Norrie said, 'The solicitor rang up while you were along at Tracy's. He wants to know if we've thought over the other offer.'

'What other offer?'

'I got a letter from them while you were in Aberdeen. The developer has upped his offer. I told you he would, didn't I? They never offer what they're prepared to pay at the beginning. When they think they won't get what they want, they offer more. It's a real sizable sum now.'

Looking down at a bill for sheep feed for well over £300 Catherine thought that was a sizable sum in view of what it bought them. Without looking at Norrie she said, 'And does the developer's sizable sum mean you want to accept?'

'Yes, I do, but the offer is on condition that the Crofters' Commission will agree to decrofting and the developer can get full planning permission. I know Judith would sell, so I rang Robbie and he's agreeable; it's up to you now.'

Catherine stopped what she was doing and stared into space while she rolled the pencil she was holding over and over between her fingers. Norrie waited for her to speak. 'I don't know,' she said. 'You've put me in an awful position. If I insist on staying put I shall always feel that I have denied our children, but I hate the thought of someone destroying the valley, because that's what will happen. These little houses that people struggled to build and rear a family in will be pulled apart. There are too many of them in ruins in Shetland already. I must be getting old because I hate change. I'm sorry, but I'll have to think about it.'

'That's up to you,' said Norrie. 'But don't take too long.'

Catherine went back to her paperwork. She went on sorting paid bills from invoices until, bit by bit, her hand slowed and she stopped. 'The thing I don't like about it is that they don't tell you everything. And if you don't ask or make a fuss you're never going to know what they're up to. They might have already got outline planning permission, but if they don't get full planning it will all have been for nothing. They feed information to us in dribs and drabs. It's like holding a carrot in front of a donkey. I really think it's time to get some advice.'

'I agree with you, in fact I was going to suggest it myself, but don't forget that nothing happens till we agree to sell. They can do nothing until then.'

'But if we say we'll sell do we have to sign anything? I mean, are we committed or could we change our minds?'

'I think if we sign the contract we'll be bound by that. It's like buying a house, isn't it? When the contracts have been signed it's all tied up and legal. We'd have to agree a date to get out then.'

'Like I said, we ought to get some advice.' Catherine went back to her paperwork and for a while the slither of paper against paper competed with the patter of rain on the window until, not stopping what she was doing, she said, 'I suppose that if all went well, with the sort of money you say they're offering, nobody in their right mind would want to back out, would they? You remember you said there'd be enough to build us a house and to give some money to Allen and Peter? I guess that must be still true, if not more so.'

Norrie looked at her. The changing expressions on her face told of the tumult in her mind. She put her elbows on the table, crossed her arms, leaned forward and gave a sigh. 'I've been here so long,' she said, 'I feel as though I've taken root. It's been my stage, where my life has been played out. But I suppose it's time now for me to exit stage left. I wonder if I'll get bouquets or brickbats.' She gave a little laugh. 'I've thought and thought about this and I have to say that it would be selfish of me to deny the children a good start in life, so I'm going to give in and say that I'll sell too.'

'That must have been a hard decision for you to make,' said Norrie. 'I know how attached you are to Deepdale, but I'll do my best to make sure you won't regret it.'

'Regret it? Of course I shall regret it, but others have to be considered and I learned long ago that we can't always have our own way.' Catherine sat back in her chair. Suddenly she slapped the pencil she was still holding down on the table. 'I can't believe I've just given in. What have I done? What have I let us in for? How long would it be before we have to move and what about the sheep? What are we going to do with them? And there's so much muck and bruck about the place it'll take forever to clean it all up. Oh dear, it'll be such an upheaval.'

'It's too soon to worry about that. There'll be more than enough time to get ourselves organized.'

'But Norrie, think about what you'd be giving up. You'd have to sell all your machinery, your tools, everything. How would you *really* feel about leaving Deepdale? And it's not only me and you; it's Peter and Rosie and Tracy and Paul too, don't forget they're going to have to find somewhere else to live.'

'Tools and machinery can be replaced. I wouldn't miss them. I suppose I'd miss the valley, but not as much as you. I know some people live and die in the place they were born, but that's folk that never go anywhere, afraid of their own shadows, they are. That's not me, I'd settle down anywhere.'

'But *where* will we go?' There was rising concern in Catherine's voice.

'We'll start worrying about that when the developer's got his planning permission. We can't be certain of anything until then and if you're going to start wishing you hadn't changed your mind I'm not going to talk about it anymore.' Norrie stood up. 'I'm going to find something to eat. Do you want anything?'

Catherine didn't and the subject was dropped.

Norrie had been right; negotiations with the Crofters' Commission were lengthy and when they had finally agreed on decrofting the land it was the turn of the planning office to deliberate and the weeks continued to drift by. Catherine helped lift the potatoes and when the barley was ripe she walked behind the binder and stooked the corn. When the last of the harvest was in it was time to think about Christmas. She was not looking forward to it. Rosie was going home to her mother for the last few weeks of her pregnancy and, as she was due early in the New Year, would be there for Christmas. Peter was going with her. Allen and Karen had their own flat in Lerwick and there was little doubt that they would spend Christmas day with her parents. Robbie had said he would probably be on shift, which left only Judith. It was more than likely that she would be singing at some party or other, and Catherine ruled her daughter out as no more than a casual visitor. How could less than twelve months bring about such drastic changes?

'We'll not keep on so many sheep,' said Norrie when they were sorting out their breeding stock. 'This is the best time to sort out the old ones; they'll sell better now than they will later on. We'll put the rest through the marts when the time comes. The developer won't want them.'

'What am I going to do with no sheep to look at?' said Catherine. 'Ever since I started I was hoping one of my boys would take them on. Did I spend all that time learning and building up the flock just to sell them to someone else?'

'We'll get somewhere where you can keep a few,' said Norrie. 'Just pick out the ones you want and put a mark on them. You could still go on breeding pedigree rams and I'd be there to help you.'

Tentative plans began to be made regarding the move. The grapevine, that lightning-quick spreader of news, had already put a rumour in circulation that the valley of Deepdale was to be sold. As to what was going to happen there, what was going to be built or what it was to become, no one was sure. But, as rumour would have it, it could be anything from a housing estate to a holiday village, or even a nudist colony.

Tracy called on Catherine. 'I've heard the rumours,' she said. 'Do we have to start looking for somewhere else, or is it too early?'

'Nothing's settled yet,' said Catherine, 'and until it is even I don't know if I'm going to have to move, but I'll let you know what's happening as soon as I do. I won't keep you in the dark.'

'The trouble is that there're so few places to rent and I'm really getting to like living in Shetland. Paul is too. He's into birdwatching now and he's fascinated with the history of the place. I've had to borrow books from the library for him and he's always got his nose in one when he's home. I think he'd like to stay here permanently.'

'You could think about buying a house, then. I'd like you to stay. When the kids were small and I had the sheep to look after I didn't have the chance to go out much and I haven't got many friends, so I'd miss you if you went too far away.'

'We'll have to see what we can do about it, then, won't we,' said Tracy.

Twenty-Seven

WITH ONLY CATHERINE and Norrie to share the day, Christmas in Deepdale passed quietly. It was tea time when Judith breezed in.

'I can't stay long, Mam,' she said. 'I'm going to a party tonight. Look, I brought your presents. A glam nightie for you, Mam, and, well, I didn't know what to get you, Dad, so I got you a new wallet. I thought you might want to keep all that money you're going to get in it. I hope that's okay.'

'That's fine,' said Norrie, and when Catherine took her present out of its wrappings she said, 'This is lovely, but it's too pretty.'

'You'll wear it,' said Judith. 'And don't ever let me find that you've put it away in the drawer. It's time you got rid of those awful old pyjamas you wear.'

'But I like them, they're comfortable.'

'Yes, and now you've got central heating you won't need them. You've got no excuse and next time I come I shall ask Dad what you've done with them.'

'And I shall tell her,' said Norrie.

'How is Dominic?' asked Catherine. 'Have you heard from him lately?'

'He says he can't understand why nothing's come of the recording I made and that he's going to chase it up. But I wouldn't hold your breath. Sorry, Mam, but I've got to go.' As she kissed her mother goodbye, Judith said she would come again soon.

Rosie's baby, a boy, was born on New Year's Day. Peter, his voice bubbling with excitement, phoned his parents to tell them. 'He weighs eight pounds, Mam. He's a lovely bonnie boy. We're going to call him Kyle. He's got a lot of black hair and . . . you've got to come and see him, Mam.'

'Of course I will. I'm so happy for you, Peter,' said Catherine. 'How's Rosie? Is she all right'

'She's fine. Her mam and da are here, but they'll be going home soon.'

'All right, Norrie and I will come right away.' Catherine put down the phone and turned to Norrie. 'Rosie's had her baby,' she said. 'It's a little boy. You're a granddad and I'm a granny!' Then she laughed. 'We've joined the doiters. They'll be coming to pick us up to go shopping on the doiters bus next.'

'Don't be daft,' said Norrie. 'I can't see you losing your marbles, ever.'

'Well, I hope I don't. But come on, let's go and see the baby.'

Having flatly refused ever to learn to knit there was no traditional shawl or tiny knitted garments for Catherine to give to Rosie. Not that it mattered, for Rosie's mother had made that contribution, and Catherine took chocolates and promised to babysit whenever required. Norrie put a silver coin in the baby's hand and smiled with satisfaction when it held on to it and didn't drop it. 'He'll do well,' he said, and laughed. 'He already knows how to hang on to money.'

'Do you want to hold him, Mam?' said Peter.

'I thought you'd never ask.' Peter placed the baby in his mother's arms and, as she cradled it and looked into the tiny face and held the little hand in hers, she said, 'He's beautiful.' She held him a while longer then handed her grandson back to his father. 'I love him already, but I'm forgetting his mother.' She turned to Rosie as little Kyle was put back in his cot. 'You will never have to ask if I'll look after him,' she said. 'I'm so glad Peter chose you for his wife.'

It was several weeks before Peter and Rosie returned to Deepdale. Tracy called to see them and crooned over the baby. 'How lucky you are,' she said. 'It seems I'm destined not to have one, so you can hand him over to me any time.' Rosie smiled and said she thought there'd have to be a toss-up between her and Catherine, but that she thought that she'd keep him to herself for a while.

February brought east winds and snow and Catherine worried when Norrie set off for work on icy roads. He said she had no need to worry, because he and another man shared their transport week and week about, and he was never driving on his own. So Catherine donned her waterproof jacket and leggings and walked out to tend her animals. There were no parents to write to now so she wrote to Janet. She spent time with Rosie and little Kyle or with Tracy. But she didn't want to impose on the young ones too often and found that the hours spent on her own dragged, and she was lonely.

'I wonder what's happening about the plans for this place,' she said to Norrie one evening.

'I can tell you that,' said Norrie. 'And it isn't much. Geordie Halcrow's boy works in the planning office and he knows who's drawing the plans. The man's ill and they say that he's likely to be away from work for some time.'

'Who's Geordie Halcrow?'

'He's the man I share transport to work with.'

'Well, how did his boy know who was doing the Deepdale plans?'

Disbelief showed on Norrie's face when he looked at his wife. 'Haven't you lived here long enough to know that nothing is secret? Everybody knows we've had an offer for the valley and those in the planning office know that plans will have to be drawn. So they poke their noses in to find out who does what.'

'I could believe that.'

'I already told you these things can drag on for ages. I expect it will be autumn before we get out of here.'

'Hi Catherine, where are you, me dook?' Tracy was fighting the wind that was trying to prevent her from closing the front door. Closed at last she leaned against it. 'Does this wind ever stop?' she said as Catherine, with a broad smile on her face, came through from the kitchen.

'Now and then, but March has only just started so it'll get worse yet; we've got the equinox to come. You'll have to put up with it for a bit longer.'

'Why should the equinox make any difference?'

'It usually blows a gale then. You can be sure we'll have one.'

'Oh. I don't really mind the wind, but it wouldn't be so bad if it wasn't so cold. Um . . . I was wondering if you were going to the drama festival at the Garrison. I've heard it can be very good. I thought I'd go but Paul doesn't want to and it would be nice to have company.'

'Yes, I'll come with you,' said Catherine. 'I have been before but Norrie grumbles if I ask him to come with me. Men don't seem to have any liking for drama, do they?'

'Is there any news from the developer or whoever it is?'

'I was talking to Norrie about that the other day,' said Catherine. 'He said he'd heard that the man drawing up the plans had been taken ill so everything's on hold for a while.'

'That gives us some breathing space, then. I've been looking at the ads for houses. Paul is as taken with Shetland as I am, so we're thinking about buying. Why do they all have a price and offers over afterwards?'

'That's the way they do it here. If you look at a house and you like it you tell the solicitor you're interested. You don't have to do anything then until they decide there are enough people who would like to buy. They decide on a closing date then and that's when you have to write down your offer and submit it in a sealed envelope, usually by midday that day. Best offer wins.'

'My lor', that's a bit of a gamble. What happens if you can't sell the house you've already got? How are you going to pay for something else? Back home you never offer what they're asking. Always under and then you beat about the bush till you can agree. Mm. We shall see, then.'

'Are you sure you want to stay here?' asked Catherine. 'It's not only the weather that's a drawback. Sometimes when you want to get off the island you can't, either because there's a gale blowing and the boat isn't running or the planes are fog bound.'

'When you've lived in a place like Manchester, and I mean in the heart of it,' said Tracy, 'this place is heaven. Paul is a bit of a twitcher and he's getting that excited about being here and able to watch for migrating birds. Me, I can take 'em or leave 'em, but I'll see neither hide nor hair of him when they start coming through. I've been thinking I might get myself a little job somewhere later on. But not for a bit. I'm just enjoying being here at the moment.'

'So there's no point trying to persuade you that you'd be better off back home then,' said Catherine. 'I'm glad about that because I would miss you if you went away.'

'And I'd miss you too. You're like us, down to earth, call a spade a spade sort of folk, I like that. So when *you* move you'd better not go too far away.'

At that, Catherine laughed. 'Don't be daft; you can't get too far away here. The main island's only seventy miles north to south so even if I went up to North Roe I'd only be an hour's drive away. Not that I'm going to go there, mind you, you might as well be on a separate island as there – that place really is isolated.'

'That's good. Now, what about the drama festival? Whose car are we going to go in?'

Tracy still drove the car that she had rattled down into Deepdale that first time in, and remembering it Catherine said, 'I think it had better be mine.'

Twenty-Eight

WHEN THE MONTH of March gave way to April the winds that had scoured Shetland died away. April, month of spring flowers and showers of rain did bring showers, but not the ones expected; these were showers of snow, borne on a cold north wind. The sky filled with grey clouds, and snowflakes danced on the breeze, gently at first, but then filling the sky with a whirling, swirling mass. The land it fell on was slowly warming up and the snow that fell on it quickly melted away.

Tracy Finney, red hair covered by a woolly hat, her body insulated by layers of warm garments and feet encased in fur boots, plodded to Catherine's house. She hammered on the door, opened it and called out, 'Hi, Catherine.'

Catherine was in the kitchen. She had loaded her washing machine and switched it on. It was old and tired from constant use and it whirred, clanked and rattled. Due to the noise, and concentrating on what she was doing, Catherine was unaware that Tracy had come in till the girl stood beside her. She jumped in alarm. 'Heavens above,' she said. 'You did give me a fright.'

'Sorry about that,' said Tracy. 'I didn't mean to, but that thing . . .' she pointed at the washing machine, which was now emitting a high-pitched scream as it spun its contents, 'that thing's lethal. Get rid of it.'

'It works,' said Catherine, 'why should I?'

'Because one of these days it's going to explode and when it does you will be drowned under a mountain of froth. It would be a very nasty death.' Tracy laughed as she spoke. 'I can see me coming in and finding you lying on the floor in a puddle of water with your fingers all turned into witch's fingers and I don't know what else.'

'Go on with you, Tracy,' said Catherine with a chuckle. 'Just listen to it now.' Spin cycle stopped, the machine turned gently back and forth and the only sound that was coming from it was a pleasant hum. 'You see? It's no monster.'

'I wouldn't trust it,' said Tracy. 'Is it coffee time?'

'When you're here it is,' said Catherine. She put the kettle on while Tracy fetched mugs. 'What did you really come to see me for?'

'I was wondering if there were any lambs yet.'

'I haven't been out to look yet. Peter or Norrie do the early rounds and neither of them said anything.'

Kettle boiled and coffee made Catherine was about to hand a mug to Tracy when the washing machine started on a fast spin. The clothes inside it had somehow gathered together in a lump and were being thrown around the drum. Rocking from side to side and banging against the unit it had been fitted into the machine began to vibrate rapidly and as it did it moved forward.

Tracy, mouth open, stared at it then, grabbing Catherine by the arm she shouted, 'Run, run for your life, it's coming to get us!'

When Norrie and Catherine had driven the in-lamb ewes into the barn Tracy had tagged along. The sheep were divided into small lots and penned till they gave birth. It was much better for the ewes to lamb under cover and much easier to tend them. No one had to walk round the parks at night to see if any needed help. Tracy had been so excited that she was going witness the birth of a lamb that she found it hard to keep away from Catherine's house.

'You would tell me if you had any, wouldn't you?' she said.

'There's none yet that I know about,' said Catherine. 'But now that the boys have had a look at the washing machine and it behaves itself, we'll go and have a look. I'll just get my coat.' She was pulling on her boots when the phone rang. 'Pick it up, will you, Tracy? You're closer to it than I.'

'It's Norrie,' said Tracy as she gave Catherine the phone.

'Hi Norrie, what's the matter?' said Catherine. When she gasped Tracy looked at her and saw the mouth open and the eyebrows raised. 'Well that's all we need,' Catherine went on. 'Who told you? Geordie I suppose . . . . Okay . . . . Thanks for nothing.'

'Sounds like you got bad news,' said Tracy.

'I wish I had *never* agreed to the sale of the land,' said Catherine. 'I knew it was wrong from the start. It's taken months already and now the man who was drawing the plans has upped and died. He was off work sick for ages. I suppose someone else will have to be found to do them now.'

'But does that really matter?' asked Tracy. 'I mean, it'll be a pain for the developer, but it'll give you, and me, longer to get used to the idea of moving.'

'That's just it. It's prolonging the agony. If anything else goes wrong I swear I shall think seriously about backing out. Nothing's signed yet, so we're not bound to sell.' As she zipped up her coat and pulled on a hat Catherine turned away to look out of the window. She stood there for a few moments, obviously deep in thought. Then she turned round, a grin on her face, 'Come on, let's go and see if anything's happening in the maternity ward.'

The doors to the barn, on the south side of the building, were wide open. Tracy asked if they were meant to be and Catherine said that they were; sheep needed a flow of air. Even with the doors open there was a warm atmosphere and a strong smell of wool, silage and sheep dung. From time to time there were deep guttural bleats from some of the ewes and, disturbed by the arrival of the two women, the rustle of straw beneath their feet as they moved around.

Catherine, followed closely by Tracy, walked along the side of the pens. As she did she cast an expert eye over her sheep, looking for any sign of impending birth. From the corner of one of the pens came a reed-like bleat. 'Wait there,' she said to Tracy. 'I think we have a lamb.' Catherine climbed over a hurdle and into the pen. 'It's not long been born,' she said when she found the lamb lying in the straw, 'and I think there's going to be another.'

'Another? What, twins?' said Tracy.

'Yes. I'll get the mother out and into one of those small pens over there if you'll help me.' Catherine pointed to where small individual pens had been constructed. 'Open the hurdle at the front of it then come and open this one.'

Tracy did as she was asked and Catherine, carrying the lamb, coaxed the mother to follow her by imitating the lamb's bleat.

'Wow,' said Tracy when mother and baby were installed in their own pen, 'isn't the baby tiny. Why is it that colour? I thought lambs were white.'

'It will be when the mother has cleaned it up. It's been lying in a bag of fluid, you know, and that's what makes it that colour.'

There was a second lamb. Catherine stayed in the pen beside the ewe while Tracy watched from outside it. 'She doesn't make any noise, does she?' she said as she watched the ewe straining to push the lamb out.

'For a very good reason,' said Catherine. 'If she was out in the wild there would be predators ready to steal the lamb as soon as it was born. Any noise would attract them.'

'If that was me, I'd be yelling my head off,' said Tracy. 'You've seen them programmes on television, haven't you? The language some of them women use, well, it would do justice to a stoker. Oh look, two little feet.'

Two little feet were followed by a nose, then a head, and seconds later the body of the lamb slithered out onto the straw on the floor of the pen. Catherine reached out to remove the membrane from the nose of the little animal. As she did it sneezed. The ewe got up from where she had been lying and turned to look at her offspring. She began to lick it and clean the birth fluids off of it, as she did she spoke to it, her voice a soft whickering that came from her throat.

It was not long before the lamb, on shaky legs, was standing up. Instinctively, it staggered along its mother's side till it reached her udder and the life-giving fluid it contained.

'It's sucking strong,' said Catherine. 'It'll be all right. We can leave them to bond together now.' She had been kneeling beside the ewe, and now she stood up. 'What did you think of that, then?' she said.

'Wonderful,' said Tracy. 'I'd never seen anything being born so thank you for letting me watch.'

'I can do more than that,' said Catherine. 'I can teach you what to look for so you will know when a ewe is in labour and then you can do my job if, for some reason, I can't.'

'That would be great. I'm so excited. I shall have something to talk to Paul about when he comes home. Can I come along tomorrow?'

It wasn't Tracy who knocked on the door that evening, but Paul. When Catherine let him in he asked to see Norrie. 'Thought you may be able to tell me what I want to know,' he said. 'I've been looking at my bird books and I think I've seen a merlin, but I can't be sure and I wondered if you knew.'

'It's no good asking me. I can only recognize blackbirds, robins and sparrows and I'm not sure how much Norrie knows. He'll be back in a minute; he's just gone to check the sheep. We're in the middle of lambing.'

'Tracy was telling me about that. She said you let her watch a lamb being born; she was so excited about it. But it must be run of the mill for you, isn't it?'

'You might think so, but every birth is a wonder to me. I think it's a minor miracle, but I'm not sure the men think about it that way. Ah, here's Norrie now.'

Norrie kicked off his boots by the back door.

'Paul wants a word with you,' said Catherine.

'Oh, does he? And what can I do for you, young man?' said Norrie.

'I thought birdwatching would be a good hobby to take up. So I've been studying my bird books and I think I've seen a merlin. But of course I don't know. Would I be right?'

'You probably are. Let's see, it's the middle of April now, another month and they'll be thinking of nesting. You should join the RSPB. They'll give you all the information you want. I think one of the blokes lives near here. I'm sure they're in the phone book – give them a ring.'

'Thanks, I'll do that . . . Mr Williams, I don't know anything about farming but if you ever need a hand with anything, you only have to ask.'

'That's very good of you. There's nothing at the moment, but we can always do with an extra hand at harvest time.'

Twenty-Nine

JUDITH CAME HOME for the Easter weekend. Catherine took her to see Rosie's baby, but when she expected her daughter to croon over the plump, happy little boy that Kyle was, she was disappointed. Judith looked into the pram, smiled and said what a bonnie child it was, but when invited to pick it up she backed away. 'I'm not good with little ones,' she said. 'For some reason they just look at me and cry. See?' she pointed at the baby, whose mouth had begun to turn down and whose eyes were bright with tears, 'didn't I just tell you?'

'Poor little thing. What did you do to it?' said her mother.

'Nothing, I did nothing. It happens every time. I swear I'll never look at another baby again.'

'Never mind, my peerie bairn,' said Rosie as she picked her baby up. 'Judith loves you really.'

'Of course I do,' said Judith and, 'Of course she does,' said her mother.

Peter said Judith's face would frighten anyone, especially when she got mad because Dom hadn't got her a recording contract yet. 'He's forgotten you and found someone else,' he said. 'You'll have to pack up and go to London and do it all yourself.'

'I would if that developer would get up off his backside and pay us. I've been trawling the net; London's a very expensive place to live. I can't go without a decent amount of money in my pocket.'

'What about going down to Southampton and staying with your Aunt Janet? I'm sure she'd have you. You could get on a train and get up to London in an hour or so,' said Catherine. 'Wouldn't that be a help? You could probably get work in Southampton while you were waiting.'

'No thanks, Mam. It's London I want to go to, not Southampton.'

'Well, you might like to think about it.'

Peter, usually the one who listened and said nothing, continued to tease his sister. 'Judith will go to London and be busking on the underground,' he said. 'A very rich record producer will find her and . . . no, he won't make her famous he'll keep her for himself because Dom has . . . aah, no!' he yelled as Judith threw a cushion at him and walked out.

'That was unkind of you, Peter,' said his mother. 'Can't you see that she's upset about it? Why couldn't you keep your mouth shut? Dom hasn't gone off with anyone else. At least, I don't think he has. Judith says he still keeps in touch. But, thanks to you, I shall have to go now and see if I can cheer her up.'

The rest of the weekend passed quietly. Catherine tried but failed to lift Judith's mood and ruefully admitted that she was glad when the girl went back to her flat in Lerwick. Having her home for a few days had not been a success. Judith had changed. The way she behaved when confronted with Rosie and Peter's baby made Catherine wonder if her daughter would ever marry and have children of her own. Sadly, she thought it unlikely.

The busy few weeks of looking after the ewes as they gave birth was nearly over, but every morning after breakfast Catherine went out to the barn to see if all was well. It would only be one more week before the beginning of May and the parks would be filled with the gambol of lambs. She had done her rounds and was on the way back to her house when a movement at the top of the track into the valley caught her eye. She looked up and saw men there, one with a red and white painted staff. She guessed that they were surveyors measuring the track. Normally, she would have watched from a distance for a while, then left them to it and got on with her work. But today she was curious and, putting down the bucket she carried, she went to talk to them.

'What are you doing?' she asked when she reached them.

'Why would you want to know?' said one of the men.

Catherine gave the man an icy stare before she replied. 'I have every right to know, which is why I asked,' she said. 'This valley belongs to me and my family and, unless you have been sent here to work, you are trespassing. So will you please tell me what you are doing and why?'

'I apologize for me mate,' said the older of the two men. 'I take it that you're Mrs Williams, and if I'm right, you're in the process of selling the land to a developer.'

'Yes, I'm Mrs Williams,' said Catherine.

'We've been sent here to survey the access road.'

'And what do you find?' said Catherine.

'At the moment, without even doing a survey, I can see that to widen it, which is what will have to be done, will cause a lot of problems. Is this the only road in and out?'

'Yes.'

'Hm.' The man rubbed his chin. 'Would you mind if we looked around to see if there's anywhere else we can make secondary access?'

'As long as it's only that and you don't disturb the sheep, I don't suppose I have any reason to stop you.'

'Thank you. We'll do what we've got to do here first and look round later. I promise we won't get in your way.'

The men did not get in her way and Catherine neither heard them about their work nor saw them go. A week went by before there was anything to remind her that they had been there. The reminder was in the form of a letter from the developer's solicitor. *Problems have arisen regarding the access road. Work is in hand to try to solve them, but unfortunately this is going to delay the contracts being drawn up. Andrew Patterson regrets the inconvenience, but for the time being there is nothing to be done till the surveyors have come up with a solution.*

'I'm beginning to think that this development was never meant to take place, Norrie,' said Catherine after she had read the letter out to him.

'I knew there would be snags. Didn't I tell you it would take a long time? This is only the beginning. Better prepare yourself for more.'

'But it's like living on a knife edge. We can't make any plans because we don't know how long this is going to take or how much money we're going to get. In fact, I've a good mind not to sell. Money doesn't bring happiness.'

'It's not their fault that there's a problem with the access; they know they'd be lucky if everything went according to plan.'

'If they expect to have a lot of traffic in and out everything hinges on the road being suitable, so they should have looked at that in the first place,' said Catherine. 'And if they didn't take a proper look at it, it *is* their fault.'

There was a knock on the door. It was Paul. 'Can I come in?' he said.

'Yes, of course you can,' said Catherine.

'I'm not interrupting anything, am I?' Catherine shook her head and Paul went on, 'I thought you'd like to know that that bird is a merlin. But you're not going to like this because, well, it's a protected species. Um . . . there's more . . . there are two of them flying around here now. I guess they're a breeding pair.'

'Well, that's all right, isn't it?' said Norrie. 'I like birds; I don't go around shooting them.'

'It's not that. It's just that if they are a breeding pair and they decide to nest in the valley, which seems very likely. . .' Paul hesitated and stopped. 'Well, it would mean that it would be against the law if they were disturbed.'

'What you're really saying is that no building work could go ahead till the little ones had hatched and left the nest. How long would that take?'

'Incubation is thirty days,' said Paul. 'I'm not sure how long after they've hatched it would be before the little ones could fly, but a few weeks I'm sure.'

'Oh, my God,' moaned Catherine. 'That means that they couldn't use any heavy machinery to dig out the hillside. Even the noise of the tractor echoes round the valley; it would be hell with their great machines. And you know what this means, don't you, Norrie? It's going to be the middle of July before they can even make a start.'

'I seem to remember telling you that I thought we wouldn't be out of here before the autumn. I think I'll revise that and say we'll still be here next year.'

'I'm sorry if I brought you bad news,' said Paul.

'Not your fault. Where did you learn all that about the bird?' asked Norrie.

'I joined the RSPB like you said.'

'So it's my fault then. If I hadn't said that, you wouldn't have known what a merlin was, none of us would have been any the wiser and the work would have gone ahead. Oh well, as the Yanks say, that's the way the cookie crumbles.'

Thirty

THE MONTH OF May was temperamental. One day the sun shone and the next day it rained. And so it went, day in and day out. But by the middle of the month the weather made up its mind what it was going to do and the wind shifted and blew from the south. Catherine put on a jacket, fetched her hoe and set about working between the rows of carrots in the rig. Hoeing was a job she liked. It was a repetitive job, the action of lifting the hoe and bringing it down with just the right amount of force to cut into the ground and sever any weeds, became automatic and freed her mind to wander where it would. So she worked on, conscious of birdsong, the whisper of the ever present wind and the clink of the hoe blade against a stone. She was aware of and savoured the smell of fresh earth as she turned it over with her hoe. She saw the bugs, the little creepy crawlies and the occasional fat worm that appeared and disappeared as she disturbed the rich black loam. She was there on the rig when the postman brought the letter.

'I hope it's not bad news,' he said as he looked at the solicitor's logo and the official office stamp on the envelope.

'So do I,' said Catherine. It's a good job it isn't a postcard, she thought, or the whole neighbourhood would know what it said. She took the letter indoors and put it on the mantelpiece. Although she really wanted to open it, if it was bad news she didn't want it on her mind all day. It could wait till Norrie was home. She picked up her hoe from where she had left it and went back to the rig.

She had been working for some time when she heard her name being called. She looked up to see Paul Finney at the door of his house. He began to walk towards her and beckoned her to come to

154

meet him.

'What's wrong, Paul?' she asked when they met. 'Is there a problem?'

'No problem,' he said. 'At least not for me, but it might be for you. I've been watching the merlins. They are breeding. They've built a nest and the female's sitting on it. She's up there on the side of the hill. Here, have a look.' He handed her a pair of binoculars. 'She's over there,' he said as he stood beside her and indicated the direction in which she should look.

Catherine put the binoculars to her eyes and scanned the area Paul pointed out. 'I can't see anything,' she said.

'She's well camouflaged, but keep on looking and you will. There's a big white rock about ten yards to the right of her and a bit higher. When you find that, come on down and then scan left . . . .'

'Oh, there she is,' said Catherine. 'My golly, you'd have a job to spot her if you didn't know where she was.' Catherine continued to look through the binoculars for a while then she handed them back to Paul. 'You must have been watching her every day,' she said. 'How long has she been sitting?'

'Three days now.'

'Have you climbed up to have a look at the eggs? Or is the nest too difficult to get at?'

'I wouldn't want to disturb her, she might forsake the nest, and anyway, I'm not a climber,' said Paul. 'I've got no head for heights so I couldn't get up there, it's too steep.' He indicated the birds' nesting place. 'I'd rather have my feet on the ground, that's why I'm an engineer and not a pilot. But I would have liked to have been one.'

'An engineer's job is important, though, isn't it?' said Catherine. 'I don't suppose many pilots know how an engine works. Thanks for letting me see the bird. I'd never have spotted her myself. You're right, of course, the fact that they're there is going to be a problem, not for us, but it is going to delay everything for the planners and builder. But that's life. When did it ever run smoothly?' She gave an exasperated sigh. 'I suppose I shall have to tell the solicitor so he can let the developer know.' Then she looked at Paul. 'Why are you home and not at work?'

'It's me day off. Tracy's sweating it out in the kitchen, she's always baking something. I'm sure she'd like to see you so why don't you come and have a coffee with us?'

'Thanks, I will. And you can tell me more about what you've learned about the birds.'

'This came this morning, Norrie.' Catherine handed him the solicitor's letter. 'I wonder what they've got to say *now*?'

Norrie slit the envelope open. 'Let's have a look and find out,' he said.

Catherine watched his face as he read the letter and saw how he twisted his lips then lifted a hand to tug at his beard. 'What is it, what is it?' she asked.

'Here,' said Norrie. 'You read it.'

She took the letter from him. 'My God,' she whispered as she read. When she'd finished she sat and looked at it for a while. Then she looked at Norrie. 'I suppose Judith and Robbie will have had a letter like this too. Hadn't we better get the kids together to talk about it?'

'I suppose we had, but I shall read them the riot act if they don't behave better than they did the last time. You'd better get hold of Robbie first,' said Norrie. 'With a bit of luck he might be home.'

Catherine dialled the number and stood to wait while it rang. Melody answered and when asked, said that Robbie would be home in a couple of days and yes, she would tell him to ring home, and no, she wouldn't forget.

'I don't trust her to remember,' said Catherine. 'You know what a scatterbrain she is. I shall ring again if he doesn't ring me.'

But Melody did remember, she did tell Robbie and he did ring. He had had a letter too. 'I hope we don't have a repeat of that last family gathering,' he said when his mother told him she wanted them all together to discuss the outcome of their letters. 'But it would be nice to spend a few days with you.'

'I don't see why I should have to come,' said Peter. 'I don't want anything and I certainly don't want to have to sit there and listen to Ju and Robbie having a shouting match.'

'You've got to come,' said his mother. 'It wouldn't be right if you weren't there.'

Judith was delighted that something was happening at last. 'We'll finally be able to get on with our lives,' she said. 'I'll be there.'

So the meeting was arranged and though Allen and Peter were not directly involved their parents insisted that they attend.

They sat round the table, Norrie at its head. 'The developer's solicitor has sent letters to your mother and I and Judith and Robbie, with the offer from the developer. I was quite surprised at the amount. . . .'

'I wasn't,' interrupted Judith. 'In fact I expected more and I shan't sell for that. He'll have to up his offer again.'

'Judith,' admonished her mother.

'Oh, come on, Mam. You forget that he's going to make a great deal of money out of this, so the less he can get away with paying us the more he stands to gain. No, just for now, I'm out.'

'What do you think, Robbie?' said Norrie.

'I have to say I agree with Judith. And though I don't know how much he's offered you, I guess it's in line with what he offered me, so I'm surprised that you appear ready to accept.'

'I haven't said that we were going to accept,' said Norrie. 'In fact that's the reason we asked you all to come here so we could talk it over.'

'Peter and I haven't got a clue what sort of money you're talking about and if you're not going to tell us, we might as well not be here,' said Allen.

'Okay,' said Norrie. 'We had no intention of keeping it from you. He's offered your mother and I, because our properties are jointly run, a hundred and twenty thousand pounds. I don't know if Judith and Robbie are prepared to tell you how much they've been offered; that's up to them.'

'My offer was sixty thousand, because of the house,' said Judith.

'And mine was forty-five thousand,' said Robbie. 'That's because it's only land – the ruin doesn't count.'

'It's a lot of money,' said Allen. 'You could do a lot with it. Build that new house, Dad, and get a new car. In fact you could give up work and retire.'

'Well we don't have to decide straight away,' said Catherine, 'and even if we said yes, they couldn't start work for another couple of months. They can come and have a look, which they have done, but something's happened which means they can't even stick a spade in the ground.'

'Why not?' chorused Judith and Allen.

'Because Paul Finney has discovered that a pair of merlins that are nesting on the hillside opposite his house is a protected species and nothing must be allowed to frighten them off. That rules out earth movers and heavy machinery and work will have to wait till the young have fledged, and that will take another couple of months.'

'Trust Mother Nature to get in the way,' said Judith. 'So, we shall have to wait till the birds have flown, hmm, but that gives us a breathing space and in the meantime we'd better put a letter together to refuse this offer and ask for, what, another ten, twenty per cent on top of what they're offering now?'

'You're being greedy,' said her mother.

'No, Mam, I am not. He probably won't agree to it, but he'll maybe give us a bit more.' Judith looked at her brothers. 'Do you lot agree?'

'I do,' said Robbie.

'Why look at us?' said Peter.

'You're not going to be left out,' said Catherine. 'Your dad and I will see to that.'

'Are we agreed on something then?' asked Norrie. 'Are we going to draft a letter?' He looked round at his family and as he looked at each one in turn each head nodded in agreement. 'Right then,' he said as he stood up. 'I'm for a cup of tea. Where did you put the bannocks, Catherine?'

Thirty-One

HAVING DECIDED THEY wanted to stay and make their home in Shetland, Paul and Tracy Finney were working hard to save enough money to put down a deposit on a house. Tracy had taken a job in the town to boost their savings with what she could earn. She went off in the morning and didn't come home till late afternoon and Catherine was again on her own for most of the day. She missed her friend's cheerful chatter and the gossip over a cup of coffee. She missed her children too and often pondered on how quickly they had all left home.

Norrie told her she should go out more: 'You're turning into a recluse,' he said. And she knew she was and that she should take herself out because there was nothing to stop her. But her life had centred on her family, her sheep and the croft, and she'd never had the time or the inclination to join any woman's group. She now had no desire to start; instead, she concentrated on tending her sheep, looking after the house and keeping the rows of carrots, neeps and cabbages in the rigs weed free. Occasionally, when the weather was fine and the wind temperate, she climbed the hill, wandered along the peat banks and found a dry place to sit while she listened to the song of the larks and watched the clowning, tumbling, flight of the peewit. The hill was the place she went when she wanted to be alone, where her peace of mind was restored and anything that troubled her lost its threat.

A letter to the developer's solicitor, telling him that the decision not to sell for the amount offered was unanimous, had been written and posted, and every day since then Catherine waited for a reply. It was slow in coming, but eventually there it was and the offer had been considerably increased. There was no need for a family gathering to decide what to do this time, and phone calls to Judith and Robbie confirmed that they agreed that the offers should be accepted. So it was done, and now they waited for the cheques that would make them all better off.

The month of June came in with fine days and on every one Catherine took her binoculars to watch the merlins' nest. From time to time she was lucky to see the birds change places, for they shared the brooding of the eggs. Every day she went to look because she wanted to know exactly when the eggs hatched. It would take another four weeks after that before the chicks fledged. It was the middle of June; they must break out of the shells soon. But even if they hatched next day it would still be the middle of July before work could start on Deepdale.

Catherine had milked her cow and was carrying the pail of milk to her house when she heard the sound of a vehicle. Looking up she saw a builder's truck coming down into the valley. She took the milk indoors then went back outside. The truck had stopped by her house and a man was getting out.

'Good morning,' he said. 'I saw you going in. I hope you don't mind, but I just wanted to come and have a look at the site and remind myself what I might be taking on. I've been contracted to do some of the work here.'

'Well you're not going to be able to start for some time. You know that there's a merlin nesting here, don't you?' said Catherine. 'It's a protected species and you aren't going to be able to do anything until the little birds have flown.'

'Oh yes, and Patterson is livid that his plans have to be kept on hold because a bird is sitting on a few eggs. But that's the least of his troubles,' said the man. 'This is not going to be an easy place to work.'

'Why, what's wrong with it?'

'The draughtsman who drew the plans needs to have his head examined. You've only got to look at the place and the fall of the land. The sewage system won't work. But you can't tell 'em. They sit in their little offices and draw lines and think that's okay. Architects should do a practical course, get their hands dirty and know what works before they're ever allowed to put pen to paper.'

'But you must have looked at the plans and if you already knew about the snags, why did you think about taking on the job?' asked Catherine.

'To tell you the truth, lady, I'm beginning to wish I hadn't.' The man spread his arms to indicate the whole valley. 'Just look at it. It's a beautiful place. It would be a crying shame to fill it with little wooden boxes for people to rent for their holiday. It'll ruin it. But then, Andrew Patterson is a very powerful man, he knows the right people, if you know what I mean, so it's very rare for anything or anyone to get in his way, and if they do they're soon dealt with.'

'I don't like what you're saying,' said Catherine.

'Sorry, darlin',' said the contractor. 'But I've got to tell it like it is. For your sake I just hope everything's not yet carved in stone.'

When Catherine pressed him for more the man clammed up and would say nothing. 'I've said too much already,' he said. 'I'll wish you all the best and say goodbye to you, mam.' He touched his forehead, smiled at her and walked away.

Troubled by what the contractor had said and wishing that she had never agreed to sell her share of the valley, Catherine waited impatiently for the letter from the solicitor confirming that the deal was complete and containing the waited-for payment. But it was too late now to revoke; contracts had been signed, and there was no turning back.

'How much longer are we going to have to wait for that money?' asked Norrie when day after day went by and there was no letter.

'I don't know. I would have thought it would be here by now.' She had told him about the contractor and the conversation she had had with him. 'I hope we've done the right thing, but I'm not sure now.'

'It's taking too long, something's wrong.'

'I think you're right,' said Catherine. 'I keep thinking about what that contractor said. He didn't have a very good opinion of Patterson and I had the impression he was thinking of pulling out of doing the work here. That would hold things up further because they'd have to contract another firm, and that takes time. But, on the other hand, it might just be because they're waiting for the all clear regarding the birds.'

'That wouldn't stop them paying us. When we get the cheque we'll have a month in which to move out. They can't start work till we do, so the birds aren't going to make any difference. It's a good job I made them settle for leaving the sheep on the higher ground or we'd have had to have a sale on site, and you never get the right price then because folk know it all has to go.'

'Well, I expect that now we've talked about it we'll get the money tomorrow. Come and have your tea,' said Catherine.

She wasn't going to let Norrie see that she was worried, but she was. If the developer was anxious to secure his purchase of the property surely he would have responded quickly to their letter of acceptance. He hadn't, so there *must* be something wrong.

Catherine was pulling carrots for supper when Tracy called to her. It was Wednesday and the shop she worked in was closed for the afternoon so she was home early. She walked across to where Catherine was working and stood at the top of the row Catherine was in. 'Have you had the radio on today, Cathie?' she asked. Tracy had started to adopt the shortened version of Catherine's name. It was the way Catherine's mother had addressed her; no one else did that, not even Norrie.

'No, and I've been outside most of the day,' said Catherine. 'Why, was there something special on?'

'Um, it was something I think you ought to know and something I would have thought you knew already,' said Tracy, 'but you obviously don't.'

Catherine laughed. 'What is it?'

'Well, it's no joke, for a start.' Catherine looked up at Tracy and was surprised to see the serious expression on the young woman's face. 'How would you feel if the whole deal over selling the valley fell through?' said Tracy.

'Fell through? What do you mean?'

'Just that. No big deal and no fat cheque. I was helping out with the bookwork in the back office this morning and the boss has a radio there. We were listening to the news. That developer, Andrew Patterson, is in a lot of trouble.'

'*What?*' For a moment that seemed to last an age Catherine stared at Tracy.

'He was developing another site and they said that the foundations that were being put in weren't being done right. The site manager had rushed the job hoping to have it done and covered up before the inspectors could get there, but they found out. Apparently, the contractor hasn't been paid and he's suing Patterson. He isn't the only one, it seems, and it's all coming to a head. Patterson owes a lot of people money, which he doesn't have, and they're saying he's going to be made bankrupt.'

Bankrupt. No deal. No cheques. No wonder the letter hadn't arrived, there was never going to be one. They were not going to have to move. The valley would remain isolated and go on as it had done for hundreds of years. Catherine began to smile. It spread across her face and she laughed and the laugh became exultant. 'Hooray!' she yelled and throwing the bunch of carrots into the air, she grabbed Tracy in a bear hug. 'You beaut,' she cried. 'It's the best bit of news I've had in a long time. Come on; let's have a cup of tea. *NO*, let's have a whisky.'

'Hold on,' said Tracy. 'You'd better hear it yourself before you celebrate.'

'Rubbish,' said Catherine. 'I've known there was something afoot for a long time. We've been waiting for settlement for ages and it hasn't arrived so hearing the man is about to go bankrupt makes sense.'

'Your kids won't be pleased.'

'That's their hard luck. Their dad and I never had a windfall to help us on our way and you can't miss what you've never had,' said Catherine. 'It's good news for you, too; you won't have to move and neither will I. So come on, we do have something to celebrate.'

Thirty-Two

CATHERINE WAS LISTENING to *Desert Island Discs* on the radio while she ironed Norrie's shirts. It was relaxing just to stand there and run the iron over the clothes. She loved the therapeutic motion of a smoothly gliding iron and the smell made by a hot iron on cotton. A smile played about her lips as she thought of the news Tracy had brought that afternoon. She had thought she might change her mind about agreeing to sell, but now the decision had been made for her and she was glad. As the weeks slipped by and nothing seemed to be happening she had grown unhappy about the whole plan to sell the valley and move away. If what Tracy had heard was right, what would Norrie say? She didn't think Robbie would be bothered but Judith would surely be furious.

Above the noise of the radio Catherine heard the sound of a car door being slammed then footsteps on the flags. She glanced at the clock. It was too early for Norrie. The door flew open and Judith came bursting in. 'Have you been listening to the radio, Mam?' she cried. 'Do you know what's happened?'

'If you mean the rumour that Andrew Patterson has gone bankrupt, yes, I had heard,' said Catherine, 'but I don't know if it's true.'

'Oh, it's true all right. That blasted Patterson *has* gone bankrupt. He must have been in debt already so what made him think he could come here and buy us out? Where did he think he was going to find the money? He's a crook and now we aren't going to get a penny.'

'Calm down, Judith. All you ever had was a promise; you've lost nothing.'

'A promise, yes, that's what men are good at, isn't it? Making promises and never keeping them. I'm pig sick about it. I was planning to use the money to go to London. I needed it to buy accommodation. I have to be on the spot; it's the only way I'm ever going to get anywhere in the music business. Dom's a no hoper; he's another one who's let me down. I've given up on him.'

'That's unkind. You can't blame him. He's very fond of you and I'm quite sure he hasn't given up on getting you accepted.'

'Fond!' Judith tossed her head defiantly. 'The man's a dago. Goodness only knows where he is or what he's doing. He hasn't done anything for me but raise my hopes and where has that left me? High and dry, that's where. And that's where Patterson has left us too. He handed out the big prize then snatched it away. But I suppose you're happy that Deepdale isn't going to be sold. I know you didn't want to agree to it. I don't suppose you'll ever leave it now.'

Catherine switched off the iron and left it to cool. 'It's no good getting mad at Andrew Patterson for going bankrupt,' she said. 'You're much better off than he is. You've lost nothing, but he's lost everything and is up to his neck in debt. He'll never be able to start a business again so how is he going to live?'

'I don't know and I don't particularly care, but it's his own fault he bit off more than he could chew. I hate people like that, they just use other people, and he's more than likely ruined the people who contracted to work for him. What did *you* think of him?' Judith had thrown herself into one of the fireside chairs. She lounged in it, her legs stretched out in front of her. 'I'm totally fed up,' she said.

'And you look it,' said her mother. 'Move your feet, I want to make up the fire.' Catherine pushed several slabs of peat into the stove. As she did so she thought back to the day Andrew Patterson sat at her table. Remembering the smart suit, the polished shoes and his misogynistic attitude, she said, 'I didn't like him at all. He treated me as if I wasn't there, as if women didn't count. He would have ignored me completely if your father hadn't spoken up. Perhaps I shouldn't say it, seeing that it's upset you, but I'm glad he's not going to have Deepdale and I'm glad he's landed himself into a lot of trouble. *If* he's got any friends they'll probably desert him and if he's got a family they'll be sure to give him a hard time. He's going to have to do a whole lot of digging to get out of the hole he's in. Would you like to be in his shoes?'

'No, I don't suppose I would.'

'Well, stop complaining then. Heavens above, there's still time for you to make a name for yourself. I don't understand why you don't just go to London anyway. You don't need a lot of money. Some folk would set off with nothing but the train fare in their pocket. You could get a job and if you were clever you might get something to do with the music industry. And you'd find somewhere to live, so why don't you go? It's not like you to hang back, what's stopping you?'

'You're getting at me, Mam.'

'Well it's about time somebody did. You're letting yourself down; it's time you stopped waiting for Dom to pull strings for you and pulled a few for yourself. Are you going to stay for your tea? Norrie should be home soon.'

'No, I'd better go, but maybe I'll come home on Sunday.'

'Mind you do then; the house is awful empty now you've all gone. Your dad's too tired at the end of the week to want to go out so I don't see many folk.'

'All right, see you on Sunday, then.'

Catherine had made a large bowl of salad and was slicing cold meat when Norrie came home. From the oven came the appetizing smell of baked potatoes.

'Have you had the radio on? Did you hear that Patterson's gone bust?' asked Norrie.

'Oh, that's stale news. Yes, I have,' said Catherine.

'And what do you think about it? I imagine you aren't going to lose any sleep over it.'

'Not a wink. I couldn't be better pleased. What about you?'

A slow grin spread across Norrie's face. 'Can't say I'm sorry.' Then he shook his head, and said, 'Well, it was a bit of a dream, wasn't it? But I'm sorry for the kids. The money would have given them a good leg up. Still, I suppose they'll have to do the same as we did and make it on their own.'

'And that's the best thing for them.' Catherine put the bowl of salad on the table. From the kitchen she fetched a platter of cold meat and a dish containing the potatoes. 'Judith came home this afternoon. She was mad as a hatter, but no doubt she'll calm down. Help yourself to what you want.'

'All this kerfuffle with Patterson has made me think. We're going to have to start making some plans,' said Norrie. 'I don't know about you but I think it's time I thought about retiring.'

'You *what*?'

'Well, I am over retirement age,' said Norrie. 'How much longer do you think I can keep on driving up to Sullom to work? And, because you can't live on fresh air, I've kept going till now because I wanted to have enough put by for our old age. But I think it's time to stop.'

'Are you feeling all right? You're not ill, are you?'

'No, I'm not ill, but I am feeling my age.'

'Rubbish, you're the fittest old man around here for miles.'

Norrie laughed. 'And you'd know, would you?'

Catherine answered that with a smile then said, 'What are you going to do with yourself if you're at home all day?'

'Well, my peerie yarta, the first thing we do is go away on holiday.'

Aghast at Norrie's suggestion, Catherine cried, '*Holiday*?'

'Why not? We never did have that holiday I promised you, oh, how many years ago was it? There's nothing to stop us now. We have Peter here to look after the flock, Allen will be there to help if Peter needs him and there's no one at home to cater for, so, how about it? Where would you like to go?'

Catherine stopped eating and put down her knife and fork. 'What's got into you, Norrie?' she asked. 'Our lives were going to be turned upside down by that *awful* man, and now he's gone you want to take his place and upset us all again.'

'For goodness' sake, woman, I'm offering to take you on holiday so stop looking at me like that and say, "Thank you very much, Norrie."' He spoke forcefully but, instead of capitulating, Catherine stared at him. 'I can't make you go,' Norrie went on, 'but if you refuse to come with me I shall go on my own.'

'You wouldn't.'

'Yes, I would.'

This was a side of Norrie that Catherine had never encountered before. 'But where would you go?' she asked.

'When I was in the navy and I had some leave, I saw a lot of things down in the south of England that we don't have here. And then there were the things that Tom Barrington talked about, twenty- and thirty-acre fields and all on the chalk. Many were the times I'd have liked to go back south and look around. But there wasn't time or money to spare. I had a wife and family to provide for. This is the first and last time I shall have that chance, so, I'd like you to come with me. I could take you to see your sisters and the rest of your family if you would.'

'I don't believe it. You want to go on holiday? You, the man who never stops work, and not only that, Norrie, it's July, the middle of the holiday season. There'll be people everywhere, crowds of day-trippers with bawling kids sucking lollies. You wouldn't like it.'

'Then we'll go in August.'

'That's worse. I can't leave the garden.'

'All right, let's say September.'

'Can't go then, that's when we sell the lambs.'

Norrie stood up and pushed back his chair. He roared at Catherine, went to her and pulled her up out of her chair. Holding her by her shoulders he shook her. 'If I say we're going on holiday we shall go whether you like it or not,' he said. 'Peter knows how to grade a lamb and it'll be good practice for him and about time he shouldered the responsibility. You can go on making as many excuses as you like, it won't do any good. We're going on holiday.'

Catherine looked up at Norrie. She began to giggle and then to laugh. 'Oh, Norrie,' she said. 'I love you when you're being so masterful.'

'Now you're taking the mickey.'

'Yes, I know. But I do love you and I will go on holiday with you.'

'Thank goodness for that, I had visions of packing you in the suitcase.'

Thirty-Three

WHILE THE MAINLAND of Great Britain sweltered in a heat wave, August in Shetland was a month of low clouds, mist and fog. At the airport workers twiddled their thumbs, waited for planes that never came and wished they could be given leave to go home, but knew they couldn't, because the fog might lift and a plane could be circling up above them, the pilot hoping for a window in the weather and a chance to land. In Deepdale, relaxed and happy now that the threat of packing up and moving out of the valley had gone, Catherine went about her work in a cheerful mood. She often visited Rosie and her baby. Little Kyle was now seven months old, sitting up and taking notice, and she loved him dearly.

'I could look after him if you wanted to go back to work,' said Catherine.

'Fine that,' said Rosie, 'but I've only just got him settled on to solid feed, so not just yet, eh?'

'Let me know when you're ready, then.'

'I will. Here, you can nurse him.' Rosie put Kyle on to Catherine's lap. 'Have you decided when you're going away?'

'It'll be next month some time. There are too many tourists about in August and I don't know about Norrie, but I'm not too happy in a crowd these days, I'm just not used to them.'

'Will you book up somewhere?' asked Rosie. 'Or will you hire a car and go as you please?'

'I think that's what we'll do, and get B&B where we can. I shall have to get some new clothes to take with me; I would swelter in my Shetland stuff so I'm going into Lerwick this afternoon to see what I can find. Is there anything I can get for you?'

There wasn't and Catherine went home, made a sandwich for her lunch, drank a cup of tea then got in her car and drove into Lerwick. She parked in a roadside car park on the edge of the town then walked along Commercial Street to the shops. The paved main street was crowded with shoppers; Catherine scanned their faces for a familiar one, saw none and, when she saw the cameras bouncing on shirt fronts, and the style of clothes that were being worn, knew that there must be a cruise ship anchored out in the sound and that passengers had come ashore. It wasn't until she was looking in a shoe shop window that someone touched her arm and said her name. She turned to look and smiled as her old friend Rose Sandison said, 'Hello, stranger. What are you doing here?'

'Rosie! How nice to see you. I was looking for a pair of sandals. Norrie and I are going on holiday next month and I need a few new things.'

'You don't mean to say you've persuaded him to leave the croft to someone else's tender care, have you? That'll be a red letter day.'

'Actually it was Norrie's idea. I wasn't keen to go but he persuaded me to, said that if I didn't go with him he'd go on his own. It will be the first time he's been off the island since the war. I couldn't believe it when he said he wanted to go. And he's going to retire – says it's time.'

'Good heavens, what's happened to him? Has all this fuss you've been having lately turned his brain? I want to hear all about that developer chap. I hear he's gone bankrupt and that's why you're not selling. It's such an age since I saw you and I want to hear all the gossip. Let's go to Salotti's and have a cup of tea and you can tell me all about it.'

The two women walked to the little café at the other end of the town. It was still known as Salotti's even though it was now owned by someone else and the name had been changed.

'I like it here,' said Catherine. 'They do lovely cakes.'

'And it's nice to be able to look out on the harbour.' They were sitting at a table by the window. 'I love the lifeboat,' said Rosie.

'It's a true life saver,' said Catherine, turning in her chair to look out at it. 'If it hadn't been for the lifeboat I might have lost Robbie. There was no lifeboat to save his father, but neither was there anyone to see what happened or to call it out.'

'That's a long time ago, Catherine. And your Robbie is not on a fishing boat now.'

'No, he isn't, he's on a drilling platform out at sea. I suppose it's safer than a fishing boat, but I don't know. I don't like it, but it's his choice.'

When the waitress had taken their order Rose leaned towards Catherine, 'Now then,' she said. 'Spill the beans and tell me all about what's been going on in deepest Deepdale.'

Towards the end of the month the mist and fog lifted, the sun shone and the blue dome of the sky was cloudless. Catherine booked flights for herself and Norrie and packed and repacked her suitcase to make sure it would hold all she wanted to take with her. Then she wrote lists of things to be done, others not be forgotten and what to feed the dog and the chickens, and gave them to Peter.

'Mam,' he said. 'I'm twenty-six years old. I'm a married man with a family. I am not a little boy.'

'I know,' she said. 'But I also know you, and even if you don't look at the lists you can't blame me if you forget, can you?'

'All right, stick them on the notice board, then.'

Ever since the children were little Catherine had used a small blackboard, pinned to the kitchen wall, as a memory aid. Meetings, appointments, school holidays were all written up on it. It was too easy to lose a note on a piece of paper, she said, but you couldn't lose the blackboard.

'Are you going to come and help me sort these lambs, Peter? Or do you have anything else planned?'

'Nothing that important,' said Peter. 'But why do you want to mess about with the sheep? I thought you were going to leave all that to me.'

'Yeah, I was,' said Catherine. 'But, dammit, I love working with them and I won't be doing it much longer so please don't deny me the pleasure now.'

'You aren't ever going to give up, are you?' Peter laughed. 'Come on, then.'

With the help of Catherine's dog they penned the sheep, sorted prime animals from those that needed to stay on the croft a little longer and put the two lots in separate parks. Catherine watched Peter at work and knew that she would have no need to worry about her stock while she was away. It pleased her to think that he was so capable, but at the same time it made her sad to think that her days of shepherding were nearly over. Would the days of her retirement be filled with hours of thumb-twiddling boredom?

They were walking down the hill on their way home when a car drove down into the valley and raced along to stop at Catherine's house.

'That's Judith,' said Catherine. 'She's in an awful hurry. Why does she drive so fast? I hope she doesn't drive like that on the road. She'll either have an accident or get pulled over by the police.' They watched as Judith got out of the car, slammed the door behind her and ran into her mother's house. 'I wonder why she's in such a tizz?'

'We're soon going to find out,' said Peter as Judith reappeared, looked around, then saw them and began to run towards them.

'Mam,' yelled Judith. 'I heard from Dom . . . oh, Mam . . . .' When she reached them she gasped, 'That recording I made . . . it had got lost, but now it's turned up again and I've got to go to London. Oh, Mam . . . .'

The girl was near to tears and Catherine put her arms round her. 'That's nothing to cry about, is it?'

'But I'm so excited.' Judith was wiping the tears from her eyes with the back of her hand. 'Dom said there'd been a lot of changes at the studio, some people had gone and new ones come in and then somebody found the recording. One of the new men there played it and when he did he loved it.'

'When do you have to go?'

'Next week.'

'So soon . . . and will you have to stay or will you be back?'

'I don't know.'

'Well,' said Catherine, 'I hope it all works out all right for you and that this is really the break you wanted – you've waited long enough. Who knows, we may see your name up in lights yet.'

'If you do have to stay down there you will keep in touch, won't you?' said Peter. 'You won't forget your little brother.'

'Of course I'll keep in touch. I'll miss you, but I shall come home as often as I can. I'll have to because I bet they don't make bannocks down in London, or mince and tatties. And that's a thought, I haven't had anything to eat for ages so is there anything in the cake tin, Mam?'

'There is, bannocks and a lardy cake and I made the butter this morning.'

'Lead me to them, then. Oh, by the way, can I have one of your suitcases?'

'I thought you had one of your own.'

They had reached the house now and Peter said, 'I hope all goes well for you, Ju. Let us know, won't you. I've got to go; I'm on shift in an hour.' He gave his sister a hug, said goodbye to her and his mother, and left them.

Catherine led the way indoors. 'Are you going to wait and tell your father your good news, Judith?' she said.

'Yeah, I can . . . hey, wait a minute, what's this, a new suitcase?'

'Oh, that,' said her mother. 'You can keep your hands off of that because you can't have it.'

'Why, what do you want it for?'

'Your father and I are going on holiday and the cases we've got are past it, so I bought a new one.'

Judith began to laugh. 'Tell me you're joking,' she said. 'You and Dad are going on holiday? Where on earth are you going? Not the Med, I hope.'

'Don't be ridiculous. Your father hasn't been off the islands since he joined the navy and went away to war. He wants to go now.'

'But where are you going?'

'The south of England. I'll send you a card. And I'm sorry, Judith, but you'll have to buy your own suitcase.'

Thirty-Four

IT WAS A lovely autumn day when Judith left Shetland, there was a light wind and the sun was shining. Norrie drove her to the airport and for once Catherine was sitting in the back seat. The road to the terminal snaked round the perimeter of the airport and as they approached the last bend and the overflow car parks, Judith said, 'Pull over here, Dad, and park for a minute or two, I want to get a smell of the sea before I go.' When Norrie had driven into the park and brought the car to a stop, Judith got out and stood gazing at the blue-grey waters of the North Sea. She breathed deeply of air that was well laced with the tang of the seaweed.

'There's not too much time to spare,' said Norrie.

'Just give me one more minute,' said Judith, 'I've got to remember this.'

A pair of noisy oystercatchers flew overhead and Judith looked up at them. 'There won't be any of them in London,' she said.

'And there won't be any of those, either,' said Norrie. 'Look, Judith.' He pointed north to where a skein of wild geese was flying, not just a skein but a gathering together of a great number of birds. Though they were quite high it was still possible to hear the sound of their voices as they communicated with one another. And they were going south.

'They're going early,' said Norrie. 'We're only just into September; I hope that doesn't mean we're going to have a bad winter.'

'Do you remember when I told you I would go south with the geese one day?' said Judith.

'Yes, and I asked if you would come back in the spring with them.'

'That's right. But there they are and I'll be flying south with them like I said I would.'

'But will you come back in the spring?' asked Catherine.

'That depends on what I find when I get where I'm going,' said Judith.

'Come on, let's go and get you checked in,' said Norrie. 'We can talk while you're waiting to be called.'

Two days after they had said goodbye to Judith, Norrie and Catherine were back in the airport. The plane they boarded took them to Edinburgh where they changed flights and got on a plane for Bristol. Early that evening they touched down at Bristol Airport. Norrie looked out of the window.

'It looks very green,' he said.

There was a rustle of movement as passengers prepared to disembark; seatbelts clicked as they were undone and thrown aside. People stood to open overhead lockers and recover belongings they had stowed there.

'Come on,' said Catherine. 'I hope the hotel's not too far away; I could do with a shower and something to eat.'

'Me too,' said Norrie. 'I'm tired. I think I shall sleep well tonight.'

'Are you awake, Catherine?' Norrie was sitting up in bed. Beside him Catherine stirred in her sleep. Norrie raised his voice. 'Are you awake, I said?'

Catherine grunted, turned over and looked up at him. 'What's the matter, can't you sleep?' she asked.

'It's so noisy. Doesn't anyone go to bed here?'

'This is Bristol, it's a city,' said Catherine. 'And we aren't even in the middle of it. Pull the bedclothes over your head and go to sleep.'

'I can't. I hear every sound. It's three a.m. and there's enough cars going up and down the road for midday.'

Catherine reached for the light switch and clicked it. She turned to look at Norrie and then laughed. He was bleary-eyed and his hair was mussed up. 'You poor old thing,' she said. 'It was your idea to have a holiday. I'll make you a cup of tea.' With a dressing gown over her pyjamas Catherine boiled the little kettle on the hostess tray, popped a tea bag into a cup and poured water over it. 'I hate these little cartons of milk,' she said as she picked at the flap that was supposed to be so easy to open. 'I'll give you some cotton wool for your ears if you think that'll help,' she said.

'No thanks.'

'Will you be all right now?' she said when Norrie had drunk his tea. 'Can I put the light out?'

It wasn't Norrie who got into the driver's seat of the hire car the next day, it was Catherine. He sat in silence as she wove her way through the traffic in the busy streets of the city and only relaxed when they were driving through Clifton Gorge towards the M5. 'That's the Clifton Suspension Bridge,' said Catherine as she pointed out the bridge in front and high above them. And then they were turning on to the motorway to join the stream of traffic heading south.

'Can we get off the motorway?' said Norrie after they had gone a few miles. 'We're not going to see much while we're on it, are we?'

At the next junction Catherine drove on to the slipway and then on to a country lane. They went to Glastonbury then to the wetlands and the willow-growing area where Catherine bought herself a willow basket. They stayed at a farmhouse B&B and drank cider that had been made from apples grown on the farm. They ate cheddar cheese and pickled onions and crusty bread and listened while the farmer talked about how difficult farming was, 'It's all these new-fangled ideas coming out of Europe,' he said. It was Norrie's turn then to tell how different his life was and how much he would like a longer growing season and not the mad gallop that it was for him.

When they had gone up to their room Norrie said, 'He thinks he's got it rough. He hasn't got a clue. Level ground to work, good pastures and what about that field of wheat he showed us . . . I'd like to see anyone grow *that* in Shetland.'

'I'm sure it's not all plain sailing,' said Catherine.

Norrie sat on the bed and yawned. Catherine looked at him and smiled. It was the first time Norrie had drunk Somerset's famous scrumpy. 'Do you think you're going to sleep well tonight?' she asked.

'I think so,' said Norrie as he stifled another yawn.

'I think so too,' said Catherine.

In the morning, after a big fried breakfast, topped off with toast and marmalade and a pot of tea, Norrie took the wheel of the car and headed east.

As they left Somerset and drove into Dorset Catherine said, 'I'd like to see the Cerne Abbas giant. It's just a little way out from Dorchester; perhaps we could stay there tonight and then we could go to Southampton. There's an agricultural show at Romsey – it's always held on the second Saturday in September. We could go to that. You'd love it.'

'Okay. Whatever you want, but how good are you at map reading because I haven't a clue where we are.'

They stopped for lunch at a public house in a pretty little village where the houses were separated from the road by a stream of water and a grass verge. Norrie was impressed by the size of the restaurant that was part of the pub. 'We could do with something like this back home,' he said.

'It wouldn't work there,' said Catherine. 'This is built with the tourist trade in mind. I expect it's shut for much of the winter.'

The waitress who brought them their meals asked if they were on holiday. When Catherine said they were going to see the Cerne giant she told them which way to go to get the best view. 'The road is awful narrow,' she said, 'so take care.'

'These roads are worse than ours,' said Norrie as he drove slowly along narrow country lanes. 'At least you can see what's coming on ours.'

The banks and hedges that had obstructed his view gave way as they crested a hill. As they began to descend, there, cut out of the chalk of the hill on the other side of the valley, they saw the giant.

'My God,' said Norrie. 'That's obscene.' He slowed the car to a stop then pulled over into a layby. He couldn't stare at the giant and drive at the same time. Obviously others had had the same idea.

'It's supposed to be an aid to fertility. In the past—'

'Don't tell me, I don't want to know.'

'It's only a naked man,' said Catherine, 'well, the symbol of one.'

'I think we'll move on,' said Norrie and, putting the car in gear, he let off the handbrake and started down the hill towards Cerne Abbas. The village had an old-world charm but Norrie wasn't inclined to stay and drove on to Dorchester. Dorchester was a pleasant interlude and because it was a Wednesday there were stalls lining the pedestrian-only streets and Catherine and Norrie drifted and dawdled and looked at and bought souvenirs.

Catherine drove to Southampton where her sister, Janet, met

them to guide them to her new home. 'You'd never find it on your own, sis,' she said. At her house Norrie sank into a voluptuous arm-chair and fell asleep while the two sisters talked on well into the small hours. Norrie eventually left them to it and went to bed.

The next morning, which was Saturday, Janet gave them each a bag of snacks to eat at the agricultural show. 'Aren't you going to come with us?' asked Catherine.

'I don't know one end of a cow from the other, it would all be wasted on me,' said Janet. 'But you go and enjoy yourselves. I'll see you later.'

The traffic going in the direction of Romsey slowed to a crawl as it approached the entrance to the show ground. Catherine was driving. She was patient. Norrie was not. 'Are we ever going to get in?' he asked.

'Eventually,' said Catherine, 'and it will be worth it when we do.'

Through the entrance at last and the car parked Catherine looked at the programme. 'Where shall we start?' she said. 'What do you want to see?'

'Take it as it comes,' said Norrie. 'There's too much to make a choice.'

So they looked at clothes and jewellery and handicrafts of every sort. They wandered in and out of marquees, admired penned sheep, goats and totally exotic long-necked llamas. They saw chickens, ducks, geese and guinea fowl. They stood at the ring side and watched a parade of prize rams, of cart horses with plaited manes and tails, of plodding pedigree bulls and then cows with calves. And always the white-coated exhibitors.

'It's not like this at home, is it,' said Norrie.

'No, it isn't. I thought it would be and that I'd have to lead my ram round the ring, which is why I trained him to a halter. I didn't know you didn't do that. But there is one thing that's the same and that's a refreshment tent, let's go.'

There were so many things to see and Norrie wanted to see them all, but as evening approached he turned to Catherine and said, 'I'm braaly tired, lass, I've had enough. I've seen it all and I think it's time to go home.'

'Good, I'm tired too. Janet will be looking out for us.'

'I mean I'm ready to go home to Deepdale,' said Norrie.

'You are? Then we'll go. Will tomorrow do?'

Thirty-Five

THE DAYS WHEN the house was full of happy, laughing people for the Christmas festival, were long gone. This year, only Robbie would be there to celebrate with his parents. Melody had left him and divorce proceedings were in progress. In London Judith's career had blossomed and work commitments meant that she would be working right up until Christmas Eve. Allen and Karen were planning to spend Christmas abroad somewhere, though why they should want to do that Catherine could not understand. Wasn't Christmas for families? Peter and Rosie and little Kyle were going to stay with Rosie's family. Catherine would miss them, for Christmas without little children was a nothing, but she could see Kyle every day, his other grandparents could not; she would not want to deny them the pleasure.

So Catherine told Tracy she was going to Aberdeen to shop for presents and asked if she'd like to come with her. Tracy said of course and when were they going? When they had gone on a shopping trip before it was only for a day and the trip had been nothing but an excuse for a bit of retail therapy. This time it was going to be different.

Heads together over Tracy's computer they booked a return ticket for a cabin on the boat, a room in a hotel and seats for a show at The Lemon Tree theatre. Norrie took them to Lerwick to board the ferry and when they landed at Aberdeen harbour and left the boat the next morning, they made for the shops. All day they shopped, taking their time to explore what was on offer. Then, showered, changed, fed and refreshed and armed with sweets and popcorn they sat through a show at the Lemon Tree.

'Well, that was good, wasn't it?' said Tracy as she and Catherine went to their beds at the hotel. 'We should do this more often. It's a pity there isn't a bigger theatre in Shetland.'

'Yes, but we wouldn't have an excuse to escape and come here if there was,' said Catherine.

'You're right, and I have enjoyed this trip.'

'Did you have a good time?' asked Norrie when the boat docked and he picked them up. 'Or,' as he looked at the number of bags they were laden with, 'is it a waste of time to ask?'

'We had a great time, it was lovely,' said Tracy. 'Cathie is a good pal.'

'You should come with us next time, Norrie,' said Catherine.

'You've no hope of that. Two's company, three's a crowd and shopping's a woman's thing. Did you spend all your money?'

'Not quite.'

'You'll come in and have a drink with us over Christmas, won't you?' said Catherine as they left Tracy at her house.

'Love to,' said Tracy.

Norrie helped Catherine carry her purchases indoors. 'I know it's a bit early,' he said, 'but I've already got your present. It's over there.' He pointed at a box-like object that had been covered with a cloth. 'I hope you like it.'

'Whatever is it?' asked Catherine as she put down the bags she carried. She went to where her present stood and pulled off the cloth that covered it. 'A television set! Oh, thank you, Norrie. You'll have to show me how to use it.'

Despite the depleted numbers that sat round Catherine's table for their Christmas dinner, it was a happy occasion. Norrie carved a roast leg of lamb while Catherine dished up vegetables and Robbie poured wine.

'I'm sorry that things haven't turned out better for you, Robbie,' said his mother. 'What are you going to do now that Melody has gone?'

'I'm going to stay on the rig,' said Robbie. 'I plan to do ten years on it and by then I will have enough money saved to get my boat. I expect I'll have had enough of working off shore by then.'

'So that means you've got another eight – nine years to do.'

'Yes, something like that, but that depends how it goes. What about you, Dad, are you finally going to retire?'

'Yes,' said Norrie. 'And to give me something to do, I'm going to fix up your mother's old house for us to move in to. Well, not just me, I shall get some help. But I thought I'd put an extension on it and make it bigger and better.'

'What? You . . . this is the first I've heard of it. When were you going to tell me?' said Catherine. 'Anyway, you can't, Peter and Rosie live there. You can't turn them out. Where would they go?'

'They can come and stay with us while it's being done and then they can have this place when we move out. They'll need something bigger soon because they're sure to have more kids.'

'I think that's a great idea,' said Robbie. 'I suppose Peter might be in line to inherit the croft, but what about Allen?'

'Allen's the odd one. He's changed since he got married. We don't see much of him now, or Karen, and I think she's the one who's keeping him away. He'll still help Peter with the croft accounts, but he doesn't really want anything to do with the animals. It wouldn't surprise me if he goes into business on his own. That would suit Karen.'

'I never took to Karen,' said Robbie. 'I got the impression that she thought she was superior to us, but I suppose I don't have to live with her so it doesn't matter.'

'That's exactly what I think,' said Catherine.

'Still, never mind them; it's been lovely to have time with you, Mam. I'm glad I could come. When I go home you can sit back and take things easy.'

'You know she'll never do that,' said Norrie.

'We're not done with Christmas yet,' said Catherine. 'Don't forget we've got presents to give to Kyle and Rosie and Peter. They'll be back on Monday.'

Kyle was not really old enough to know what was going on, but his excitement at all the presents that were showered on him by Catherine and Norrie and his uncle Robbie gave much pleasure to the adults round him. He was petted and cuddled and spoiled, and his mother said that she would put some of his gifts away, for it was too much all at once.

'You should find yourself a proper wife, Robbie, and have a handful of kids,' said Peter. 'Kyle really took to you; you'd make a great dad.'

'It won't happen while I work off shore,' said Robbie, 'but I might think about it later.'

'Well, so you should and when you do, let's have a proper wedding.'

'Only if you'll be my best man.'

'That's a deal, bruv.'

Plans for the extension and modernization of Catherine's house were drawn up and when they were passed, Norrie employed a builder to make a start on it. Norrie would oversee the renovations and work with the builder too. Peter, Rosie and Kyle came to live with Catherine and Norrie while the work went on. Catherine was delighted to have the baby in the house and to be able to look after him to give Rosie a break. The house was full again and the walls resounded to the happy laughter of the child. Evenings were spent watching television and the dark nights never seemed as long as they used to.

Every day Catherine put Kyle in his pram and wheeled him along to where the builders were working. Gradually the walls of the house grew and spread and when they were done, while painting and decorating was going on inside, Peter and his father put a fence round a patch of ground.

At last the rebuilding of the house was finished. It now had four bedrooms, a large kitchen diner and a sitting room, which led into a conservatory. Catherine loved the conservatory because she could sit there and look at the bay and the sea beyond. Tracy and Catherine went to Aberdeen to choose curtains and rugs and Rosie helped Catherine hang the curtains. New furniture arrived and was put in place and Catherine and Norrie moved in.

Life had come full circle and Catherine was back where she started, living in the house that she and Robbie's father had painted and decorated and made fit to live in all those years ago. But the house was not the same as it had been then and neither was her life, for the old folk had gone and there was no Jannie to harass her. Norrie no longer drank to excess, but just took a dram now and then, and the dear, funny Norrie was back, the Norrie who had wooed and won her. Life for them both seemed to be set fair.

Peter took over the running of the croft and it was he who made the day to day decisions, consulting his parents only when a major problem arose. Catherine contented herself with planning a garden in the fenced off area round the house.

In no time at all little Kyle, a sturdy toddler, was two years old, into mischief and a handful for his mother. And then there was another baby on the way. A sister for Kyle was born in August. Rosie called her Daisy because, she said, her face was like a little flower. And then Kyle was three and Catherine wanted to know where the time had gone.

'My days are so full,' she said, 'that I don't know how I ever found time to work with the sheep and look after the family. I wouldn't be able to do that now.'

'It's because you're happy and not under any pressure,' said Rosie. 'Time only drags when you don't know what to do with yourself.'

Tracy came to sit in the conservatory with Catherine when autumn approached and drizzle made sitting outside impossible. 'No matter what it's doing out of doors,' she said, 'it's so lovely and warm in here. Aren't you glad Norrie insisted on putting this up?'

'I am now,' said Catherine. 'But I did wonder at the time. You know what terrible gales we get, don't you?'

'Yes, but being in the valley means you're sheltered. What's Judith going to do with her house? Is she going to keep it, or do you think she would sell it to me and Paul?'

'I don't know, but next time I phone, I'll ask. You haven't found anything you like better then?' said Catherine.

'No, I don't think there is anything better than Deepdale, we've taken root in it,' said Tracy. 'We've already been here four years.'

'Have you? Is it as long as that?' Catherine was shocked. 'I lose track of time and I'll say it again; I don't know where it goes.'

'How long have you been here? You came just after the war, didn't you?'

'That's right. It was 1946, what is it now? Let's see . . . it's 1984, isn't it? Ah, that means I've lived here for . . . ooh . . . thirty-eight, thirty-nine years. It doesn't seem that long.' Catherine smiled at her friend. 'I've sort of got used to the place, so I don't think I'll ever be going anywhere else.'

Thirty-Six

'KYLE STARTS SCHOOL in a couple of weeks,' said Rosie. 'I have to buy him some new clothes. Could you look after him and Daisy for me while I go into town?'

'When do you want to go?'

'Tomorrow, if you're not busy.'

Sitting in an armchair with Daisy on her lap and Kyle tucked in beside her, Catherine read to them. When they tired of that she found them paper and crayons and watched while they scribbled and drew matchstick men, and then, while they lay on the floor and played with their toys.

'Kyle's growing so fast,' said Rosie when she came home, 'It's hard to keep up with him.' She dumped a pile of bags on the table. 'It's a pity Daisy isn't a boy, or I could hand down his clothes.'

'Never mind, be glad that he's fit and well, that's what counts,' said Catherine. 'Did you stop for anything to eat or drink in the town? I'll bet you didn't. Stay and have lunch with me, Norrie's gone off to a sale somewhere and goodness only knows when he'll be back.'

'It's good of you to help out,' said Rosie. 'I do appreciate it.'

'That's what grandmothers are for, isn't it?'

'Yes, perhaps, but I may have to put on you again presently.'

'Why?' Catherine looked at her daughter-in-law and was surprised to see that there were tears in the young woman's eyes.'

'I'm pregnant again,' said Rosie.

'But that's good news, isn't it? Why are you crying?'

'I didn't want another,' sobbed Rosie, 'but Peter did and I couldn't say no to him. It's only been a couple of months – I'm due in October.'

'They come for a reason,' said Catherine as she hugged Rosie. 'Be happy, lots of women would envy you.'

'Then lots of women can have my morning sickness,' said Rosie.

'I'm sure they wouldn't mind if it meant a baby for them,' said Catherine. 'I guess you'll want to keep it to yourself for a bit longer so I won't say anything.'

The summer passed peacefully enough. Kyle loved school and Rosie's pregnancy went without a hitch. The morning sickness did not last long and was not as bad as she had expected. Catherine said that though it might be an old wives' tale, mild sickness might mean she was having another boy. It was the girls who caused the problems.

Norrie was delighted with the news. 'I'm glad Peter's keeping the family going; it doesn't look as though any of the others are likely to. I don't think Robbie is ever going to get married again and Allen, well, I think Karen would rather have a couple of dogs than a family. Kids would be too messy for her.'

'You're right,' said Catherine. 'And Judith doesn't get on with kids. It shows and the little ones sense it, so no hope there either. I was worried about her for a while, thought she was turning the other way, but I don't think it's that.'

'Do you mind that it's only Peter whose going to give you grandchildren?'

'No point, is there? I can't get upset because my children refuse to breed.'

They were sitting in the conservatory. Norrie had been working with the sheep that morning, and Catherine had been weeding her garden.

'Why don't you go down to London and stay with Judith for a few days,' said Norrie. 'There's nothing to tie you here now.'

'I don't think that's a good idea. She works late and lies in bed till midday, it would be no fun. I couldn't go anyway; I need to be here for Rosie. She's getting near her time and we don't want anything to go wrong.'

'When is she due?'

'End of October.'

'A matter of weeks, then.'

September came and went and October dragged its heels and still Rosie was on her feet.

'It's a lazy boy,' said Catherine. 'It'll come when it's ready.'

October gave way to November and the days continued to drift by. And then it was bonfire night and Norrie built a bonfire for Kyle and Daisy. Tracy and Paul came to watch when it was lit. Peter had bought fireworks and set them off and Catherine said that he was enjoying them more than the children. But the sparklers were a success as was the supper that Catherine had prepared for everyone. There was tattie soup and baked potatoes and shortbread, drams for the adults and pop for the children.

It was when Rosie was carrying a pot of soup from the cooker to the table that the pains started. She bit her lip and said nothing, but when she helped clear the table and began to load dirty dishes into the dishwasher, she told Catherine.

'Why didn't you tell me before?'

'I didn't want to spoil things,' said Rosie.

'How frequent are the contractions?' asked Catherine.

'They're pretty close. . . .' Rosie grabbed the back of a chair and gritted her teeth. 'Uuurgh,' she groaned. 'But it'll be all right for a while.' She went on with what she was doing, but moments later she was hanging on to the chair again.

'Come on, Rosie, they're too close and you know it,' said Catherine. 'Peter,' she called, 'Rosie has to go. Get the car, and don't be long about it.'

It was ten minutes past midnight when the phone call came. 'It's a boy, eight and a half pounds, Mam,' said Peter. 'Rosie's fine. I'm coming home now.'

Catherine stayed at Peter's house to look after Kyle and Daisy and put them to bed.

'That was a close thing,' said Peter when he got home. 'We got to the hospital just in time. If Rosie had left it any longer, she would have had it on your kitchen floor.'

'Did she have an easy time, then? Oh, my lor'.' Catherine covered her mouth with her hand.

'What is it, Mam?' said Peter as a chuckle escaped Catherine. 'What's so funny? What are you laughing at?'

'Do you know what his nickname's going to be when he goes to school?'

'What?'

'I knew a boy who was born on the fifth of November and everybody called him Squib, you know, that little firework that jumps about all over the place. It was very apt because that's just what he was like.'

'Huh, well nobody's going to call my boy, Squib.'

'You want to bet?'

'I'm not listening to you.'

'Can we stay at your house, Nana?' said Daisy when Kyle had been taken to school and she and Catherine were home again. A box of toys for the children was kept in her conservatory. It was a warm place for them to play and it was easy to keep an eye on them there. At mid-morning she gave Daisy a cup of milk and a biscuit and made coffee for herself. After her snack Daisy, who had been awake since the early hours, was ready for a nap so Catherine tucked her up with a blanket and a cuddly toy. While Daisy slept she would read a book. She switched the radio on and while it played softly she began to read. But Catherine had had little sleep the previous night and soon the words on the page blurred and her eyes grew heavy. Knowing that her mother's instinct would wake her as soon as Daisy stirred she let the book fall, lay back in her chair and dozed.

'Nana, I want a pee.' Daisy was awake and so was Catherine. She took the child to the bathroom then returned to the conservatory. The radio was still on so she turned up the volume. It was one o'clock and the news was about to start. Same old stuff, thought Catherine, not worth listening to. She was about to tune into another station when the announcer's voice made her stop and listen. Horrified at what he was saying Catherine gripped the radio tight with both hands. A Chinook helicopter had crashed into the sea.

'Norrie,' she cried as she dropped the radio. 'Norrie, where are you?'

She snatched up Daisy and hugging her tight ran through her kitchen and out of the house. '*Norrie*,' she yelled, '*Norrie, where are you?*'

'Whatever is the matter?' said Norrie as, coming round the corner of the house, he nearly collided with her. 'What's happened?'

'A helicopter's gone into the sea and they're all dead.' Catherine burst into tears and Daisy, frightened by this turn of events, burst into tears too.

'Pull yourself together,' said Norrie. 'You're frightening the little one. Here, let me take her.'

Norrie took Daisy in his arms and tickled her chin with his beard. 'I'm a big, bad bear,' he growled, 'and I'm going to eat you all up.' He chattered his teeth together and Daisy, because this was a game they'd played before, forgot her tears and laughed. 'Now let's go and find some toys,' said Norrie and carried his granddaughter back indoors.

'Where did you hear that a chopper had crashed?' said Norrie when Daisy was busy with the toy box.

'It was on the radio. I only heard a bit, oh, Norrie.' Tears ran unchecked down Catherine's face. 'What if Robbie was on it.'

'Stop panicking. Hadn't we better find out where and when it happened?'

Thirty-Seven

'YOU WERE WORRYING about nothing, Catherine,' said Norrie. Tracy, who was at work, had heard the news and, thinking that it might upset Catherine, phoned to see if she was all right. Norrie had answered and was glad to get a less garbled account of the crash than Catherine had given him.

'You see,' he said to his wife, 'if you had waited you would have known that Robbie could not have been a passenger, because that one was based here.'

'Oh, but that's worse. The Dan-Air crash was bad enough; it took Peter ages to get over that. If they bring the dead bodies back to the airport he'll have to go through all that again.'

'We'll just have to be there for him then, won't we? He's got the new baby, though, that'll help to take his mind off it.'

The fact that the chopper that had crashed did not service Piper Alpha, but the rigs in the Brent Oil Field, a considerable distance from it, did nothing to allay Catherine's fears for the safety of her son. Robbie still had to board a helicopter and be flown out to the rig and one aircraft was as liable to crash as the next. Norrie did his best to reassure her that nothing bad was going to happen to Robbie and gradually Catherine's fears subsided. Rosie came home with her baby a few days after the crash and the little boy proved to be the distraction that Catherine and Peter needed. Catherine had cared for Kyle and Daisy while Rosie was in hospital, but the new baby was a precious bundle to hold, drool over and love.

'What are you going to call him?' said Catherine.

'We thought maybe George, but I'm not sure,' said Rosie.

'I like George,' said Catherine. 'It's a good strong name. And is this going to be the last?'

'I hope so . . . well, actually it's going to have to be if Peter wants me to work with him. You know what it's like to juggle family and work, don't you?'

'Tell me about it,' said Catherine. 'But I'll always be here to help and you know Tracy would fall over herself to look after your little ones.'

'It's a pity she can't have any of her own,' said Rosie, 'especially as she's so good with mine.'

'Well, that's the way it goes,' said Catherine. 'How is Peter?'

'He's awful quiet. I've tried to get him to talk about things, but he clams up and says I don't need to know.'

'It was a dreadful thing to have to cope with, especially as he had to deal with moving dead bodies once before. I expect he'll talk when he's ready.'

That was how they left it and Peter, never the most talkative one, grew more and more reserved. When his mother, as innocently as she could, asked him how he was, he smiled at her and tapped the side of his nose. 'I'm all right, Mam. You don't have to worry. I'm not going round the bend. I've got something on my mind that's nothing to do with the crash. You'll find out soon enough. Okay?'

Catherine and Tracy took it in turns to look after Rosie's children. They bought books and read to them and Tracy, who could knit, made them jumpers and socks with wool that Catherine bought. Overall, the children were thoroughly spoiled. Not by their mother, though, who believed in discipline and wielded her rod, not with a hand of iron, but with love.

Rosie and Peter brought their children to spend Christmas Day with Catherine and Norrie. Old enough now to know that Christmas meant Santa Claus, a Christmas tree and presents, and not old enough yet to realize that it was all a con by their parents, Peter's children brought joy and laughter into the house. Under the Christmas tree Catherine piled all the presents she had bought. She asked Norrie to dress up as Father Christmas, but he flatly refused.

'It would take them less than a second to recognize me,' he said. 'It would spoil Christmas for them for evermore.'

And though the magic of Christmas was there in the excited faces of the little ones as they tore the wrappings off their presents, in their wonder of the tree and the twinkling lights that were on it,

Catherine had to agree that the magic must be preserved for as long as possible.

'It's a long time since we had little ones here to fill stockings for, isn't it?' she said, when Peter and Rosie had taken their tired little children home. 'It's been a lovely day, but I'm tired too, so I'm glad they're gone.'

'If you're tired it's your own fault. You always did do too much for others. You're retired, so slack off a bit.'

'Why? Would you have me any different?'

'I suppose not.'

Catherine and Norrie were invited to Tracy and Paul's for Boxing Day and Catherine was made to sit down and be waited on, Tracy would let her do nothing. 'Were none of the others free to come home to you this year?' she asked.

'Judith and Robbie were working and couldn't get time off, though Judith says she's coming home later in January. And Allen, well, Allen's married to Karen and ah . . . we don't see either of them very often.'

'That's a shame, but that's kids for you, isn't it?'

'Yes, they've to go their own way and we have to let them. It's Kyle's birthday at New Year, he'll be six, but he'll be at his other grandma's. We shall have a party of sorts ourselves; I always like to see the New Year in. You'll come, won't you?'

'Try to keep us away.'

The New Year party was like another Christmas Day; the decorations were still up and the Christmas tree still flourished. Rosie had stayed with her parents but Peter had come home as he still had to go to work.

'I have to do more and more of the accounts these days, Mam,' he said when he followed his mother into the kitchen. 'It's a good job Rosie's switched on, because Allen seems to be losing interest.'

'But you can't hold down a job and do all the work with the sheep without a bit of help. Do you want me to have a word with him?'

'Not really. I've been thinking about it and . . . well . . . what I'd like to do is try to get a job as shepherd somewhere in Scotland. That way I'd probably get a house to go with it and I wouldn't get all the hassle of paperwork, but . . . .'

'But what?' said his mother.

'Well, that wouldn't be fair to you. If I left and Allen didn't help, how would you manage?'

'Mm, I'll have to think about that one. Let me talk to your father.' Catherine had opened the oven door and brought out a tray of sausage rolls. 'Put these on a plate, will you,' she said, 'while I find some paper napkins.'

No more was said about Peter leaving Shetland – no need to put a damper on the party, thought Catherine. And it wasn't till the clock struck twelve that all five of them stood outside under what was, for once, a bright moonlit sky, linked arms and sang *Auld Lang Syne*, before going away to their beds.

Judith came home at the end of January. She was alone and her mother asked her where Dom was and why he hadn't come with her.

'He's not a little dog that I drag round on a lead, Mother, and neither is he my boyfriend,' said Judith. 'He's a mate, that's all.'

'But it's plain to see that he's very much in love with you,' said Catherine.

'Then he should know better.'

'Surely you don't work so hard that you don't have time for a boyfriend.'

'They come and go, Mother, they come and go.'

'What do you mean?'

'It's just about impossible to decide who's genuine and who's not. I know I'm not the top dog, but fame of any sort isn't all it's made out to be. Men like to be seen with me and it's nothing about being in love or being a couple, it's just reflected glory.' Judith sounded bitter.

'Then don't write Dom off just yet,' said her mother. 'I'm quite certain he has your best interests at heart.'

'Well, if you insist, next time I come home I'll bring him with me.'

'I wish you would. Have you decided whether you want to sell your house to Tracy yet? I asked you months ago. It's about time you made up your mind.'

'I might as well, I suppose. I had thought about keeping it, but I don't think I'll ever come back here to live. Where's Dad?'

'Do you have to ask? He's either out looking at the sheep or he's making a straw kishie in the barn.' They were in the conservatory. Judith lolled on a settee. She had lost weight and with it much of her energy. 'Would you like to go for a walk?' said her mother. 'It's a bit cold but the wind's not too bad.'

'No, I'd rather stay here.'

'You're too thin, Judith. You're not eating properly, are you?'

'Don't lecture me, Mam.'

'You'll make yourself ill and then where will you be?'

'Home with you, I expect.' Judith smiled at her mother and added, 'I would hope.'

'Oh, I give up,' said Catherine.

Thirty-Eight

WINTER DAYS NEVER seemed to be as dark or the nights as long since Norrie had bought the television set. Catherine's favourite programmes were of murder and mayhem.

'Why do you watch that stuff?' he asked.

'Because it's not for real,' she said. 'I like the suspense.'

On Saturdays Catherine had Peter's children to stay overnight. She played with them and taught them the board games she had played with their father and bundled them in beside her on the settee to watch television.

Tracy came too and brought her knitting. 'What do you think of this?' she said. She handed a knitting pattern to Catherine. 'I thought I might make that.'

'But it's a first size, Tracy,' said Catherine. 'Little George is nearly five months old, it won't be big enough for him.'

'Oh, it isn't for George.'

A smiling Tracy watched the doubtful expression on Catherine's face turn to one of surprise and joy. 'You're pregnant. Oh my dear, I'm so happy for you. When is it due?'

'The doctor said the sixteenth of September, or thereabouts. We're only just into March now so I've got six months to get used to the idea. I'd given up, you know, thought this day would never come. I blame Rosie, must have caught it off of her.' She laughed. 'But I'm so thrilled and Paul's daft with pride that he's going to be a dad. He treats me as though I'm made of spun glass. Imagine it, ten and a half stone and tough as old boots. Still, it's nice to be made to feel precious. I'm a bit nervous about it though.'

'You don't have to be, go and talk to Rosie. I'm sure she'll be able to answer all your questions and put your mind at rest. Things have changed since my day, but I'm here too, so you're not alone.'

Tracy picked up her ball of blue wool and her knitting needles and started to cast on stitches. Catherine watched as the young woman deftly began her piece of knitting. 'We want a boy,' said Tracy. 'But I wouldn't mind a girl.'

'You can have a scan and find out what it is,' said Catherine.

'But that would be like knowing what your Christmas present was before you opened it.'

'That's one way of putting it.'

'I've waited long enough to get pregnant,' said Tracy. 'Surely I can wait a few more months to find out what the sex of my baby is.'

Patience is a virtue, so the old saying goes, thought Catherine. It seemed that Tracy had it and it was something she was going to have to cultivate. It wasn't *that* long before Robbie would be home. On her fingers she counted the months she had to wait: eighteen. In the meantime there would be another baby to welcome to the valley, another Christmas to celebrate and then time would fly and she would have to prepare for Robbie's homecoming. How wonderful it would be to have another celebration with all the family there.

Throughout that summer Catherine and Tracy spent many companionable hours together. Catherine took up her embroidery again while Tracy knitted a layette of small garments.

It was nearly the end of September before Tracy found out what sex her baby was. After a long hard labour she was delivered of a boy. Family came to visit, a small noisy crowd of parents and a sister. Catherine smiled as she remembered how her own mother had arrived and tried to take charge. It was not the same for Tracy's mother, there was no barrier of dialect or in-laws to contend with, only Paul, who smiled, went to work, and left them to it.

And then in no time at all it was Christmas and New Year and time to start feeding the ewes because what they could pick of the grazing was very little, and a sprinkle of what Norrie called 'bag meat', a mixture of cereal grains and vitamins, did not go amiss. Flock numbers had been cut to reduce the work load for Peter, who now worked at Sullom. Lambing started at the end of March. Norrie still helped out, but increasing age had brought rheumatism, which made for painful joints and, much to his annoyance, slowed him down.

When they were in the thick of lambing Peter took time off work. He did the night shift; Catherine and Norrie shared the work through the day. At the end of April it was over, and parks all around were filled with happy gambolling lambs. Peter went back to work and Catherine and Norrie to their now quiet life.

It may have been quiet for Norrie who did nothing but potter around the place, walk round the sheep and check the fences, sometimes sit in the barn and make kishies, but for Catherine things were different. As the sun lifted higher in the sky and summer seemed to hold out a promise of not being far away, she looked at her house and decided it needed a spring clean.

'Can't you sit down and take things easy?' said Norrie when he found her on a step ladder taking down curtains to wash.

'No, I can't,' she said. 'Don't you realize Robbie comes home soon?'

'But that's ages away.'

'No, it's not. It's the end of May already and he finishes at the end of July. That's only eight weeks. I wanted to get his bedroom redecorated and you know how time flies.'

It was no use trying to tell her that there was no need for her to get things looking spick and span for the boy, thought Norrie, just the fact that he was home would be enough. He wouldn't know or care that she had gone to all that trouble. But Norrie said nothing and for the next few weeks absented himself from the house as often as he could. There was no room for him and the man with ladders, buckets and brushes that Catherine had engaged to paint and decorate. When he saw that the decorator had finished and was putting his tools in his van ready to drive away, he said to Catherine, 'Are you happy now it's done?'

'Yes,' she said. 'I'm so excited. Robbie will have the chance to make a new start, and he'll be here with us to do it.'

'But he wants to go back to fishing, how are you going to cope with that?'

'I can't stop him, can I?' said Catherine. 'So I'll have to live with it.'

She had cleaned and washed and polished till the house was as fresh and neat as a new one. No more could be done and gradually the days slipped by till at last there was nothing to do but wait.

*

Norrie had set a wooden bench in a sheltered spot against the wall of the house. Catherine sat on it now and looked at her garden. She had planted shrubs to protect tender plants against the unrelenting winds that swept across the islands, and had planted snowdrops and crocus under them. In February she had watched as the snowdrops flowered and the green spears of crocus parted to allow purple and yellow flowers to emerge. Daffodils and tulips had flowered and died, but the honeysuckle's wandering vines, looped in and out of the wooden bars of the garden fence were coming into flower now. It also climbed a trellis fixed to the wall of the house.

How lucky she was to have all this, a nice house, her children doing well, three lovely grandchildren and Norrie, especially Norrie.

The only fly in the ointment of her contentment was Allen and his choice of wife, Karen, who, from the absence of endearments, made it plain that she thought a crofter and his wife were not her social equals. Her attitude made it difficult for Allen to visit his parents but, unhappy though she was about it, Catherine had to accept that the boy had no choice.

Judith worried her. The girl made no secret of the fact that she didn't like small children; neither did she deny that she had no steady boyfriend and Catherine wondered again if her emotions led her in a different direction. Maybe it was just that her career took precedence. Again, there was nothing her mother could do.

Peter was not academic and did not have a soul-searching desire to become famous in any way. All he wanted was to work with animals and spend his life on the land. Being married to serene and sensible Rosie, and having his children round his knee was all he asked. His attitude to life was calm and unruffled, which made those he met feel glad to know him, and made his mother love him all the more.

And then there was Robbie, child of her first husband, who wanted more than anything to have his own boat and to be a fisherman. She had tried to persuade him not to, but his heart was set on it, which was why he had taken a job on an oil rig where he could earn the sort of money that would help him buy his boat. He had it all planned. He had said he would stay on the rig for ten years and then leave, that ten years was nearly up. Catherine couldn't wait to have him home.

Thirty-Nine

CATHERINE WAS DISHING up scrambled eggs, toast and grilled tomatoes. 'Put the TV on, will you, Norrie,' she said. 'I'd like to see the news.' She put the plates containing their breakfast on the table then turned to look at the TV.

Norrie turned it on and stared like a man transfixed. A mass of leaping flames filled the screen. 'My God, that's some fire,' he said.

The view widened and more of the fire could be seen. The legs of an oil rig, big and black, stood outlined against the fire above and the scarlet glow of burning oil on the sea below. What should have been the structure of a rig, the derricks, metal work, helicopter landing pad, bulk of offices and the living and sleeping quarters of two hundred men, was a ball of fire. Greedy flames consumed all, leapt high and danced a macabre dance. Clouds of thick black smoke wreathed, writhed and billowed above the fire.

A solemn voice gave a commentary.

Catherine stood as though glued to the spot. 'What did he say? Piper Alpha . . . *destroyed*?' She closed her eyes, clasped her hands together, took a deep breath then, letting it out said, 'No . . . it's some other rig . . . not Alpha.'

Norrie turned to her. 'Oh God, it *is* Alpha. I hope Robbie's off shift.'

Catherine, her face blank, stood watching the scene on the television. 'No,' she said, 'he's not. I know.' Her voice was calm and level. 'But he'll survive. God cannot be so cruel as to take him from me too. He *will* come home. Believe me, he *will* . . . come . . . home.' Turning away she sat down at the breakfast table. 'Now come and eat your breakfast, Norrie.'

Norrie continued to look at the scene of devastation for a while then at his wife. How could she be so unfeeling? Hadn't she heard what the announcer had said, that so far there were only sixteen survivors? The chance that Robbie was one of them was so remote as to be almost impossible. If he had been one of the lucky ones his mother would have been told by now, for all this had happened the night before and if they hadn't been watching something else they would have known then. She was in denial, that's what it was. Unable to accept what had happened she was refusing to believe it. He would have to watch her, for when she realized that Robbie was probably gone, well . . . then the dam would break. He sat down and looked at the eggs on his plate. In the short space of time since he had turned on the TV, the eggs had congealed and the tomatoes had gone cold and mushy. He no longer felt hungry and pushed his plate away.

'I'll just have a cup of tea,' he said. 'I don't want anything to eat.'

'Don't be foolish,' said Catherine. 'Eat up.'

Norrie pushed back his chair. 'What's got into you, woman?' he shouted. 'Are you heartless? Don't you realize what's happened? Your son was on that rig. It's a ball of fire. He's either burned alive or drowned and you tell me to eat up.'

'Sit down, Norrie and don't shout at me,' said Catherine. 'Robbie can swim. He will have jumped into the sea and he will come ashore.'

Norrie sprang forward, took Catherine by the shoulders and shook her. 'Face facts Catherine. Wake up. But you *won't*, will you? You think there's going to be a miracle and Robbie's coming home.' Distressed and angry with her, he continued to shout. 'Don't you know that the jump would have killed him; the platform is a hundred and seventy foot above the water.' She had not resisted him and under his hands she was as putty. 'Oh God,' he moaned, 'that poor boy.' He let go of her and sat down. 'I loved him like my own.' Tears filled his eyes and ran silently down his face. He did nothing to stop them.

'Calm down, Norrie.' Catherine reached out to pat his hand. 'I know you want to prepare me for the worst. But we don't know yet that Robbie's missing and until we do I shall *not* give up hope. This is not the time for hysterics. We have to stay calm and wait till we have news.' She stopped and gave a little smile. But it was a smile that was not quite sure of itself. 'He will come home,' she went on. 'I am convinced of that. I *cannot* lose him.'

Perhaps there was some sense in what she was saying, thought Norrie, but how could she remain calm in the face of such a disaster? Was he panicking and jumping to conclusions or was he being sensible? Surely being prepared to hear the worst must take the sting out of it when it comes? There were so few survivors – what chance had Robbie of being one of them?

The phone rang then. It was Judith. 'Hello, darling,' said Catherine. 'Yes, I know. I saw it on the television. We don't know yet. . . . No, there's no need for you to come home. Norrie's here and, no, I'm not a screaming wreck, I'm all right . . . . Yes, I'll let you know. Goodbye.' It was the same when Allen rang, the same answers and the same refusal to allow him to come home. 'What did they think they were going to do?' said Catherine as she put the phone down. 'There's nothing any of us can do but wait.'

Norrie grieved for a son that wasn't his, grieved for a wife who was turning a blind eye to the probability that her son was dead. How long would she be able to maintain this resistance and what would happen when the truth hit her? Someone from the oil company would ring and tell them if Robbie had or had not survived, and someone had to be there to take the call. He had to be the one to hear the words, not Catherine. While she cleared the breakfast things he picked up a newspaper and sat down to read.

He heard Catherine rinse the dishes before putting them in the dishwasher, the splash of water in the sink, the clash of china as she stacked plates, cups and cutlery. He heard the slam of the dresser drawer, the rattle of cutlery and then she was coming to join him.

'Why are you sitting there reading last week's paper?' she asked. 'Aren't you going to go out and walk round the sheep?'

'No, Peter can do that.'

'It's not like you to sit about; can't you find something else to do? Or are you going to stay indoors and get under my feet all day?'

'Can't you just let me sit here and read the paper in peace for a while?'

'But it's last week's.'

'I know it is. You can say what you like, I'm going nowhere till I know what's happened to Robbie.'

'Where are you, Mam?' said Rosie, holding her baby in her arms and Daisy by the hand. 'I came as soon as I could.'

'Why, what's the problem?'

'Um . . . have you seen the news this morning?'

'Yes. And I expect you're wondering why I'm not in floods of tears. I don't know whether Robbie is dead or alive. Someone will be sure to ring and let me know, but if he's dead I won't believe it until I see his dead body.'

'Oh, well there's no more to say then,' said Rosie. Daisy had climbed on to Norrie's knee. 'Read me a story, Gramps,' she said.

'All right,' said Norrie. 'Catherine, can you make us some coffee?'

While Catherine was in the kitchen, Norrie said, 'She's in denial, Rosie. I fear the worst and I'm afraid of how she'll react when the news comes. I don't want to leave her alone so could you stay with her for me to have a break?'

'Of course I can and the little ones always like coming here.'

'She won't let Judith or Allen come home, though they both wanted to.'

'It's shock. It affects people in different ways.'

'Talking about me, are you?' said Catherine. The tray she carried contained coffee mugs, a cup of juice for Daisy, and some biscuits.

'Of course we are, darlin'.'

'Cooee, hi, where are you? Oh, there you are. Good morning,' said Tracy.

'Have you come to sympathize as well?' asked Catherine.

'Why would I do that?'

'Haven't you seen the news?'

'No, our TV's up the creek. Why, what's happened?'

'Piper Alpha has been destroyed by fire.'

'*What*? Oh my God. Where's your Robbie? Is he safe?'

'We don't know yet,' said Norrie. 'We're waiting to be told.'

'Oh, Cathie, me dooks, come here.' Tracy threw her arms round Catherine and hugged her tight. 'Oh me darlin', what can I say?'

'Nothing,' said Catherine. 'Until we're told that he's been taken from us there's always hope, and I will *not* give up.'

'You're being very brave.' Tracy looked at Norrie and saw the raised eyebrows and the slight shrug of the shoulders. So, all was not as it should be. Tread carefully, Tracy. 'Well, I'll not stay as you have a houseful,' she said. 'But you know where I am, don't you. Bye.'

Forty

MISSING, PRESUMED DEAD, was the message.
'I told you, didn't I?' said Catherine. 'He's only missing. He'll be on a life raft somewhere waiting to be picked up. They would have had life rafts, wouldn't they? Are you drinking whisky, Norrie? I thought you'd given it up. I'd like one.'

'You? But you don't like my malt.'

Catherine waved her hand impatiently in the air. 'Just give me a tot, Norrie. What does it matter what it is?'

Norrie fetched a glass from the kitchen and poured a tot for her. To his surprise she picked up the glass and tossed it off in one. 'You did that like a hardened drinker,' he said. Had she been drinking secretly?

Catherine gave a brittle laugh. 'I'm not a drinker, never have been. It's just that I like a dram now and then. It's relaxing, so I'll have another, please.' Norrie chewed his lip and stared at her. 'Ah, don't look at me like that,' said Catherine. 'You drink now and then so why shouldn't I? I don't make a habit of it.'

But it wouldn't take much, thought Norrie. Screwing the top back on the bottle he made a mental note to keep an eye on the level of what was in it.

They were sitting in the conservatory and though the heat of the day had dissipated, the room was still pleasantly warm.

'Dom phoned,' said Catherine. 'He said he was sorry to hear what had happened, and then he said Judith was working too hard. He sounded worried. It seems she's afraid not to accept every booking the agent makes.'

'She doesn't realize what a good friend Dom is to her,' said

Norrie. 'I wish she'd see that. I'm not at all sure this singing career is a good thing. I know, well I suppose I do, that she's getting good money, but that's not everything. Still, we don't have to worry about her while Dom's around.'

'I'm not going to. She's a law unto herself. It would be a waste of time.'

'I wish you'd let her come home. We see little enough of her.'

'Why should I? There's nothing she can do and I've got Rosie and Tracy close by if I want company. And there's always you.' Catherine drank the last of the whisky in her glass. 'I'm going to bed.'

The days when every waking hour was filled, when there was always some job to be done, and when sleep claimed Norrie as soon as his head touched the pillow, were gone. Now that retirement reduced his working day he often woke in the night and lay staring into the darkness.

He had followed her to bed and fallen asleep, but now was awake. He shifted position then realized that the bedclothes on Catherine's side of the bed were disturbed. He put out a hand to feel for her. She was not there. Ah well, she would be back in a minute or two; she had maybe gone to the toilet or to get herself a drink. There was a full moon and cloud shadows drifted across the ceiling. He lay and watched them. Catherine was taking her time. He waited, but as the minutes ticked by and she did not return he got out of bed. On the landing he called her name. There was no reply. The bathroom door stood ajar. She was not there. He went back to the bedroom and pulled a pair of trousers over his pyjamas, a thick jumper over the jacket. He searched downstairs, but there was no sign of her. Where had she gone? He put on boots and a coat and let himself out. She loved the hill and often went there, but surely she hadn't gone there now. He turned his gaze towards the bay and what he saw there made him sigh with relief. A figure was seated on the rocks.

'I missed you,' he said as he stood beside her. 'What on earth do you think you're doing here? You'll catch your death of cold dressed like that.'

Catherine was wearing a dressing gown over her nightdress, bedroom slippers on her feet. 'I'm not cold,' she said. 'Well, perhaps just a little bit.'

'But why are you here?' asked Norrie.

'I'm waiting for Robbie.'

'What makes you think. . . ?'

'Oh don't be stupid,' interrupted Catherine. 'He knows the way home. He learned all about navigation at school. He'll have got hold of a boat somewhere and he'll sail in this way.' She indicated the space between the headlands.

Norrie crumpled and sat down on a rock beside her. He hung his head. Oh God, give me strength, he prayed. Then he put his arm round her.

'I'm sure if he came and saw you sitting here half-dressed he'd be mighty cross. "He knows the way home," you said, so he knows where to find you. He would expect you to be at home, which is where you should be right now. Why don't you come back with me and wait for him there?'

For a moment or two it seemed she might refuse, but then she said, 'Perhaps you're right.'

From time to time Norrie took the whisky bottle out of the cupboard. To his dismay the contents shrank visibly.

'Have you been at the whisky, Catherine?' he said. 'If you haven't someone else has, because the level's gone down.'

'It was all there was,' said Catherine. 'I've got a bottle of Vodka now.'

At first she took one after supper. And then it was two. And then Norrie didn't know how many because he wasn't always there to watch her. She began to wake bleary-eyed and to neglect her house and garden. He tried talking to her.

'Darlin', I don't mind if you take a drink, but you're taking too much and it's not doing you any good. If Robbie came home,' – God forbid that he should say so, knowing that it was never going to happen – 'if he came home and saw you looking the way you do, I don't think he would be very happy.'

She stared at him with dull, blank eyes, and he knew she had not registered a word he had said.

'I don't know what's taking Robbie so long to find his way home,' she said. 'Perhaps he's stranded on one of the skerries. I shall tell him off for making me worry when he does get here.'

'I'm worried about her, Tracy,' said Norrie when the young woman called. 'She was never a drinker, but now she's at the bottle any time of day. I have to keep an eye on her because she wanders off and I've found pans left cooking and beginning to burn. I can't keep an eye on her all the time.'

'She's not going to do any harm to herself is she?'

'I don't think so. She will have it that Robbie's going to come home and she goes out looking for him. I hate to say it, but she won't accept that Robbie's dead. I try to talk to her but she won't listen, and once I thought she was going to attack me for even suggesting it. I don't know what to do.'

'Have you called the doctor in to look at her?'

'She won't hear of it, screamed at me when I suggested it.'

'Then all you can do is to keep an eye on her. I'll help; I can come along and bring the baby and my knitting,' said Tracy. 'If she decides to go up on the hill she has to go past my house, so I'll try and keep an eye out for her.'

As the weeks went by and August faded into September Catherine withdrew more and more into herself. She stayed away from the hill, promised Norrie she wouldn't go there now the weather was not so good. 'I won't find Robbie there anyway,' she said. 'It was the sea he loved.' And every day, come wind, rain or shine, she went to the beach. 'I have to wait for him here.'

She turned on the TV, but, sunk in a chair with the vodka bottle on the table beside her, paid little heed to what was on the screen.

'How long is this going to go on, Dad?' asked Peter when he caught his father cooking a meal while Catherine slumped in chair.

'I don't know, son,' said Norrie. 'I've tried everything to snap her out of it, but nothing helps so there's nothing I can do but look after her. Rosie and Tracy are very good. I couldn't do it without them.' He lifted the lid on a pan of potatoes and added a dash of salt. 'Go home to Rosie; I'll shout if I need you.'

The kitchen was warm. A couple of pans on the cooker bubbled away happily. Somewhere a clock measured time. From the sitting room came the drone of voices and the music of a TV programme, but otherwise there was nothing to mar what passed for peace.

When it came, the scream was ear splitting and the explosion loud. It made Norrie drop the plates he was holding.

'Catherine,' he cried as he ran, 'what is it?'

She stood in front of the television. Her body shook violently and her face was contorted with grief. 'He's dead, Norrie. I saw him. Why did they show him to me like that?'

'Like what, my darlin?' Norrie gathered her into his arms. She did not reply but wilted against him. He looked at the television set. There was a gaping hole in it, a vodka bottle embedded in the debris. Then she was clawing at him, lifting her head and, eyes wide and staring, gave a cry that was the agonized howl of an animal. 'Hush,' whispered Norrie. 'It's over.' But she wasn't listening; she was gone, had become a rag doll and would have slid to the floor if he hadn't held her close. He laid her on the settee.

'What's happened, Dad?' It was Peter. 'I was outside and I heard screaming.'

'I don't know why, but your mother's just killed the TV. She seems to think she saw Robbie on it. God only knows what's going to happen when she comes round. I think you'd better call the doctor. Tell him it's urgent.'

Norrie swept Catherine up in his arms and carried her up to bed.

Forty-One

NORRIE SAT BY the bed and watched his wife as she slept. It was not normal sleep, but sleep brought on by alcohol. When the doctor asked him how much he thought she had drunk, he shook his head and had to admit that he had no idea.

'In that case,' said the doctor, 'I can't give her anything, but I'll leave some sedatives with you that you can give her later on. But wait as long as you can for the alcohol to clear her system.'

Norrie had no intention of leaving Catherine's side until he learned what it was she could have seen to reduce her to such a state of anguish. So he stayed till Rosie joined him and insisted that he take a break.

He went downstairs and looked at the wrecked TV. The neck of a vodka bottle pointed at him from the debris. The set had imploded. Catherine must have thrown it with considerable force and accuracy to have done so much damage.

'Hi, Norrie, how's Catherine? I know I'm being nosy, but I saw you had the doctor here.' Tracy, who knew that the door was always open, had walked in.

'Hello,' said Norrie. 'Yes, we did have to send for the doctor. Catherine's sleeping at the moment. Rosie's with her just now.'

Tracy gave a loud gasp. 'My goodness, what happened to your TV?'

'It got broken,' said Norrie. 'Catherine saw something on it, I don't know what, but she had hysterics and threw a bottle at it. Now we have to wait till she tells us what panicked her. Whatever it was, it might have done some good.'

'Perhaps that was what was needed,' said Tracy. 'She was going to have to accept the truth sooner or later, wasn't she? If you want anyone else to sit with her remember I'm available any time. I'd do anything for Cathie.'

'I'll remember,' said Norrie. 'Now I'd better send Rosie home and get back to Catherine myself.'

Wearily Norrie plodded up the stairs. Rosie sat quietly while she watched her mother-in-law.

'What do you think happened, Da?' she asked when Norrie joined her.

'I don't know, lass, but whatever it was I believe it's made her accept that Robbie's dead, and perhaps that means that she'll recover.'

'I do hope so. I'd better go now,' said Rosie. 'Peter's looking after the bairns. I'll bring you some food later on. Spend your time with Mam.'

Norrie sat down on the chair Rosie vacated. How long was Catherine going to sleep? He'd been here for hours and sleep was trying to claim him too. Outside, the wind whispered through the naked honeysuckle vines. Inside, all was quiet save for the regular in and out of Catherine's breath. She sighed and stirred and Norrie sat forward in his chair. 'Catherine,' he whispered.

There was no reply, he waited, and when there was still no response, he relaxed and sat back again. There was no telling how much vodka Catherine had drunk, so there was no telling how long she would sleep. Remembering his bachelor days, Norrie recalled sleeping a full twelve hours after a wild drinking session. If Catherine was going to sleep that long he'd better be prepared to sit there for the rest of the day and half the night. It was still only afternoon and not time for bed, but oh, it was where he would like to be. He looked at his wife. She was so sound asleep that surely it would be all right for him to doze a while.

Catherine stirred then turned over and opened her eyes. She looked at Norrie, sound asleep in his chair. What was he doing there? And it was still daylight so why was she in bed? She turned back the bed-clothes. Only her shoes had been taken off. Dimly she remembered the doctor being there, telling her that everything was going to be all right. But there was something else, something that had upset her . . . it was . . . it was . . . what was it? She couldn't remember.

Then there was the floating sensation . . . and nothing more.

But she was awake now and Norrie was watching her. He'd been watching her forever. Everybody watched her, at every hand's turn there was someone there, behind her, in front of her. They never left her alone and she'd had enough. They'd say, 'What are you doing, Catherine?' and it was none of their business. Very gently and quietly she lifted the sheets off her and put them aside, swung her legs out of bed and stood up. Walking carefully, so as not to wake Norrie, she moved past him, out of the bedroom and down the stairs. In the kitchen she put her feet into her outdoor boots and put on her coat and hat. She lifted the car keys from the hook and let herself out of the house. The car was not in the garage but standing outside. She unlocked it and got in, slotted the key in and turned on the ignition. Gently and in first gear she rolled the car past the house, then, determined that she was going to let no one stop her she gained speed and drove past Peter's house and Tracy's and up out of the valley. On the main road she turned left and a few minutes later turned off and on to one that led only to the hill and some long abandoned peat banks. She drove as far as she could then stopped the car, got out and began to walk.

The day was dying and light fading. The surface of the road she walked on had deteriorated badly from lack of use. The stony surface petered out and gave way to a grassy track. Still she walked.

They can't watch me here; they can't look at what I'm doing all the time. They can't come and pretend that they've only come to visit when really they think I'm going out of my mind, and they need to keep an eye on me. They won't believe me when I tell them I'm sure that Robbie is going to come home. He is, isn't he? He didn't die in that fire, did he? Tell me he didn't.

A skinny little hill ewe appeared out of nowhere and stopped to stare at the woman who had invaded her territory. 'Go away, I'm not talking to you,' Catherine shouted and the animal bounded off at the sound of the raised voice.

What am I doing, talking to a sheep? Stupid sheep!

The coat Catherine wore was long, waterproof and windproof. She was glad she had it on for the wind was keen. She walked on, stumbled a little on the uneven surface, but kept walking. What am I doing here? she thought, where am I going? She slowed her steps then stopped. She was in the midst of the hills now. On either side of her, hillsides rolled away to right and left. Above her, a moon, not quite a half, climbed the sky. It wouldn't give much light, but then, with its help, neither would the night be inky black. Stars were beginning to twinkle. There were noises, but she wasn't alarmed for she had come here to think. Tucking the bottom of her coat beneath her, she sat down.

Vodka was odourless on the breath, she had been told. Well, that was all right as long as you only had one or two and kept the bottle hidden. But if you didn't care if anyone saw you drink, why do that? She had been drinking earlier in the day. They said that if you drank enough it would blot out your troubles. It hadn't done that for her, it had only made her stupid and made Norrie despise her. Yes, she knew he did, for hadn't she felt the same about him when he had taken to the whisky?

She had wanted to blot out her troubles, wanted to go on believing that Robbie would come home, didn't want to believe he was dead. But that was before that film on television. She had paid little attention to it until she had seen . . . the body . . . floating in the water. It had rocked up and down with the motion of the waves and, fuddled with drink as she had been, as the picture became clearer she had thought it was Robbie, her Robbie, drowned as his father had been. Suddenly the fog that clouded her brain had cleared and she knew that Robbie had perished and was never going to come home again.

She had not wept for him then, because the enormity of knowing was too much. She had screamed, yes, she had screamed, but that hadn't made it go away, and she had thrown the bottle, but all that had done was destroy the television set. Then Norrie was there and she vaguely remembered being carried up to bed, the arrival of the doctor and his brusque words, before drifting into nothingness.

But she cried for him now.

The tears came slow at first, for in her heart she knew that she had grieved for him already, her refusal to accept from the start that he was dead had made her hide it. But now, there was no one to hide it from, and soon the tears came thick and fast. Reaching out, she threw her cries into the accepting arms of the empty hills, heard them echoing back and forth. She wept till she was spent, then, lying back and turning on to her stomach, she sobbed into the moss of the peat-covered hill.

*

When Norrie slid sideways and would have fallen, he woke up. Opening his eyes he looked at the bed.

Catherine had gone.

But not far, please, not far. She'll be in the bathroom, surely. But she wasn't. Norrie hurried down the stairs and called her name as he went into the kitchen, the sitting room, the conservatory. She was nowhere. Maybe she was upstairs in the room she had set aside for Robbie. He hurried back up, his rheumatism making him stumble.

The room was empty.

Downstairs again he looked to see if the coat and boots she wore to go out were still where they should be. They were not. He looked then to see if the car keys were still hung on their hook; they too had gone. It must have been the sound of the car that had stirred him.

With a sob he covered his face with his hands and slumped on to a kitchen chair. There was no telling where or in what direction Catherine had gone. What hope had he of finding her before nightfall?With sudden decisiveness, he stood up, tore out of the house and headed for Peter's place. He burst into his son's house just as the family was sitting down to tea. 'Come with me, Peter. Your mother's run off and I've got to find her. She's taken the car. I can only think she's gone up in the hills somewhere. I've got to find her before it gets too dark.'

'Okay,' said Peter as he grabbed his coat.

'Take a torch,' said Rosie, 'you may need it.'

They searched the hill where the Deepdale peat banks were, walked and called her name, called again and again, but only got answers from sheep. 'She's not here,' said Peter. 'Let's try the next hill; there's a road a long way up. No one goes up there to dig peat any more now they've got central heating.'

With Peter driving they followed the old road to the peat banks on the next hill. 'There's our car,' gasped Norrie as it showed up in Peter's headlights. 'She won't be far away now, I'll find her.' He had the door open and was out of the car almost before Peter had brought it to a stop. 'Wait here.'

He set off briskly, but slowed down when his rheumatics hampered him. As he went he prayed that Catherine had not strayed off the roadway and on to the rough grass of the hill. He would never find her if she had. When the road became a grassy track he began to call her name; no answer came, but he pressed on. In the heart of the hills he found her, a crumpled heap lying on the ground. He knelt beside her and put his hand on her shoulder.

'My peerie yarta, I've come to fetch you home,' he said.

She turned and looked up at him, eyes red from her tears. 'Oh, Norrie, Norrie,' she cried. 'Robbie's dead, you know.' Tears filled her eyes and overflowed. 'I know it now. I didn't want to believe it, but it's true.'

'Yes, my darlin'. I know it too. Come, stand up.' He stood, and taking her hands helped her to stand beside him. 'We have to grieve for him,' he said. 'But we have to be glad that he was ours, if only for a while.'

For a while neither spoke then Norrie said, 'Dry your eyes, my darlin', Peter's waiting for us. Let's get back to the car.'

Peter saw them coming and went to meet them. 'I love you, Mam,' he said. 'We all do. Come home now.' He kissed her. 'I'd better get back to Rosie.' Then he got in his car and drove away.

A few minutes later, Norrie and Catherine followed him.

Forty-Two

'NORRIE.' SOMEONE WAS poking him. 'I'm sorry,' said Catherine. 'I'm really sorry.'

'What for?'

'For smashing the television set. It was because—'

The ringing of the telephone interrupted her. 'Save it for later,' said Norrie. 'I'll get that.' Everything was going to be all right, he thought, as he shuffled down the stairs. Catherine had accepted that Robbie was dead and their lives now had a chance to get back to normal. He picked up the phone, 'Hullo, hullo?' he said.

'Sorry to call so early.' It was Dom. 'It's not good news, I'm afraid. Judith's had a breakdown and the doctor says she needs a complete rest. I was wondering how things are with you and whether it would be all right if I brought her home.'

'Of course, you must, just let me know when you get a flight and what time you want picking up,' said Norrie. 'It's just about the best thing that could happen at the moment. I'll explain when you're here.'

'Great, I'll be in touch, then. Thanks.' And Dom rang off.

Catherine stood at the bottom of the stairs. 'Who was that?' she asked.

'That was Dom. Judith wants to come home for a few days.'

'Wants to, or needs to?'

'She needs to come, actually. She's had a breakdown. Dom will bring her. Do you think you could cope with that?

'Of course she must come. I shall have to look after her; I suppose she's run down. Will I be able to cope? You tell me.'

'I think looking after her would be good for you.'

'So do I, but don't you want to know—'

'Not now. You can tell me later on when we're both ready to hear it.'

'My dear girl, just look at you,' said Norrie as he took Judith into his arms and hugged her. 'You look like a scarecrow. When did you last eat?'

'That's anybody's guess,' said Dom.

'Well, we'd better get you home and feed you up. Your mother will have a fit when she sees you.'

'How is she, Dad?'

'Recovering, thank God. I was hoping you might cheer her up, but it will be a case of the blind leading the blind if I'm not mistaken.'

'I think looking after Judith might be just the thing her mother needs,' said Dom, who had collected their bags from the carousel. 'It will give her something else to think about.'

Norrie, who had gone to the airport to meet them, was pleased to see how Dom was looking after his daughter. He knew that Judith would think nothing of working till she dropped and she needed someone beside her who would try to make her put the brakes on. There was no doubt that Dom was the one to do that.

It was November now, and dark November days were bad enough without the snow and ice they brought, so Norrie drove carefully. Judith was in the front passenger seat, huddled in a long padded coat, which she had pulled round her. When they reached Deepdale, she said, 'How are you getting on with the folk in my house?'

'They're lovely. You'll like them. The wife is a good friend to your mother. I don't know how I'd have coped these last few months without her.'

Catherine came out of the house to greet her daughter. 'Hello, Mam,' said Judith as she was swept into her mother's arms. 'Long time no see.'

'And whose fault is that?' said Catherine. 'I've been here all the time.' She smiled when she saw Dom. 'I'm glad you've brought Dom.'

'Correction, Mam,' said Judith as they went indoors, 'Dom brought me.'

'Good for him. You need someone to look after you. I have a meal ready for you, so get that coat off and come and sit down.'

Catherine busied herself with putting food on the table while Norrie showed Dom and Judith their rooms. When Judith came back and was about to sit down, Catherine, who was carrying a pile of plates, put them down with a thump. 'My goodness,' she said. 'Are you anorexic? Because that's what it looks like.'

'Don't go on at me, Mam. I mustn't get fat or I won't get any bookings.'

'But—' Catherine began then stopped. 'We won't talk about it now, but we will later on. Let's eat.'

When the meal was over and Judith had gone to her room, Catherine said, 'What's been going on, Dom?'

'Judith collapsed at her last gig. The doctor said it was malnutrition and sheer exhaustion. I had to do something, because I knew she wouldn't, which is why I rang and asked if I could bring her home,' said Dom.

'I'm glad you did.'

'She won't turn down anything the agent offers. She does too much and she doesn't need to. The public love her, but there's such a lot of competition; the young girls are stick thin and Judith thinks she has to be the same.'

'But it doesn't suit her. What's she doing to herself? Is she on a diet?'

'No, but I don't suppose you know what her life is like. Engagements take her all over the place so she travels a lot. Meals are often something that has to go in the microwave and when you're tired you don't want to eat so you don't. And that's just about it. She just isn't eating enough.'

'I see. So I shall have to look after her and get her back on her feet. Are you going to stay? It's nearly Christmas, had you got anything planned?

'I'd love to stay, Mrs Williams. I love being here.'

'Okay. I'd be happy to have you, on one condition, though, and that is that you call me Catherine, or Mam, like the kids do.'

'Then I'd love to stay . . . Catherine.'

They were sitting at breakfast. 'Your lifestyle is so different to mine,' said Dom. 'We're at breakfast and it's still dark, and Judith tells me that when it does get light it won't last long and it'll be dark again by three o'clock. Don't you get fed up with it?'

'We're used to it,' said Norrie. 'But we're so busy in the summer that maybe we need the dark days to rest up.'

'But you still have livestock to look after.'

'Yes, but there's not much to do in the winter except feed them, and that's easier now that we have silage and don't have to struggle to make hay.'

'Mam used to be the shepherd,' said Judith. 'She started our flock of Cheviots and won prizes with them.'

'But I don't do it now,' said Catherine. 'Peter has taken over and Norrie helps him, so I've been made redundant. Does anyone want more toast?'

'None for me,' said Judith. 'Do you know what a Cheviot is, Dom?'

'A breed of sheep?'

'That's right,' said Norrie. 'But we've got Shetlands and cross-breeds too. If you like you can come with me when I walk round them. We've had a frost but it's a fine day, just the right weather for walking.'

'I'd like that,' said Dom.

'Has everyone had enough to eat?' asked Catherine and to protestations of being full to the brim, she started to clear the table. While Norrie and Dom were putting on jackets and boots she and Judith saw to the dishes.

'Come and talk to me,' said Catherine when they'd done. 'I want to know what you've been doing with yourself.'

In the sitting room a fire was already burning in the grate. It was fired with peat and a straw basket full of it stood by the side of the fire. 'When did you get to light that?' asked Judith.

'Your father did it. I know we've got central heating, but I still like the smell of a peat fire. I didn't want oil-fired heating; it makes me feel like a traitor, more so now Robbie's gone, but it was the most reasonably priced.'

'Why didn't you let me come home when Alpha went on fire?' said Judith. 'I was devastated and you must have been too.'

'I think I went on to auto-pilot. I couldn't cry. I could not, *would* not, believe that Robbie could have died in that blaze.'

'Not even when they told you he was missing?'

'Even then I wouldn't let myself believe it, I *couldn't*. I kept thinking he was cast adrift on a raft or an island and that he'd be found and rescued.'

'I *wish* you'd sent for me. I wish now I hadn't waited to be asked, I should have come home anyway.'

'I don't think you could have helped. I'd set my mind on him coming home. Norrie couldn't make me change it, so I don't think you could have. I tried to stop Robbie going to sea on a fishing boat so I wasn't going to accept that the sea had got him anyway.' There was anger in Catherine's voice, but there were tears in her eyes. 'Norrie tried to make me understand that Robbie was dead, but I fought him off and the longer it went on the more I believed he'd come home. I was convinced that he would walk through that door as if nothing had happened.'

'But he didn't, did he.'

'No.' The word was said in a whisper. 'And then I went looking for him. Norrie caught me on the beach one night, but he didn't know about the other times. He slept sound, I made sure of that, because I used to put some stuff I knew would make him sleep in his bedtime drink.' Catherine turned her head and stared at the fire. Judith said nothing, but waited for her mother to continue. 'And then, my love,' said Catherine, her attention still on the red embers of the peat, 'life was so empty. You were away and Karen kept Allen close and he rarely came home. There was only Norrie. Peter was busy with his work, with the sheep and his family. And I started to drink. Not much. At first one was enough.' She was playing with her hands now, her head bent to watch as she turned the rings on her fingers. 'And then it was two, and then as much as would make me forget. Your poor father, he had an alcoholic for a wife, me, who got mad at him when he drank too much.'

'What stopped you then? You don't drink now.'

'Your father hasn't told you?'

'No.'

Catherine turned to look into the fire again and after a few minutes turned to face Judith. 'I was sitting here,' she said, 'with a bottle of vodka on the table beside me, yes, vodka, because someone said you can't smell it on your breath and I thought no one would know. As if the fact that I carried the bottle round with me wouldn't give me away. Anyway, there was a film or something on the TV.'

She stopped talking, swallowed hard and took a deep breath. 'I haven't told anyone this because the memory still hurts; even your father doesn't know. I wasn't really watching the television, it was just background noise.' And then the words came out in a rush, falling over one another, wanting to be told. 'But then I saw water and waves and something in the sea and then it looked like a body, and I thought it was Robbie. And I screamed and I didn't want to believe it and I threw the bottle to make it go away. I smashed the set and then Norrie was there and the next thing I remember was waking up in bed. Norrie was watching over me. He was asleep and I got out of bed. I had to get away. They were all watching, you see. All the time there was someone there and I couldn't stand it.'

As she spoke the tears came, and with the outpouring, the shuddering heart-rending sobs, the anguish of remembering and re-living a traumatic event. She buried her face in her hands and Judith, heartbroken at witnessing her mother's grief, gathered her in her arms and held her till the storm lessened.

'Oh Mam,' said Judith, her own tears running free. She was on her knees in front of her mother holding Catherine's hands in hers. 'You should have let me come home. It wasn't right for you to bear all that yourself.'

'But I wasn't thinking straight, was I? There's one thing I regret, and that is that there's no grave and I wasn't able to say goodbye to him. And then I think about all those other women who lost husbands and sons. But the worst is over and now I've got to look after you.' The suspicion of a smile played about Catherine's lips. 'I think I'd better go and freshen up or when your father comes home he'll think we've been fighting.'

Forty-Three

'Now that you're here,' said Catherine, 'and Peter has decided not to run away to Scotland, we'll have a family party. Tracy and Paul will join us.'

'Won't that be a lot of hard work for you?'

'No, Rosie and Tracy will cook and Norrie will be in charge of the drinks.'

And now the day of the party had come. Catherine had been banished from her kitchen. Rosie, Tracy and Judith were cooks in charge. A joint was in the oven and potatoes peeled and ready to put in the pan to roast. Norrie and Peter had taken Kyle with them to look at the sheep and Catherine had Rosie's little ones to look after. Daisy sat on her grandmother's lap to listen while Catherine read a story, and little George gurgled contentedly in his carrycot as did Tracy and Paul's son, Charlie. Dom, who had also been banished from the kitchen because he was a visitor and not expected to help, sat with Catherine.

'Would either of you like a glass of wine while you're waiting?' asked Tracy. 'At the rate we're going I think dinner is going to be late.' She laughed. 'Rosie's already pie-eyed, and Judith's not far off.'

'I knew I shouldn't have let you loose in my kitchen,' said Catherine. 'I think I'd better come out and see what you're up to.'

'Oh no, you don't,' said Tracy. 'You're to sit there and do as you're told. Now what's it to be, a nice glass of chilled white?'

'Yes please,' said Dom, 'and Catherine will have the same.' He smiled at her. 'You will, won't you?'

'Thank you, Dom,' said Catherine. 'I might as well.'

'See who we found outside,' said Norrie as he and Kyle came in.

'How are you, Mam?' asked Allen as he kissed his mother. Karen smiled and said she hoped Catherine was well.

Kyle clamoured for her attention. 'We're going to slip the rams tomorrow,' he said.

'Granny doesn't need to know that,' said Allen.

'Oh yes, she does,' said Kyle. 'When I go to the sheep with Da, Granny always wants to know what's going on, don't you, Granny?'

'Yes, of course I do. Where's Peter?'

'He's just coming.'

Though Catherine did her best to involve Allen's wife in the conversation she found it very hard to get Karen to join in. What was the matter with the girl?

'Here's your wine, Mam.' As Peter had come through the kitchen he had been handed two glasses of wine and told to deliver them. 'Did you know what you were doing, letting that lot out there cook the dinner?'

'Thank you,' said his mother. 'I didn't have much choice, they threw me out. How are they getting on?'

Peter turned to Dom. 'Glass of wine for you? As for how the cooks are doing, Mam, well . . . don't ask me,' he said.

'Allen, did you know that we nearly lost Peter? He was going to look for a shepherding job in Scotland?' said Catherine.

'Yes, I did,' said Allen. 'He talked to me about it. He was still thinking about getting a farm, but it wasn't the right time for me. I'm sorry, Peter, but . . . um . . . well . . . I may as well tell you. The reason I couldn't come with you is because I'm going to be setting up my own business.'

'What? Why haven't I been told about this?' asked Catherine.

'Because it's only just been settled, Karen's dad is helping me. Karen and I are going to be partners.'

'I thought you were already.' Norrie laughed.

Tracy, banging a tin tray with a wooden spoon marched in, 'Dinner's ready. Come and eat.'

In the kitchen the table had been extended to its full length. Small children were put into high chairs, babies looked at and changed and fed where and if needed. On the table dishes of steaming vegetables had been placed while a large joint of beef, waiting for Norrie to carve, stood on a dish on the worktop.

'Can I sit next to you, Catherine?' asked Dom.

'It would be my pleasure.'

Dominic pulled out a chair for her then waited until she had seated herself. 'I should have brought presents,' he said.

'Oh no, Dom, this is not a Christmas dinner, just a get together for the family while Judith is home. You'll be taking her back to London soon, no doubt.'

'I think she's ready to go back to work. She's certainly looking better.'

With food-filled plates and wine glasses topped up, conversation was hard pressed to compete with the clatter of cutlery and the clink of glass. But it flowed as memories were shared, new projects discussed and plans aired. Catherine looked round her table at which, for the first time since she and Norrie had moved into the new house, her whole family, bar one, sat there. She smiled as she looked at the high colour of Rosie's face, not all of which was due to the heat from the cooker. Judith and Tracy seemed to have much in common but Karen, aloof and cold, spoke hardly at all. Allen and Peter were keeping up a continuous conversation and she guessed it had to do with the croft. Norrie caught her eye and smiled at her. And then there was Dom. She stole a glance at him, then chuckled and touched his arm. He turned to look at her.

'You don't understand a word they're saying, do you?'

'No, I don't.'

'That's because, apart from Tracy and Paul, they're all Shetlanders and when they get together they speak in dialect. It's daunting, isn't it? If you come here often enough you'll get used to it.'

The young women were moving, clearing away plates and dishes as they emptied. Then Judith carried a steaming Christmas pudding to the table. 'Have you got the brandy bottle handy, Dad?' she said.

He had. He unscrewed the top and poured some on the pudding.

'Don't, Granddad,' said Kyle. 'You're going to make it soggy.'

'Oh dear, I'd better do something about that then,' said Norrie. 'I think I'd better set fire to it, don't you?' Kyle's eyes grew round as Norrie put a match to the pudding. But as wispy blue flames wreathed around it, the boy's horror turned to delight.

'Ha ha,' laughed Kyle. 'Granddad's burning the pudding!'

Catherine stood up. 'I hope you will excuse me; I don't want pudding.'

A pool of light surrounded a small table lamp in a corner of the conservatory. Catherine sat down in an armchair facing the windows that looked towards the bay. They were set low and, by the light of a full moon, she could see past the rocks, the beach and the bay and through the headlands to the sea. Moonlight lit a pathway that reached all the way up to the beach.

Behind her and from the kitchen she could hear the laughter and excited voices of the younger members of the family. There would be sore heads in the morning, she thought, for all through the meal wine had flowed free. It had been a long time since her children and their partners had been together; they had every right to celebrate.

'I brought you a liqueur.' It was Dom. 'I thought it might make a fitting end to the meal. May I come and sit with you, or would you rather be alone?'

'I spend a lot of my time alone, Dom, so please stay. Have you had enough of trying to decipher what they're saying?'

'It is difficult to understand,' he said.

'It took me a long time to know what they were saying, but it's second nature to me now. Did you bring a drink with you?' Dom shook his head and Catherine went on. 'I can't get Judith to tell me much about what she's doing. It bothers me. Do you know where she's living and what it's like? Does she have a boyfriend?' Catherine sipped her drink.

'She has a flat, not very big, but property in London is very expensive. As to boyfriends, they come and go; she never seems to stay with anyone for long.'

'She told me that all they want is to be seen with her, and she thinks it's just to get their photos in the paper. She won't admit it but I get the impression she's not happy. What do you think? You will tell me the truth now, won't you?'

'It's not quite like that; singing is everything to her. She loses herself in the song when she's on stage. It comes across and that's what makes people love her. I think it's that she finds fame hard work. Media folk can be shallow, always pushing for the next big thing. It's a fight to stay at the top.'

'Oh. Tell me if I'm wrong, but you love her, don't you?'

'I do, and I'll always be there to protect her from the sharks.'

'You're a lovely man, Dom; I'm very fond of you.'

'I'm fond of you too. I admire you; it seems to me you've had a very hard life but a very interesting one.'

'Interesting? What? Stuck here in this valley for forty years? Chasing sheep? Bringing up a family and cursing the coming of oil, that's interesting?'

'Yes, it is. You came from a city and stayed. Judith took me to the croft house museum and said that the house you had to start with wasn't much better, if what you told her was right. Not many would have put up with that. I couldn't. It's nice to come for a holiday, but Shetland has nothing else to offer me.'

'You're wrong, Dominic. Shetland has a lot to offer; a slower way of life for a start, and the peace that you won't find in the hustle and bustle of city life. At first I thought the place was backward and behind the times, but there was a good community spirit. People helped one another, they had to – they didn't get help from social services like people get nowadays. Oil has changed everything. People look for better wages and an easier way of life.' Catherine smiled and shook her head as the memories tumbled in. 'They're entitled to it. Peat banks were allocated to houses, so every year the man of the house had to cut enough peat to last for twelve months. And I can tell you from experience that it's a damned hard job. Not many people cut peat now; they've got oil-fired central heating. Blast the oil.'

'What? Hasn't the oil industry brought a lot of wealth to the islands? Don't you think that's a good thing? You have good roads, entertainment centres, swimming pools and a lot of new houses. When Judith took me on a tour of the islands I didn't see that many of the old croft houses were still lived in.'

Catherine sat forward in her chair, her hands gripping the arms of it. 'Yes, oil may be responsible for all those things happening. But who has had to pay for it? Not the oil barons. Davy Jones demands payment for what the oil companies are stealing from his locker, and it's the birds and wildlife that are killed when the oil tankers spill their cargo into the sea that pay. *Esso Bernicia* collided with the mooring at Sullom. It took years to clear that up. Men have to pay with their lives too. There was the Dan-Air crash when seventeen oil workers died. A Chinook helicopter crashed a couple of years ago; forty-three passengers died then, only two were saved. You know about Piper Alpha, and who is going to forget that? One hundred and eighty seven men died there, only sixteen survived. *That's* the price of oil.'

Dom pulled back. 'When you put it like that . . .' he said.

'And there will be more,' Catherine went on. 'Don't forget other tankers have foundered; *Torrey Canyon* and *Exxon Valdez*, for instance, and it won't stop there. There will be others. It's easy, isn't it, to press a button and have nice clean heating in your house. I wonder how many people wonder what the real cost of it is? Or do they know and then want to forget about it? But I'm on my hobby horse, Dom, and I'm boring you.'

'No you're not,' said Dom. 'It's obvious that you're passionate about the oil industry and what it's done. You're lovely and though people may want to forget the cost of oil, I'm sure that *you* will be remembered for a very long time.'

'You think so? I've done nothing special with my life, nothing to set me apart. Will I be remembered? A couple of generations, maybe, but that's all. Whatever we've done, whatever we've achieved, be it something or nothing, our lives are nothing more than footprints in the sand, my dear, there till the next tide comes in and washes them away.'